A LADY MADE for MISCHIEF

A Spirited Spinters Sweet Regency Romance

ROBYN CHALMERS

Cover Art by Carpe Librum Book Design

Edited by:

Theresa @Cookie Lynne Publishing

Lia Fairchild @Your Best Book Editor

Proofing & special insights by Debbie Phillips @ DP+

JOIN MY READERS GROUP
https://www.robynchalmers.com/newsletter

CHAPTER 1

IT IS A TRUTH, UNIVERSALLY ACKNOWLEDGED, THAT A PERSON ENJOYING A SOLITARY HOBBY MUST BE IN WANT OF A MORE WORTHWHILE OCCUPATION

Mrs. Marianne Eastwood stood in the doorway of the sitting room, a white mobcap covering her gray curls. Her oldest day dress was covered by a large, dimity apron of dubious vintage. "Charis, dearest, have you finished that drawing yet?"

She was too polite to say it out loud, but she considered time spent painting could be put to better use.

"The curtains need to be pinned up so we can get the mold off that dining room wall. It smells to high heaven, and I can't stand it a moment longer. Your father has not shaved. Not that I want him to with the way his hands shake. But he needs to. Come now, you don't have time to paint."

Very well, so she *would* say it out loud.

Charis smiled and looked down at the fictional boudoir she was creating. The basis of the room was done, and the chaise lounge under the window had the first wash of azure. *Pretty.* The watercolor could dry, and she would come back to it later. Hopefully.

She really should not be painting at all. Unless she could figure a way to make an income from it, her watercolors should be relegated to a pleasant pastime rather than the all-consuming passion they had become.

If she *could* create an income, then they could move from this wretched place. Since Father had been forced to sell his commission, each year had seen them move to poorer houses in progressively worse streets of Hartley Green. Their most recent shift had put them outside the village altogether, down by the canal. The reason for the cheaper rent became clear when autumn settled in, and mold appeared on the baseboards of every room. She had even lost a pair of shoes at the back of the wardrobe to it. It was damp, cold, and dreary, no matter how much they cleaned.

It was holding back Father's recovery. It had to be.

Charis washed the paint from her brush so it wouldn't harden the bristles as it dried. "I'll start with Father."

"Good. I'll make up the vinegar wash for the wall and meet you back here in a half-hour."

Before she could go, the sound of horses and wheels crunching on the gravel outside the cottage made them both turn in alarm. Mother ran to the window, drawing the curtain slightly and then leaning back so she would not be seen. "Oh, heavens. It's Lady Hartley." She flitted around the room, gathering books and plates with crusts of toast on them into a basket. "Bess! Bess! Come help us," she yelled toward the kitchen.

Charis joined her in the frenzied tidy up. "Drat. She has the worst timing."

"How can you say that? You never know what bounty she might bring. Where is Bess?" Mother pulled off her apron and her mobcap and plunged them into the basket, too, then patted her hair down.

Charis left the room, only to collide with the maid as she entered the hall. Bess dashed past her and picked up the overloaded basket where it sat before Mother. "I knew I should have come in here this morning. Her ladyship likes to visit on Thursdays." Bess was the queen of hindsight, always claiming she knew

2

the cake should have come out of the oven earlier, or that a particular chicken was not going to fit in with the flock.

The Marchioness of Hartley was known by all in the village of Hartley Green to be kindly and generous. Nevertheless, her visits were always a source of anxiety for everyone concerned. Nobody liked the nobility appearing on the doorstep unannounced.

"I'm never sure why she visits at all. Papa may be ill, but we are not quite a charity case," Charis said softly. It no longer felt like the truth.

Mama stopped in her tracks, blinking rapidly. It normally meant she was thinking hard. "You know why. She was present at your birth and was instantly smitten with you. I wouldn't complain that she's taken an interest in you, my girl."

It was an old story. And it still didn't explain why Lady Hartley continued to visit, even though Charis was almost twenty-one. She pulled off her own apron and stuffed it into the basket before Bess left the room. "Then we really should be calmer when she visits. Her ladyship must think we live with eternally rosy cheeks, when in fact it's just because we flap around before she arrives. Most unbecoming." As true as those words were, Charis could not help but smile as they settled their skirts on opposite ends of the sofa, calmly opening books.

"Your poetry is upside down," she said with a grin.

Mother flipped the book around. "Yes, of course." She shrugged. "Although it makes as little sense to me either way."

A few moments later, her ladyship sailed into the room, carrying a basket of her own. There would definitely be no old crusts wallowing at the bottom of it.

The Marchioness of Hartley was somewhere in her mid-fifties and matched the prosperity of her position with a sensitive and dutiful soul. Today, she wore a soft cream walking dress embellished with expensive Brussels lace. Over that, a deep-green velvet cape trimmed with ermine cocooned her. She managed to look both rich and cozy.

"My dears, the glasshouse at Friar Park has produced the first oranges from the tree we got from China, and I thought I should bring you some. Also, I found a jar of this lovely blackberry jam in the back of the larder." She pulled the delicately embroidered cloth off the top of the basket and walked to the table where Charis had been working, then placed the small oranges in a bowl she spied there.

Charis watched with horror as Lady Hartley's attention was snagged by her watercolor drying on the table. Her head tilted to one side as she inspected it. "What is this? When did you become so good at painting, Charis?"

She picked it up at the corners.

Charis felt the blush on her cheeks. "I … I am not very good at drawing people. Or even landscapes, really. But chairs and rooms I am tolerably good with."

"Tolerably good?" Lady Hartley's eyes turned wide. "This is as good as anything I've seen in *Ackermann's Repository*. Such an eye for composition you have. I can already imagine myself reclining on that chaise lounge. What beautiful detail, so elegant, so very fashionable. How ever did you come up with the idea to drape the lounge like that?"

"It is meant for a boudoir. Somewhere to read in the morning, before one is ready for the world." Half the fun was imagining how she would live in the rooms herself. To be the kind of lady who lounged around until the sun crept up in the sky with nothing better to do than read a book. No chickens to feed, no vegetable patch to tend. No darning, no scrubbing. *So, a fantasy.*

Mama smiled with pleasure, always happy when somebody found her only daughter talented. "She recently helped her cousin, Mrs. Beckworth, update almost every room in her house in Surrey. Charis drew the plans, and together they scoured the catalogs and created a most beautiful residence."

Lady Hartley nodded. "I suppose with his fortune at their disposal, there was no limit to their imagination."

Charis nodded, still feeling a small burst of joy at the memory. "Indeed, it was the most fun I am ever likely to have. But pray tell, what is *Ackermann's Repository?*"

"I shall bring it for you next time. It is a new magazine, a repository, as the title suggests, of all things fashionable. News, politics, design, and even furniture. Ashcroft sent it to me. He knows how dearly I love a good periodical, and this was the very first issue!"

Her soft tone spoke of quiet delight and pride.

Lord Ashcroft was her eldest son, who resided in their town-house in London for the majority of the year. It was very rare to see him in Kent, and if one did, it was at a distance, galloping across the field on some splendid beast of a horse.

He was most handsome, but not in a conventional way. His features were not regular, his nose too big for his face, but paired with his high cheekbones, it didn't seem to matter. His eyebrows were thick—but also dark and winged. Somehow, the sum of the parts made a sublime whole. He was always dressed to perfection and entirely polished. Put that together with dark, windswept hair and a strong jaw, and every lady in the area near swooned when he was around.

Until he opened his mouth.

Then one realized that, although he was brilliant, he was serious in a way that made one *hope* to faint, if only to escape his dark eyes boring into one.

The poor man.

It was not his fault the ferocity of his intelligence made everyone else feel deficient. Or that he focused on politics to the exclusion of all fun. No amount of coats by Weston, silk waist-coats, or crisp cravats folded in a "mathematical" could make up for that. He was also quite abrupt, his manners bordering on rude. He did not tolerate a fool, and she secretly suspected he thought everyone was a fool.

Two years ago, he ran for a seat in the House of Commons in

the 1807 election. He won, of course. Now his time was spent almost exclusively in London. Her Father followed Ashcroft's career in earnest because he fought in the Commons for something close to his own heart: the welfare of soldiers. Everybody said it was because his younger brother, Timothy, had come home wounded, but Charis had a sneaking suspicion it was because he wanted to be over there himself, being a dashing Captain of the Guard. He'd drive Wellington mad within a week.

But his mama loved him. And a lady would one day love the title that came with all that intensity.

He might not remember, but they had spoken three times. Twice at the local assembly, before he won his seat, and more recently outside the pie shop before Christmas as he awaited his mother.

The interchange had gone something like:

Nod. "Miss Eastwood."

Slight curtsy. "Lord Ashcroft."

End.

He wasn't rude, per se; it was simply that he had no polite conversation to enchant one with. Or perhaps he just could not be bothered trying with her, since they moved in very different social circles. Or rather, the Eastwoods had no real social circle at all, both of her parents preferring their own company more and more as they got older.

But she had a full and happy life, and her designs entertained her.

Lady Hartley still stared at Charis's painting, lost in thought. If she wasn't careful, she would have some of that azure paint staining that pretty cream dress. Charis reached out a hand to take it from her. "It is still wet."

Lady Hartley looked up as though she had forgotten Charis was in the room entirely, but she didn't give it back. "I am quite lost in the contemplation of it," she said, looking somewhat bemused. "But I think I have hit upon the answer."

What was the question? But both she and Mother nodded enthusiastically. Sometimes Lady Hartley led conversations on an unusual and circuitous route, but they always ended up at the destination she planned.

"Well, you see … I have long thought that our residence on Grosvenor Square needs freshening. But I don't want to bring in an architect. There is no need for new staircases, mezzanine levels, or ridiculous glass ceilings. No, it just needs a sharp eye and a deft hand to bring it into this century."

A spark of hope caught fire in Charis's heart. Could Lady Hartley mean *her*? "Which century does the house currently reside in?"

Lady Hartley looked at her keenly. "Why, halfway through the last one, of course, when it was built. I grant you, there is some beautiful furniture, made by Chippendale. My mother-in-law had a love of his work. But the rest of it is sadly outdated. With Ashcroft in parliament and receiving other members in the house, it is past time we did something about it."

Lady Hartley's eyes sparkled with mischief. She put the watercolor back on the table and went to sit next to Mrs. East-wood. "What say you, Mrs. Eastwood? Can you spare Charis for a month to help me? Her ideas intrigue me. If we work hard, when the Season opens I will have a brand-new house to welcome my friends into!"

Mother shot an anxious glance over to Charis and then back to Lady Hartley.

Charis nodded. *Yes, Mama, I understand.* Mother flashed her a grateful look. She would never refuse Lady Hartley, but if Charis declined herself …

Fun in London was a paltry thing when she knew her duty. "I'm afraid not, Lady Hartley. Although I am humbled both by the offer and the honor you do me, it would make things hard for Mama if I were to leave for that length of time."

Lady Hartley smiled as though Charis had commented on the

fine weather they were having. "Miss Eastwood, your opinion is not required. Perhaps you could see if your father will join us?"

She was to be overridden, was she? Charis pulled her responding frown into a serene smile. "Of course." Little did Lady Hartley know how much Mama relied on her. How much Father relied on Mother.

She was gone for but a minute, but by the time she returned to give them the news that Father was unavailable, as he was attempting to shave himself, the two ladies were clasping hands like the old friends they certainly never were.

"You are to go, my dear," Mama said with barely restrained excitement.

What on earth?

Charis searched her face but could see no regret. "Very well," she said, slowly. "If you are sure."

"A little town polish won't hurt you," Mother said.

Drat. If she'd wondered how Lady Hartley had sold the idea to her mother, there it was. Charis was to return somehow more sophisticated and alluring. Alluring to all the local bachelors who had thus far managed quite well to elude, rather than be allured. But if they'd seen her in the blush of youth at sixteen and not been interested, they most certainly would not be interested now that she had borne the brunt of caring for Father since his apoplexy. That kind of worry tended to age a person beyond their tender years.

Lady Hartley let go of Mother's hands and smoothed down her skirts. "There now. I am happy with this result. I will send over my Maria to lend her assistance while you are gone."

Oh. With more help, perhaps she would not spend the entire time worrying about them. Her heartbeat sped up, blood thrumming through her veins with excitement.

London!

Art galleries, museums, beautiful buildings, and wondrous shops. Everything she'd ever read about. The trip of a lifetime.

Happiness burst from her, lighting up her smile. "All I hope is that I can help you, Lady Hartley. Nothing could bring me greater joy after all the kindness you have shown us over these years."

A grand London townhouse to draw and redecorate. What could be better? Perhaps if she could do it quickly, she could return before Mama was too frazzled.

"Very nicely said, my dear." Lady Hartley stood, seemingly energized by the visit too. "Wonderful. We shall leave Monday next week. Is that too soon?"

Someone cleared their throat at the door. They all turned around.

Father.

He leaned against the door jamb. It might look nonchalant, but Charis knew it was more from necessity. He smiled, lopsided as usual. "Did I just overhear that you are going to London with Lady Hartley?"

"If you'll give your blessing?" Mother asked, as if they hadn't already decided.

He shook his head sadly, but there was merriment in his eyes. "Only if you promise to eke every last ounce of fun from it." He shuffled forward. "I suppose your mother will find this a good excuse to buy new dresses and fripperies."

Lady Hartley picked up her basket, now empty of its bounty. "There is no need, Captain Eastwood. It would be my pleasure to do that as a way of thanking Charis for the hard work I assure you she will do."

"Too good," Father murmured, and Charis knew he would hate the idea of anyone buying dresses for her. He was proud.

She noted the tiny cut he had made on his neck trying to shave without her. He was getting better at shaving with his left hand, but she still wished he would have waited.

If they missed her too much, or if she missed them, she could always come home. She'd make sure there was always

9

enough coin in her purse to take the stage back to Hartley Green.

Lady Hartley departed, leaving them looking at each other in bemusement. As if they had just experienced a tiny whirlwind and survived. Mother's expression was one of pure excitement, her cheeks flushed, her eyes bright.

She cupped Charis's face in her hands. "My dear. Such an opportunity." She glanced at Father. "We will need to visit the milliner, Captain Eastwood, no matter what Lady Hartley says. Charis needs a new bonnet."

Charis was loath to disagree, but it was best to nip this kind of expectation in the bud.

Mother's fingers were freezing, so Charis pulled them from her face and warmed them between her own. "Please, Mama. I will not find a husband in London. If I have not found one going to assemblies and parties over the last few years, nothing is going to change just because I am in a new location. All the good men have gone to war."

Really, she knew it was her, not the dearth of men. She saw when they whispered behind their hands for no reason, cringed when gentlemen said, "Ha, ha, I must look up when I dance with you," and asked her if she had a new ball gown on when they knew for certain she did not. They all knew the family was poor and suffering, and they didn't want to catch the disease by association.

"But, my love—"

Charis dropped her hands. "It pains me, as you well know. I have come to terms with my future. Do not make me hope for more. I beg you not to expect it."

"Your daughter begs you, wife." There was a stern note in Father's voice. "What will happen will happen, and no amount of new bonnets will change it."

Mother flattened her lips into an unhappy line. "You shall still have them."

Father winked at Charis.

Good.

She didn't want to spend her time in London angling for a husband who wasn't there. She was going to hone her skills in room decoration. Surely working with someone of Lady Hartley's standing would enable her to find other ladies interested in the same service?

The way forward was through her own industry, not finding a man to save her.

Monday week arrived with speed.

Charis's old bonnet now had a pretty green ribbon with silk ivy leaves, and the new one was a very fetching straw covered in soft pink velvet, trimmed in deeper pink velvet ribbon. It had white silk flowers on the left-hand side at the ear and was by far the prettiest she had ever owned. Her clothes were washed and pressed, her boots polished, and her satin evening slippers cleaned. She couldn't think there would be much call for those unless … "Do you think Lady Hartley will take me to a ball?"

Mother looked up from where she had placed tissue paper over the top of Charis's one and only ball gown. "I don't see why not. While you were out of the room, Lady Hartley promised me she would be on the lookout for eligible gentlemen. I'm sure she will do a much better job than I have thus far." She frowned, and a pucker appeared between her brows. "The last few years have been … terrible, and we have lost sight of your future. I hope this trip might, in some way, give you something back. If I'm honest, I hope you'll meet a lovely gentleman who will fall in love with you and cherish you just as we do." She brushed a tear from her eye.

"There now, Mama." Charis pulled her into an embrace. She was a good foot taller than her mother and so, in some ways, it felt like she was the parent consoling the child rather than the other way around. "I'm sure there will be many lovely gentlemen in London, but I will find other opportunities in any case."

Mother glanced up, wariness in her expression. "What do you mean 'other opportunities'?"

This was not a conversation Charis wanted to have. If Mother still thought she might find a husband, she would only be upset to hear that Charis had an ulterior motive. "Oh, nothing. Just that London is a very exciting place. Who knows what will happen?"

Mother nodded, although her eyes were still narrowed. "Speaking of opportunities, I must warn you against one."

This sounded interesting. "Father and I know that you will behave with propriety at all times. You have been raised in a good home. You are a gentleman's daughter and the equal of anyone you shall meet. However ..." She shut the traveling chest, which had Father's initials, which were coincidentally the same as her own, and sat on the side of the bed.

"What is it? You can tell me anything."

"I am just thinking about how best to put this." She patted the spot next to her, and Charis obediently sat. "Please, if you can help it, do not fall in love with Lady Hartley's son." She exhaled. "There now, I have said it."

Charis couldn't help bursting into giggles. "Fall in love with Ashcroft? I think not. Have you ever had a conversation with him?"

"Only briefly. However, he *is* very handsome. His mother often tells me how he has the best of his father's physique and the best of her amiable spirit."

Charis couldn't help laughing again. "The last thing that gentleman can claim is amiability. Trust me, it will be all I can do to have him grunt good morning at me at the breakfast table. Even if he *were* interested in me, I could never attach myself to a man like that."

Mother looked at her, her eyes narrowed once again. "Do you mean that? Because I have been worried that living under the same roof might make you susceptible. And I must tell you that Lady Hartley's generosity would most definitely not extend to giving you her eldest son. She may be charitable and generous, but she has high hopes for his match."

It was somewhat lowering to be warned off him in this way. Because what lady did not want the wealthiest, most handsome man to fall in love with her a little, even if they were ill-tempered, and she would never return their regard?

"In that case, allow me to promise you I will not fall in love with him. Apart from that lovely physique, he has not much else to recommend him."

Mother looked at her wryly. "You would not be the first young lady to fall in love with the man's title and his holdings."

Charis shook her head. "And in any case, would it matter if I did? Say, for example, I spent two weeks there and fell irredeemably and hopelessly in love? I very much doubt he would even notice. I understand you don't want to make things uncomfortable with Lady Hartley, but Lord Ashcroft has not so much as looked in my direction any of the times we have met. You may rest easy."

Mother nodded "Good. Father also wanted me to warn you not to leave the house unchaperoned. Always take a footman or a maid with you. It is not like Hartley Green, where you can traipse around unaccompanied. And he also asked me to give you this …" She drew a small brown suede pouch from her pocket. It jingled. Charis took it from her mother's outstretched hand and opened it to see five gold coins shining inside. Guineas. Money they certainly could not afford. "Thank you, Mama. I should refuse these, but I know I shall need them, so I'm very grateful. I have only a few shillings of my own saved up."

"There now, we could hardly let you go to London without a money bag. If you need more, I'm sure Lady Hartley will furnish you with a small amount that we can repay."

Charis shook her head. "That won't be necessary. This is more than enough." She would bring back as much of it as she possibly could. Money like this was not to be frittered away.

There was a knock at the door, and it swung open to reveal Father standing with a large box in his hands. "All ready to go?" He had been a constant source of joviality and enthusiasm for her trip. She hadn't realized how responsible he felt for their lack of diversion in the last few years.

"Everything has been darned to within an inch of its life, and Mother has given me three new handkerchiefs, beautifully embroidered, and five guineas, which is far too much!"

Mother brushed her praise away. "There now, it was the least we could do."

Father stepped into the room and held out the box to Charis. It had a brass handle screwed into the top and smelled faintly of beeswax.

She took it from him. "What is this?"

"It's a little rough. My skills aren't what they used to be, and I had to work fast. I figured you would need to transport your paints and brushes. Correct?"

He always ended sentences with "correct" as if he were still a captain and she was an ensign. Brusque and brooking no argument. "Correct, Captain." She saluted with a smile.

Charis opened the box to find trays where one could place small cakes of watercolor, and another tray for brushes. He had taken the liberty of packing all of her art supplies into the box where they sat neatly in rows, ready for transport. Her heart lurched at such a personal and thoughtful gift.

"Oh, I love it. It is just the thing." Tears welled in her eyes, and she didn't try to stop them. "You really are the very best parents. I will try my best to be a credit to you."

Father patted her shoulder, his warm smile better than a blessing. "You do us proud wherever you are, my dear. All you have to do to please me is have a wonderful time and come home with a pocket full of stories to entertain us for months to come."

Mother lifted an eyebrow, and if Charis was interpreting it correctly, it was that she expected Charis to come back with a fiancé rather than entertaining stories.

She looked at both of them. "I will not let you down."

One way or the other, she would pull this family out of the poverty they were sliding into.

CHAPTER 2

WHERE LADY HARTLEY'S TRUE PLAN IS
REVEALED AND MISS EASTWOOD IS SHOOK

Charis rode backward in the Hartley traveling carriage. The pale green interior cloth was of the finest merino, with silk lace trim and tufted buttons that matched to perfection. It was a far cry from the creaky gig Father used to drive, that found every pothole on any road. Taking in the bare-leafed trees and fog settling on the distant hills, she shivered. The hot brick at her feet was not enough to counter the chill from the glass. They would be lucky if it didn't snow on their journey.

"My dear, stop looking at the boring countryside and look at these instead." Lady Hartley pulled a periodical from a pile she had next to her and opened it at her bookmark. "We could have it all planned by the time we reach London."

The next few hours flew by. So many magazines, brimful of ideas. Charis frowned. Usually, all she needed was one source of inspiration to build her design around. Like a painting or a carpet. Not a hundred ideas thrown at her like darts to a board with the expectation she could make a masterpiece of it.

Charis countered by showing Lady Hartley passages and images from her last birthday present, a copy of *Household Furni-*

ture and Interior Decoration by Thomas Hope. The bible for all her dreams and always an excellent source of inspiration.

"What a lovely book. So elegant. Goodness, which direction do we go in? Classic Greek, Roman, Egyptian or a mix of all three? I barely know."

Charis rubbed her temples. The combination of constantly looking up and down while traveling was not conducive to one's well-being. The recent rain had made the road muddy, and the wheels made a squelching noise beneath them. "I think I will need to see the house to know which of these directions we should take. I appreciate you saving all the pictures, though. It will make inspiration so much easier."

Lady Hartley flicked a few more pages and then closed the copy of *The Mirror of Fashion* she was looking at. "This is my eternal problem. I see so many ideas and then get confused."

Charis smiled. She would never have guessed. "I will make sense of it all, never fear."

"At least I have limitless funds, my dear. That should make it easier." She looked out the window, her brow creased, the feather on her burgundy velvet turban jolting with the bumpy road. "Goodness, what a dire road. So rutted. We must stop reading now before we feel quite ill."

Charis exhaled. *Thank goodness.* She didn't want to cast up her accounts in such illustrious company. She peered at the small clock that swung from a ribbon. Almost three. Less than an hour of travel left. If she kept her gaze firmly on the horizon, she might just make it.

The miles rushed by, and they soon reached London, putting an end to all talk of decoration. The horses slowed, giving Lady Hartley the opportunity to point out fascinating tidbits of the places they passed. "This is St. James Street. The gentlemen think it belongs to them. There's a coffeehouse or club every five yards. And there is Hoby, the bootmaker. I always expect to see

Ashcroft coming out of there. He has more Hessians than a Hussar."

She pointed out Boodles and White's. The meandering of gentlemen on the street seemed to bear out her observation. "But never fear. There is much for us here, too. The best undergarments can be found here. I always replenish my stock when I am in town."

Everybody looked elegant and genteel. This was no place for the girl who cleaned out the chicken coop and kept a basket of darning to bring in a few extra coins. She was in a different world now, and the only familiar face was someone who fit into this world to perfection and couldn't possibly understand this feeling of displacement.

The closer they came to their destination of Grosvenor Square, the more impressive and palatial the residences became. Charis alternated between clutching her skirts and being fascinated by the packed street. She had never seen so many shops as there were on St. James Street. Her hands trembled. Was it the cold? Or was the enormity of this visit and her task finally hitting her? She clenched her jaw.

Lady Hartley looked at her, concern in her eyes. "There, my dear. This is supposed to be diverting for you after looking after your father, not distressing. Think of it as visiting me in Hartley Green. No different. You will be fine."

Considering the Eastwoods only ever visited Lady Hartley for her yearly grand ball—which made Charis fretful for days in advance—this comment missed its mark. "I only hope to be of help to you."

Lady Hartley reached out and patted Charis on the knee with a kind smile. "Actually, there is something else you could help me with. It will be a great favor, but it might be amusing for you, too."

"Oh?" Did Lady Hartley need a companion? It seemed unlikely given her vivacious personality. But what else could it be?

"It's Ashcroft."

Ashcroft and a favor? This made no sense. Especially not if she kept Mother's warning in mind. It would make more sense for her to keep well out of his lordship's way.

Lady Hartley searched Charis's face, as though she might find the answer to her problem there. "This is very delicate, and I rely on your discretion, but I *must* make a good match for him. Someone elegant and sophisticated who will be a magnificent political hostess." She paused, as though choosing her words carefully. "But let's just say my son is shy. I've watched him at balls. He dances once, and then he's into the anteroom to talk politics with the most boring men imaginable. He will never catch the wife he needs if he continues on in this fashion. He is almost thirty, it is high time he took this responsibility seriously."

All true. "But how can I help?" She knew Lady Hartley wasn't suggesting *she* was that lady. Not for a moment.

"You're a lively girl. You have no problem conversing with anyone, at any level. Some might call it impertinence." Her kind smile belied the insult. "But I have always liked it. And I trust you to spend time with him without setting your cap at him."

"I have managed not to thus far," Charis replied dryly.

"There, you see? I want you to liven him up. He used to be so witty as a youth, but now he works around the clock and grows more somber each time I see him. I would like you to rekindle his joie de vivre. Flirt with him a little. Can you?"

The thought of purposely doing such a thing was nerve-racking. She pushed her hands into her muff, clutching them together. "I don't know. Why would he want to spend time with me? We have nothing in common."

This was a complication she had not sought. Perhaps if she'd known Lady Hartley's plan, she would have fought to stay home instead of being excited to come.

"Leave that to me."

Something awfully like nerves fluttered inside. "Can you not find someone else?"

Lady Hartley waved that thought away. "He knows I would never match him with the Eastwoods. Your family has no political connections. That's what makes you perfect."

How lovely to be so ineligible that Lady Hartley trusted implicitly her son would never contemplate marriage with her.

"*Must* I flirt? I don't want him to think I am setting my cap at him when nothing could be further from the truth."

She shrugged. "Bah, flirting is nothing more than a pastime for the nobility. He'll think nothing of it. No harm will be done."

No harm done, indeed. Not when the only person making a fool of herself was Charis. She wouldn't refuse to do it, but it felt wrong to flirt with a serious man without meaning it.

It proved one thing, though: Lady Hartley would ask anyone anything if she thought it would help her son. And wasn't afraid to use Charis to do it. Perhaps that soft ladylike exterior hid a spine of steel. They rode on in silence, Lady Hartley sure she had received Charis's full compliance and Charis feverishly thinking of increasingly crazy ways she could extricate herself.

They turned left onto Grosvenor Street, the greenery of the park ahead of them. She would most definitely walk there each day, maid or no maid. "I've read this is the largest square in London."

Lady Hartley smiled as though vaguely surprised. "Is it? I suppose it is."

It certainly seemed like it, with a circular leafy park in the middle, and the most beautiful houses built around it.

The horses slowed and glided to a halt in front of a townhouse. It was three stories high and had a brown brick facade. The front door was framed by tall Corinthian columns and painted glossy black.

This was to be home for a while.

How could she belong here? She would need months of

preparation to even try. But there was no way to prepare. She was to be thrown in. Her stomach was a jumble of nerves, her mind a rush of excitement. It was very confusing.

But you know who you are, and that's all you need.

She was the daughter of Charles Eastwood, captain of the Queen's Dragoon Guards, English hero, and the man who led the attack against the French in the Battle of Beaumont in 1794.

That was the level of bravery in her blood. She had nothing to fear here.

The area in front of the townhouse was spotlessly clean, the usual road debris and dust gone, as if the house had forced it away through sheer grandeur. The door opened, and a tall, austere-looking man dressed in livery, stepped through it. He came down the steps, his long legs looking almost spider-like, put two fingers in his mouth, and gave a curt whistle. Four footmen appeared and worked to unstrap their luggage.

In all the mayhem, it could have been easy to miss Lord Ashcroft saunter down the stairs. But then, towering well over six feet, he was hard to miss.

He opened the door of the carriage, thrusting his hand inside to help his mother out. "How lovely of you to visit. I received your letter only yesterday, so there was no time to reply and let you know the house has no need for improvements."

His voice was deep, so deep it sent a thrill through her. How had she not noticed before? Probably because he'd barely strung three words together in her company, much less whole sentences.

Well, now she was noticing. Not that she was supposed to.

Lady Hartley took his hand and stepped out of the carriage, balancing carefully on the wooden block placed at the curb. "Pish posh. You may or may not remember this is *my* home. Your father and I are happy for you to live here, of course, but it is ours to repair. I come here every year, and every year it has been looking sadder. I fully intend to do something about it."

"And Father has stayed behind?" Lord Ashcroft looked over

his mother's shoulder, and his eyes widened when he saw Charis in the carriage. "But you have brought a companion. Miss Eastwood, a pleasure." His frown, quickly covered, suggested he was anything but happy to see her. Perhaps he imagined having her in the house would take more of his time than he wanted to give.

But he remembered her name. That was surprising, if Lady Hartley hadn't mentioned Charis accompanying her.

He reached into the carriage again, this time to help her out. His bare hand was warm, and his grip was strong. Heat flowed through her glove and up her arm. Charis exhaled. What a strange thing. Their eyes met briefly and his flared as if in surprise.

He deposited her on the curb and then let her go. She immediately clasped her hands together as if to hoard the heat that had flowed from him.

Lady Hartley led the way into the townhouse. Charis followed her and behind both of them, Lord Ashcroft trailed.

"At least you have missed the rains. You would not have been going anywhere or doing anything for so much of January. It's been ice and rain and floods all month. The bridge at Eton was swept away entirely."

His voice was completely delicious. While thinking on it, she stumbled, and immediately felt his hand at her elbow, steadying her. "There now, Miss Eastwood."

The modest exterior was deceptive, for as soon as she walked through the front door, Charis's mouth opened and refused to close. It was magnificent. She swallowed the lump in her throat. "When was this house built?"

Lady Hartley waved her hand. "Oh, I don't know, the 1750s?"

Lord Ashcroft came to her side. "It was 1726, to be precise," he said flatly.

She did not know if this was the general style of houses built in 1726, but to her, it looked like something the Prince of Wales would live in, or at least the Duke of York.

There were ornate embellishments everywhere, from friezes on the walls to twin staircases sweeping up either side of the entry hall, with swirling wrought iron banisters. They drew your eye to a ceiling many stories up, painted a blue sky with clouds and cherubs that looked like the work of an Italian master.

And this was only the entry hall.

The rest of the house was likely to blind her with its grandeur and beauty.

"As you can see, the house is in lovely condition. I'm not sure why you are fixing something perfect in every way." He said the last words slowly, one at a time, to make his point.

Lady Hartley shook her head emphatically. "Where you see perfection, I see vulgarity. These days we like to see a more restrained palette, more beauty and less florid ornament. And the carpets are shabby throughout. That I know for certain."

He leaned an arm on the balustrade, the casual pose at odds with the spark in his eyes. "I disagree entirely. Certainly, it is of last century—"

"Early last century." She pouted. "You speak as though it were the blink of an eye. Everything is so outmoded."

He raised an eyebrow. "They built everything here to stand for a hundred years or more. Do we discard things that are perfectly good to pander to our vanity?" He spoke calmly, but there was a flash in his eye that made Charis take an involuntary step back.

It was silly to be shocked by the way he argued with his mother as though she were an equal and not a gentlewoman to be cosseted. Father often treated Mother like a fragile waif, as though she didn't carry water from the well every day.

But Lady Hartley seemed used to it. She took a step forward, holding out her hands, waiting for her son to take them. "Our vanity! You go too far, Ashcroft. I merely wish my surroundings not to jar my sensibilities." Lady Hartley smiled as he took her hands, seemingly unable to resist her entreaty. It felt manipulative somehow. But perhaps she was reading too much into it. Or perhaps that was how Lady Hartley always countered his arguments. "I can see you have most decided views, and I will get too angry if I have to listen to them. Tomorrow, you will take Miss Eastwood on a tour of the house, outlining what you love about it and the things you would like kept." She turned to Charis. "Will you take notes, my dear? I would hate it if we inadvertently pulled out a fireplace that Ashcroft holds dear to his heart. I must admit, Son, you surprise me with your devotion to this old pile."

He looked from his mother to Charis and back again, possibly trying to establish why she was involved. Then he shrugged. "It is more a devotion to my comfort and a sincere wish not to be disturbed."

Lady Hartley smiled mischievously and pinched his cheek. "I assure you, we intend to be *very* disturbing during our stay here."

He tipped his head back and looked at the ceiling. "That's what I am afraid of. How long will this take?"

Oh dear. They really *were* uninvited guests. Lady Hartley had not cleared their stay with her son at all. Did she have to? It felt like, yes, she did.

"Two months, until the Season opens. But Charis will only be here one, I think. Did I not tell you?"

"You may have overlooked that pertinent piece of information," he said with a slight shake of his head.

She cocked an eyebrow. "I'm not sure why it would bother you. You spend half your life in the Commons and the other half in your club. We will stay out of your way, I assure you. And if we are not out of your way, we promise to be entertaining. You work too hard."

"Nothing tends to happen if I don't."

He nodded, as though by doing so, the conversation was at an end. "Your usual chambers are ready, and you can show Miss Eastwood to the green chamber. It will need to be aired, but

Lambley will have someone come to lay a fire and bring her a tea tray. You must both be tired after your journey."

With a bow, he strode across the hall and opened a door, through which Charis could see a bank of filled bookcases. The door closed with a resolute click.

How on earth was she supposed to flirt with *that*?

CHAPTER 3

WHERE MISS EASTWOOD RISKS HER
REPUTATION TO DRINK CHAMPAGNE

A footman led Charis upstairs to her bedchamber, which was indeed ... green.

Deep-green curtains, deep-green festoons, deep-green bed covers under a deep-green canopy. The walls were, of course, deep-green-patterned paper that made her eyes water.

In fact, it was such a forest, there was every chance she would wake up in the morning with roots herself.

Green chamber indeed.

At least it had the happy effect of chasing away the last of her nerves. The entry hall, with its classic Italian lines and sheer grandeur, had struck fear into her heart that she would have nothing to help Lady Hartley with.

But this room gave her hope. She sat on the side of the bed and smiled.

A maid arrived, dressed in a blue-striped dress and a large white apron. Her brown hair frizzed from the sides of her white cap, and the blush on her cheeks deepened when she dipped her curtsy. "I'm Mary. Mrs. Douglas says I am to help you while you visit. I am very good at braiding hair." The breathless quality of this pronouncement suggested Mary was very excited about her new role.

"I am pleased to meet you, Mary. I'm sure you'll find me quite self-sufficient, but I am grateful for any help you have time to offer." She took a seat at the desk while Mary unpacked her belongings into the wardrobe. Thankfully, she was brisk about it and didn't look closely at the worn garments. That would have been mortifying. Charis could imagine the talk below stairs. *Miss Eastwood's dress is worn right through!*

She had two good dresses that would pass muster. A white muslin walking dress with contrasting pink pelisse, and an evening dress in blue silk that had been worn to countless assemblies. However, the rest of them, she would have been happy to leave back in Kent.

But one must have *something* to wear, so along they came.

With any luck, Lady Hartley would leave Charis to paint and design at home and forget all about her silly plan to draw Lord Ashcroft into fun.

Dinner came on a tray. Then Lady Hartley poked her head around the door. "I am out to dinner with friends, but thought you would prefer a quiet tray after our trip. Rest up, my dear. Tomorrow will be a big day."

Even though Charis had just finished thinking she didn't want to be out for the evening, a stab of dismay made her blink. Perhaps she was not to be taken out? Was she a guest, companion, or more like a servant? Best not to have any expectations until it became clear.

And perhaps best also to make plans for herself. Mama had said she could travel out alone with a maid or footman.

"Spending the evening with my book and a cozy blanket suits me perfectly."

"Good girl." She put her hand on the knob, about to leave, but turned back. "Ashcroft has agreed to show you around the house tomorrow at eleven, so make sure you have your wits about you so he doesn't bamboozle you. He has a way of making one agree with his every pronouncement. It's almost like magic. Breakfast is anywhere from nine onward in the garden room."

Any slight from being left out of the evening's entertainment was trumped by the relief of not having to get ready for them, and the delicious dinner tray. It was loaded with chicken consommé, a dinner roll, roast beef with boiled potatoes, and a small crystal bowl of trifle. To finish, there was a tiny glass of port, something she had never tried before. It was sweet and rich, and she sat back in the chair, slightly dizzy, letting its warmth spread through her.

She would spend the rest of the night with her book by the light of a six-stem candelabra that would have made her mother faint with the luxury of it. The candles were smooth and burned with the faint smell of beeswax.

Had she meant what she said to Lady Hartley? Was she happier with a cozy blanket and a book? Did London intimidate her? She shook her head. This kind of thinking would not help. She could only be true to herself. The city could take her or leave her, and that included the stern Lord Ashcroft.

What was he doing now?

As though to answer her question, a carriage arrived at the front of the house. She went to the window, pulling back the drape. The carriage had the Hartley crest on the side of it. Ashcroft alighted the steps of the house and was just about to enter the carriage when he turned and looked up, spying her in the window. His eyes flared in recognition, and instinct told her to let the drapes drop. Instead, she lifted a hand and waved.

He tipped his cane to the brim of his hat, a small smile playing across his mouth in the lamplight. Then he called Lambley to his side, his greatcoat swirling around in the wind. She glimpsed a snow-white cravat and a dark evening coat.

He said a few words to the butler, who nodded in response.

Lambley took his long legs up the steps, and within the space of a minute, there was a knock at her door. She opened it to see Mary drop a curtsy. "Miss, his lordship has asked that I ready you to accompany him to the theater this evening."

Her hand flew to her chest. "I couldn't possibly! I'm dressed for bed."

She no sooner said it than images of the liveliness of the theater and seeing a play made her think twice. Was she here to read books or to experience things?

Mary pushed her way into the room. "You'll be fine, miss. You have that lovely blue silk. I'll fetch one of my lady's shawls from her maid, and you'll look fine as a sixpence."

Charis pulled the curtain back again, to see the footmen were walking the horses down Grosvenor Square waiting for her. "Best we hurry."

Going alone to the theater with an unmarried man seemed irregular. A young lady should be chaperoned; even *she* knew that much.

Charis pulled on her stockings and divested herself of her nightgown while Mary ran to find Lady Hartley's maid and a suitable shawl. In what had to be the fastest change in the history of ladies' toilette, Charis was handed into the carriage and sat opposite Lord Ashcroft within ten minutes.

Only the soft carriage lanterns illuminated the space, and it was impossible to read his expression. "Thank you for thinking of me," she said.

"You should not be left alone in the house on your first night. I assumed Mother had taken you out with her."

"I didn't mind. Although I would much prefer the theater than a private dinner where I don't know anyone."

He nodded, and that was the end of their conversation for a few slow blocks of Brook Street.

But the thought of ruining her London stay by not following the rules plagued her. "Are you sure I am able to venture out without a chaperone? I may not be a debutante, but I am still an unmarried lady."

"We shall say you are my cousin, shall we? I'm sure that's what Mother said you were as good as at some stage. I am permitted to take a cousin out."

She frowned. *But I am not a cousin.* Something stopped her from saying it out loud. Not wanting to go back to the house, and more importantly, wanting to go to the theater with him and enjoy the evening.

Tomorrow would be early enough to find out if she'd crossed one of society's many invisible lines. Lady Hartley would surely tell her.

"Very well, cousin. What are we seeing tonight?"

"*Man and Wife.* The first production was on January fourth, but I have not seen it yet. Sheridan assures me it is most entertaining."

"You don't sound convinced."

"I hear it is one of those plays where nobody wants to marry who they are meant to marry and they spend the entire time throwing impediments in each other's way," he drawled.

"It sounds amusing."

"It sounds silly, and I retain the right to fall asleep if I so desire."

"If you fall asleep, I shall poke you with my fan." She didn't have a fan in her reticule, but he did not need to know that. She sat a little straighter. "Cousins are allowed all sorts of liberties, you know."

"I'm sure the combined theatrical effort of Mrs. Jordan and Mrs. Siddons will keep you so occupied you won't even hear my snoring." He looked out the window as the carriage slowed. "Ah, we're here. You won't be unchaperoned for long."

Before she could ask him what he'd meant, the door was flung open, and two gentlemen and a lady entered. Charis squeezed herself into the corner.

"What took you so long? We've been loitering in the hall for an age." A gentleman with silver-streaked hair and dark intelligent eyes settled himself in. He looked to be in his late fiftieth decade, Father's age.

He was followed by a man a little younger, with light-brown hair and heavy eyebrows. His eyes were a very light blue that was arresting even in the shadowed carriage. "Good evening, Ashcroft," he said and then spied Charis in the corner. He nodded and looked to Ashcroft for an introduction.

Lord Ashcroft waited for everyone to be seated and the door shut. He turned to the lady guest. "Lady Blakely, may I introduce Miss Eastwood to you?"

She nodded. "Pleased to make your acquaintance."

Ashcroft then turned to the two men. "And Miss Eastwood, may I present Mr. Sheridan, owner of the Theater Royal we are about to visit, and a mutual family friend, the Comte de Souza."

The Comte shrugged his shoulders. "I am Comte of nothing these days, my good friend. Monsieur Trellier, will do perfectly." He nodded to Charis. "A pleasure to have another lovely lady accompanying us this evening." He searched her face, his expression turning wistful. "You remind me of someone I knew many years ago in Paris."

"I do hope that's a good thing," Charis said, then realized this poor lady may have lost her life in the revolution, and clamped her mouth shut.

"Miss Eastwood is something of a cousin from Hartley Green. She is a guest of my mother's for a few weeks."

Lady Blakely clapped her hands. "Is she? How very diverting for you. Nobody knows London's delights like our dear Lady Hartley."

"I am pleased to meet you. Will we all be in the same box tonight?" She spied an opera monocle in Monsieur Trellier's hand. "I may have to borrow that from you on occasion."

"You can see everything with it. Which is just as well because the theater is gargantuan." The Monsieur had perfectly accented English, but like so many of the tens of thousands of emigres, he had likely lived in London for years. They came from France, often with just the clothes on their backs, looking for an escape from the violence and horror of the revolution.

"Are you impugning my theater?" Sheridan pretended outrage.

Trellier held up his hand in mock horror. "No, no. It is elegant, beautiful, and a true reflection of your personal glory."

Mr. Sheridan nodded approvingly. "As it should be with the amount of blunt I've poured into it."

Trellier shrugged one shoulder, more eloquently Gallic than any accent. "Well, you know what they say about a fool and his money ..."

Ashcroft looked at Charis and gave her a wry smile Mr. Sheridan did not notice, like they were sharing a joke. "You should see them when my father is here too. It's a riot."

"We only bring Ashcroft along to outrage him," Sheridan said. "He needs our good influence."

"Or he'll spend his entire life doing good deeds and going to bed early," Trellier added.

Charis laughed. "I thoroughly concur. Look at him. He's in the prime of his life! Much too young to be so serious. He needs more mischief and less work."

Ashcroft's eyes widened. Was it because she'd said he was in the prime of his life, or that he was too serious? His gaze stayed on her, heating her, even as Monsieur Trellier continued.

"Then, my dear girl, it will be up to you when we are not around. You do have a certain look about you. Made for mischief, if I'm not mistaken."

Lady Blakely rapped him on the knuckles with her fan. "All ladies are made for mischief, mon chéri, as you well know."

"Don't give her any ideas, Monsieur Trellier. I am adequate the way I am." Ashcroft looked from Charis to each of his friends and raised an eyebrow, which only made them laugh harder.

She hadn't had such fun in an age, and it was only her first night.

The rest of the evening roared along on a wave of friendly banter. They argued about which actor was best, whether the play was any good, and if Mrs. Jordan could have been given a bigger part.

Charis drank a glass of Champagne. The bubbles and tartness made her eyes water, but it also made everything funnier, especially Lord Ashcroft's stern face when he saw her accept her second glass. "Oh, no, Lord Ashcroft, you cannot bring me out and then deny me fun."

"I cannot bring you home foxed is what I cannot do," he replied grimly.

She laughed again and he frowned.

Charis scanned around the huge theater with Monsieur Trellier's monocle. She stopped at a lady in the box across from them wearing a lavender dress draped with pearls. When the lady came into focus, she was staring directly at Charis. Her gaze was narrowed and her mouth pursed.

Charis gasped. "Do not look now, but the lady in the box directly opposite is glaring at us."

She gave the monocle back to Monsieur Trellier, who immediately lifted it to his eye. He barked out a laugh. "Don't worry. She spends her entire existence glaring at me. It is her only pastime."

Leaning into Ashcroft, she whispered in his ear. "Who is she? Why does she stare at us so?"

He patted her on the leg, a friendly gesture that had her pulse leaping and her nerves skittering. But maybe it was the Champagne. "That is my mother's friend, Lady Astley. Fear not, she is glaring at me, not you. News of my riotous box at the theater will be taken to Mother next time they meet."

It was selfish to hope she wouldn't get into trouble too. But she did hope she wouldn't.

As though reading her thoughts, Ashcroft turned to her. "Don't worry, she doesn't know who you are, so she can't carry tales back."

"Oh good. I would hate to be in trouble before I even began."

"A very good girl like you, Miss Eastwood? I hardly think so. I, on the other hand." He spread his hands in apology.

Going to the theater, making the gossips report back to his mother, keeping the company of quick-witted people. He wasn't quite the somber man she'd thought he was.

CHAPTER 4

IN WHICH CHAMPAGNE IS NOT SO MUCH FUN THE NEXT DAY

The following morning Charis wound her way down two flights of stairs, running her hand along the smooth mahogany banister and inspecting the patterns on the Turkish carpet. It had threadbare patches on each step, but that only added to its charm.

Last night's fun had left her head in a delicate state. After the performance, they had visited The Piazza coffeehouse and sat at a small table, listening to Sheridan talk about the theater he loved so much into the wee hours of the morning. She went to bed only an hour before the time she normally rose in Hartley Green. *London, what a place!*

A footman led her to the garden room, which was at the back of the townhouse. It had two enormous arched windows looking out onto a small courtyard with a fountain. Rose bushes lined the garden, but as it was late January, they were bare sticks, and the grass was icy.

But if you threw the doors open in summer, surely it would feel like the room was part of the garden itself. Which made it even more of a sin that it was papered in a blue and gold fleur-de-lis pattern.

Since it was half past nine, Charis thought she might be the only one at breakfast. However, Lord Ashcroft sat at the oval table, his newspapers spread before him. He had a pair of spectacles perched on the end of his nose. His eyesight was bad. *How endearing.* A small chink in an otherwise solid armor.

He looked up and stood. "Good morning, Miss Eastwood." He did not seem any the worse for wear from all the Champagne *he'd* imbibed. It was grossly unfair.

She curtsied. "Good morning, Lord Ashcroft." And now she would have to tell Mama that she was wrong. He did not grunt at the breakfast table. It was almost disappointing.

He waited, still standing, while she helped herself to simple bread and jam, despite the pastries, meats, and eggs set out before her.

She knew better than to ask him to be seated. He would only raise one sardonic eyebrow and continue to wait, so she made her way to the table. The footman pushed her chair in. "Tell me, what is the news of the day?"

There was no way *not* to answer, and it would stop him asking delicate questions about her bloodshot eyes.

She leaned in and noticed he was reading the *Political Register*, a publication bound to put her back to sleep, even though she had only just woken.

He grimaced as though in pain. "I'm sure you would find the contents of this newspaper less than enthralling."

Perhaps he just didn't want to talk to her.

Well, too bad for him because she liked the sound of his voice. "Then I suggest you tell me the contents entertainingly." She took a bite of crusty bread with fresh-churned butter. "Oh my, how delicious."

He steepled his hands in front of him and nodded slowly. "Very well."

He sat fully back in his chair, with a sparkle of mischief in his eyes, suggesting she'd just invited a particularly bad punishment.

"The commander-in-chief of our armed forces has apparently been using a female acquaintance of the intimate variety, a certain Mrs. Clarke, to sell commissions in the army." He said the words lightly, but she could feel the intensity radiating off him like the tension in the air before a thunderstorm. "Amusing, no?"

Charis stilled her chewing, gathering her thoughts. She swallowed. "But isn't that the Duke of York?" If he truly meant the Duke of York, then the news was less entertaining and more horrifying. If high-ranking commissions in the army could be sold to the highest bidder, it would undermine the entire king's army. "Please tell me this is something scurrilous made up by his enemies."

He took a deep breath, as if the issue already weighed on him. "That is what the Commons must discover. We are trying to figure out the best course of action. I think the only solution is to appoint a committee to enquire into his conduct."

"Are you willing to be part of this committee?" Perhaps this was why their visit was ill-timed.

He nodded. "It will be a dog's breakfast from start to finish."

"Which is being somewhat disparaging to the poor dog's breakfast."

He smiled, and she felt a stab of triumph. And, if she was honest, an equally strong stab of fascination. When he smiled, dimples appeared at the sides of his mouth. Combined with the thick lock of dark hair falling across his forehead and those spectacles, he looked ...

Her next thought caused a sharp intake of breath.

Incredibly handsome.

Somehow all his intensity, the poetic hair hitting his shoulders, the too-big nose, and the too-wide mouth were just right with his high cheekbones. There was also a sprinkle of freckles across his nose like a small reminder this enormous man had once been a boy. Perhaps a part of him still was.

He did not go back to reading his newspaper, but let his head rest on the back of the blue chair, which matched the blue curtains and the blue wall.

So much blue.

However, he blended right into it, with his dark navy coat and crisp white cravat. She should stop staring at him like he was an exhibit at a gallery. It was because she had never been in such close quarters with a man like him. Young, strong, potent. It was hard not to stare at the way his eyebrows were like arrows, his jaw like something hewn from stone. The only soft thing about him was his eyes. They were dark honey in the morning light.

She waved a hand, hoping he hadn't noticed her prolonged inspection. "Please continue to read. Pray, don't let me interrupt you."

He must've heard the sincerity in her voice, for he continued, although now he read parts of interest out loud. Some of it went right over her head—not being involved in matters of parliament, as he was.

However, there was something heartening about the fact he thought she could appreciate it. She let his voice wash over her as she took bites of bread.

Occasionally, there was a slight tremor in his voice, a surfeit of emotion in an otherwise flat reading. It must be a thing of wonder to hear him on the house floor. His voice would boom throughout and probably wake up a half-dozen members from their daily nap. The thought made her smile.

"What did you make your maiden speech on?" Speeches in parliament were known to go for four or five hours, so what subject enthralled him that much?

His gaze snapped to hers in surprise. "I thought you would know, having a veteran in the family."

"Oh, yes, of course I know. Father could speak of nothing else for weeks. He was so proud of you. The welfare of soldiers, was it not?"

He nodded with a smile. "Precisely. For all the good it did them."

"Ah, now, change only comes in small increments. But if they aren't talking about it, then it will never happen at all."

He stilled, his knife raised over his plate, blinking at the bacon there, then up at her. "Precisely. One must start somewhere."

She finished her breakfast and folded her napkin, placing it on her plate and drinking the last of her chocolate.

He noticed and folded the newspaper. "Come. I believe it is time for me to give you the grand tour. Let us start with the dining room, which is on your left as you came in the front door yesterday, but which you may have missed. I will lead the way." He looked over his shoulder, expecting her to follow. "You will see nothing needs to be changed."

His curt opinion put a stop on the silly idea he was the most attractive man she had ever met. *He only had to open his mouth. Remember?*

"I have brought my notebook." For she was sure he would have a *lot* to say. "I am sure there is *much* to be done."

Theo Wren, Earl of Ashcroft, could not fathom why Miss Eastwood, daughter of a retired army captain from Hartley Green, was suddenly in charge of the refurbishment of his townhouse.

Which needed no refurbishment.

What was Mother's game?

Instead of following him to the door as he'd requested, she wandered to the windows, looking out over the frosted court-yard. "How long has your family owned this house?"

He turned to her, admiring the way a small cluster of curls framed her face. Her hair was a deep gold that could look blonde or brown, depending on what light was available. This morning, with the winter light streaming through the windows, it was the color of the eighteen-year-old oaken whisky he kept in the library.

But she was waiting for an answer. He blinked a few times, trying to remember the question. Ah, right, how long had they owned the house? "Nobody on Grosvenor Square owns their house. We lease. My grandfather extended it for eighty more years."

She trailed a hand along the flocked wall papering. She liked to touch things. Yesterday she had run her hand over the marble statue in the hall. "It seems a strange thing to put so much effort into a grand home and yet not actually own the building. You would not think of it in a country estate."

He shrugged. "The Grosvenor family has owned this area since the sixteen hundreds. I can understand them not wanting to sell it outright."

"Oh, of course. I am not used to London ways." Her smile was self-deprecating, but there was a twinkle of mischief in it.

Which led him to his next question. "I am about to be impertinent and likely bordering on rude."

She stopped, eyes narrowed. "Then perhaps you should reconsider whatever it is you are about to say."

Should he? As he thought about it, he noticed she had long curling eyelashes fringing her light-blue eyes. He liked her eyes. They were a fine shade of aquamarine with a golden halo around the iris. They sparkled when she smiled. He closed his eyes briefly and huffed. He had obviously been in dry political circles for too long to notice such things.

"No. I shall forge ahead because I want the answer. In my work, badgering is the only way you get the answers you need."

"Badger away then, your impertinent-and-likely-bordering-on-rude lordship."

A smile escaped him before he'd noticed or given it permission.

A sharp mind, too. She became more interesting again. Then again, ladies with sharp minds found him excruciatingly boring. She would get there, too, eventually.

"I was merely wondering why you, in particular, were chosen to assist my mother in her improvements. Do you have some skill in this area?"

She frowned and stopped short, turning to him. "Now, if I say I have skill, you will find me boastful. If I say I don't, you will think me sorely qualified. I can't win, so I shan't answer. You will just have to find out for yourself."

Then, happy with her response, she continued on with a lightness to her step that suggested his question had not bothered her at all.

She was tall. Not so tall he couldn't see the elaborate braids atop her head, but most ladies tended not to reach his shoulders. If they danced, he would be able to look into her eyes easily.

He led her toward the front of the house until they reached the entry hall, then stopped. "You have seen the entrance hall." He looked up at the amazing mural on the ceiling and the walls with their classic plaster moldings. "I can't imagine it needs changing."

She nodded. "I concur. It cannot be improved upon. Yesterday, it took my breath away. It's beautiful."

He swung around, one eyebrow raised. "Ha! All may not be lost."

She looked down from the ceiling. "The mural looks Italian, but the plasterwork in this hall has a Greek influence I cannot help but admire. The two work well together. Perhaps a fresh coat of paint, and some restoration work on the marble tiles, but that is all."

He didn't want a house that looked like a jumble of different time periods. He *liked* to be comfortable. His big frame *needed* to be comfortable. Therefore, an honest, forthright conversation must be had. Miss Eastwood needed to know who was in charge. Him.

"Just so we're clear. I want none of this silly mixing of Egyptian, Greek, and Roman aesthetics."

She held up her hand as if to disagree, but he had to finish. "Please, let me say my piece. I don't want to live in the British Museum. And no gilt, this is not a palace." He took a breath. "No spindly chairs one cannot sit in, or if one does, it creaks like an old floorboard. No furniture strewn across the room. Chairs belong against a wall, as the good Lord intended. No ripping things out without my approval, no tradespeople hammering when I am trying to think. No—"

"So, essentially leave it as it is?" She looked like she wanted to roll her eyes, but there was a tilt to her mouth that was almost a smile.

"You may paint and order new drapes."

"Oh, thank you! And in which rooms am I permitted to do this?" Her voice had taken on an arch quality, as though she were teasing him. But it was impossible to be sure.

He crossed his arms over his chest. "All of them. As it pleases you. See? I can be magnanimous."

"You are the *soul* of generosity." She dipped a curtsy, looking up at him with an expression full of mischief.

In doing so, she took him back two years, to a summer assembly in rooms above The George Hotel.

He had danced with her. When it was finished, she'd dipped down into a curtsy and then looked up at him the same way. Amused and yet vexed. He was as confused about it then as he was now. But he'd forgotten all about it until this moment.

"Do you remember dancing with me at The George about two years ago?"

Her eyes widened. "Yes," she said, slowly, as though not really wanting to enter the conversation.

"You gave me the same look back then. What did it mean?"

"Truth or polite answer?"

"I suppose the two are mutually exclusive?" She laughed, a husky thing that made him blink as it settled over him like a warm rug.

"Truth, then," he added.

She nodded. "Very well. You danced with me, but spent the entire time a hundred miles away. I tried to speak to you twice, and twice you grunted like I'd poked you in the side. Then, when it was over, you told me it had been a pleasure. So, you got *that* look."

He took a deep breath. "Hmmm. I probably deserved a good box around the ears." She deserved better.

She nodded sagely. "It was tempting, but ladies must not make a scene." Her mouth twitched as though she longed to smile.

"I feel you would now, given the chance. I find I must agree with Monsieur Trellier. You are merely biding your time before you unleash ladylike mayhem."

She tilted her head to the side. "Do we all not want a little mayhem in our lives? I'm not a mushroom sitting under a tree, waiting for someone to pick me."

"No, indeed. Or if you were, you would give the innocent picker bad dreams and a sore stomach for days." He smiled, liking the thought of it despite himself. Perhaps life had been too boring of late? Reading for parliament, talking about bills and the endless gossip besetting the place. Perhaps some diversion would be welcome.

Even if it did come at a bad time. The scandal with the Duke of York was building to be the greatest the country had ever seen. If the parliament investigated in a public forum, as he thought they should, it would be a bloodbath.

And he'd be right in the middle of it.

She wandered into the dining room, leaving him to trail behind. Her breath hitched. "Oh my."

What did that mean? Did she love it or hate it? He stood in the doorway and looked around the riot of crimson and gold with fresh eyes. Hated for certain. "I rarely use this room. It is called the formal dining room, and I have had no formal occasions. I use the garden room, even for dinner." He rubbed his jaw, thinking. "Although now you are both here, we will probably use this room often. It has not changed since my childhood."

"Oh, please, no. I couldn't possibly *eat here*." She took in the glory of the gilt candelabra mounted on either side of the gilded fireplace.

He was immediately defensive. "It's not *that* bad."

She laughed as though he'd told a joke, then sobered when he didn't join in with her. "Surely you jest? How could I take a bite? This room would surely slap me for my impertinence."

It could be true. "You make it sound like a very opinionated room."

"It's not just opinionated. It's vainglorious." She turned to him, eyes narrowed. "I thought you didn't like gilt?"

"I don't. But you're right. Perhaps new drapes are not enough to save it," he said. It was more of an admission than he had any intention of making.

"Left to me, I would strip it clean, although the dining setting is lovely. I adore the backs of the chairs. They look like they have come straight from the Orient."

He trailed behind her. "Don't even think about concocting a Chinese room here. I won't have the house looking like a souvenir of someone's Grand Tour."

She turned to him, her eyes glowing. "Elements in a room should be in sympathy with each other." Her words were rushed in her enthusiasm. "The dining setting is elegant and light. It needs wall hangings to complement it. Never fear, it will be pretty."

Never fear, she said. Famous last words if ever he'd heard them. He didn't need her experimenting on the house he had to live in, and spending a lot of money to do it.

"Ignore me at your peril, Miss Eastwood." He tried to imbue his voice with the menace he normally shot at his parliamentary opponents.

It did not work on her.

She shrugged one shoulder. "Or you'll what? Send me home? Give me crusts for dinner?" She rolled her eyes. "Convince others you are a tyrant, but not me. I know who you are." With that cryptic statement, she swept out of the dining room, not waiting for his response.

"My, but you are refreshing," he said to the now empty room. "I do believe I have changed my mind and you can stay." He followed her out.

She looked over her shoulder. "I was going to, but let's not quibble."

They wandered from room to room on the ground floor, him pointing out items that had personal and historical significance to his family. Some, when he looked more closely, should likely be replaced. Although he hated the timing, perhaps Mother was right, and the house did need updating. He also liked the idea it was not to be a full-scale refurbishment, but something that would not intrude too much.

Eventually, they reached the room he did not want altered in any way. He swung the door to the library open. "This is my library."

She gasped, and this time in a good way. The awestruck way.

His great-grandfather, when taking over the lease, had instructed Chippendale to outfit the library with floor-to-ceiling bookshelves, which had subsequently been filled with books owned by generations of Hartleys.

It had thick rugs on the floor and deep, comfortable leather chairs. But the most important part was his work desk, situated so he could see out of the small single window of the room.

"And let me guess." She walked toward the window and

looked out, just as he liked to do as he composed letters. "You would like this left as it is. I would too."

In a world where people made it a personal mission to misunderstand him, her appreciation had him at a loss for words. "If it's not too much trouble. It might be a small window, but I can see the tree and watch the birds. I have one I call Lark, even though he's a wren. He's always awake before anyone. It sounds silly, but when one is up early, working …"

"It is nice to have a companion. And your family name is Wren, is it not? You must have an affinity with him."

She understood. The rest of the family enjoyed living in Hartley Green for the majority of the year, but he didn't have that luxury. It was just him knocking about the townhouse on his own.

"Your armchair looks well worn." There was a question in her eyes. *Could I change it?*

"At your peril, Miss Eastwood," he said sternly. "If you recover it, the wonderful dip in the seat that has been the hard industry of countless Hartleys will be lost forever."

Her eyes flashed with merriment. "Indeed, far be it from me to intrude on the generational work of such noble behinds." She wandered back to the window. "I do like the aspect of this room. The light is lovely."

"I am often at Whitehall, so I don't enjoy it as much as I would like. But as you can see by the table Mother has propped under the window, it is a very good place to draw."

She went to say something, stopped herself, then nodded, seeming to decide on a course of action. "If you are not here, could I please use the table when I create the designs for your mother? I feel very forward asking, but it is such a lovely space."

"Of course. Please treat it as your own." He immediately had an image of her sitting at the table, her head bent, with sunlight streaming in, turning her hair golden. He would not be there to see it. Indeed, it would probably be better, all things considered, if he wasn't.

Miss Eastwood may be lovely and have a mind to match, but sweet country misses were not made to be political hostesses. His future wife would need to be part goddess, part virago.

She'd eat the likes of Miss Eastwood like a bonbon.

CHAPTER 5

IN WHICH MISS EASTWOOD DISCOVERS THE JOY OF SHOPPING WITH AN UNLIMITED PURSE

That week, Lady Hartley's luxurious town carriage took them all over town to the warehouses and showrooms where the Ton shopped. Places she'd never dreamed of seeing when she saw their advertisements in the *Morning Post*.

On Monday it was the cabinetmaker on Aldersgate Street, where they pored over thick books of designs. New tables, chairs, and sofas for the drawing room and the garden room were ordered. An appointment was made for the upholsterer to visit them the following week when Charis had a better idea of the color palette to be used.

Tuesday took them to the art studios of modern painters on Harley Street. A painting was purchased from Turner. It was a green and hazy view of Richmond Hill that made her swoon with happiness just to look at. "Ashcroft will prefer his art modern," was all Lady Hartley had said.

Wednesday was all afternoon at Morgan and Sanders, a furniture showroom where she convinced Lady Hartley to buy a chair that turned into library steps, the very first of its kind either of them had seen.

Then it was Thursday, and they were entering the area of St.

Paul's Churchyard, the cathedral towering behind them, to visit the showroom of Pellatt and Green—glassmakers to the king. It was all very grand and intimidating.

"Aren't you glad I made you wear your sturdy half-boots this week?" Lady Hartley said.

"It was good advice," Charis replied. "I vow I have not done so much walking since Sally hurt her fetlock, and I had to walk everywhere for a sennight."

Lady Hartley pursed her mouth. "You should have said, silly child. We have horses aplenty up at the big house."

Oh, yes, she could see Father asking Lady Hartley if he could just borrow a horse for a few weeks.

"She came good soon enough," Charis replied.

Once inside, it was easy to understand why the king gave them his custom. A dozen large and brilliant chandeliers hung from the ceiling, and long tables were piled with delicate glass and china. Each small mountain looked like the slightest touch could send it tumbling. And with her luck, it would.

Lady Hartley breathed a sigh of pleasure, a sound Charis was getting used to. My lady loved to shop and liked nothing more than to imagine how pieces of her fancy could fit into the refurbishment.

"Look at the one fourth from the left," Lady Hartley said, not doing anything so rude as pointing. "I quite love it. Would it suit the dining room?"

Charis nodded. "I think it would suit any room it graced. I encourage you to order one. Then can we go back to Grosvenor Square so I can put all these ideas onto paper?" Ideas were itching to be painted, and every day they shopped was another day she didn't paint.

But Lady Hartley wanted to peruse each table and each cabinet.

"I think I shall order a chandelier for the dining room, a larger one for the entry hall, and some smaller ones for the staircase."

"I could make those work with whatever I design," Charis replied, tucking her skirts in before they hitched on an urn ridiculously placed on the corner of a table. Almost as though they *wanted* her to knock it over.

A store assistant appeared the moment the word "order" was bandied about, bowing so low Charis got an excellent view of his balding head. It glowed under the lit candelabra as though he'd buffed it with wax.

After a quick conversation, all obsequiousness on his side and brusque annoyance from Lady Hartley, who hated that kind of behavior, he left them to finish the paperwork and give them a date of delivery.

They waited by the counter.

"How long will it take you to make your drawings? I am eager to see how our days of exploring the showrooms will affect your style."

"Perhaps a week or two?"

Her ladyship nodded. "Good, very good. Lambley is organizing the plasterers for any stucco work you want done, to start next week. And the painters for the following week. I know the cabinetmaker and the upholsterer need some time to fulfill orders, so I would like to place them as soon as possible. Although I can always pay to have them done quicker, I suppose."

Things were going to move at a rapid pace, and she really would have to focus on only her painting to get it done in time.

And there would be no time for revisions if she got it wrong and Lady Hartley, or more to the point, Lord Ashcroft, hated them.

"Do you have a date you are working toward? All craftsmen need a set deadline." Not to mention *she* needed to know. The likes of the nobility often thought it was unnecessary for underlings to know the detail, but it most certainly was.

Lady Hartley blinked rapidly, as though the question had caught her off guard. "Yes," she said slowly, as though deciding how much to share with Charis. "And it ties in with the other thing I tasked you with. I would like the house finished by the start of March. Everybody will be in town because parliament is open, and I can throw a ball in the newly refurbished room. That is also your deadline to whip my son into order."

Charis drew in a breath. Lord Ashcroft lived a quiet life in London. He said he hadn't thrown any "formal events" in the dining room, suggesting he had similarly left the ballroom in disuse. In fact, he hadn't even *shown* it to her. Of course, she'd found it herself, but that wasn't the point.

"How wonderful. Have you decided on the theme? I know you haven't asked for my help, but I've always dreamed of decorating a ballroom." Perhaps it could be another way to earn income. Designing parties for society matrons. Her heart leaped at the idea.

"No definite theme yet, although I want it to be pretty and romantic. The young ladies of this Season must fall in love with the ball and with the house if they are to fall in love with my son."

Falling in love with the *house and her son*? Charis blinked. Of course, that was the aim.

How could she *be* so silly?

The house hadn't had a finger lifted on it in decades, and yet suddenly it was being refreshed and a ball was to be held. And she was being roped into making him look more attractive, both with his home and his person.

Lady Hartley had come to town to find a match for her son, and she was pulling out all the stops to do it.

Charis had just been in the right place at the right time to help her. She was free, discreet, and immediately available.

And the promise Lady Hartley had made to Mother to help her find a husband?

The very last thing on her mind. Lucky, so very lucky, she had her own plans.

Charis took a deep breath. "I'm glad you confided your goal to me. I have been looking upon the redecoration from a more political angle, thinking the house should reflect well on Lord Ashcroft as a politician, not as a suitor. This will change my direction."

Lady Hartley blinked. "I'm not sure what you mean. Surely an impressive house for a politician is the same as for a young bachelor lord in want of a wife?"

Charis shook her head. "They are entirely different. A politician's house speaks of wealth and power, understated influence, and rock-solid respectability. The house of a young bachelor lord in want of a wife is about creating a house the prospective bride can envisage her future in. It will have a nursery on the upper floors with the most delightful mural on the wall. The kitchen will boast the most beautiful range we can buy, and there should be modern water closets on each floor. A young lady and her mother will appreciate these conveniences. And, of course, everything in the first stare of elegance. That goes without saying." She paused, choosing her words carefully. "I assume you will invite the mothers of these suitable ladies to see the house during the ball?"

She looked around the room as though only just realizing the breadth of her aspirations. "Yes, most definitely." Lady Hartley looked at her through slightly narrowed eyes. "How brilliant you are. I would not have thought of that. This is obviously why I made the very intelligent decision to bring you along."

The store assistant came back. "Mr. Green says we can rush your job and have it ready for you in three weeks. We hope this is acceptable."

Lady Hartley nodded. "Excellent. Thank you for your help." It was the deferential service she had received all day, and it never failed to amaze Charis the lengths the manufacturers would go to secure her custom.

She turned to Charis. "Now, we have one more stop. There is

a new modiste in Covent Garden where I have made us both an appointment."

"My lady, you don't need to do that. I am not out in society. There really is no need."

"Apart from the theater the other night, you mean?" Lady Hartley lifted her chin to look down her nose at Charis. Or at least she tried, but since Charis was a few inches taller, the effect was ruined. "Oh, yes, I heard all about it. In the box with Sheridan, drinking Champagne and generally enjoying yourselves."

Charis winced, feeling her ears burn red. "I—"

But Lady Hartley cut her off. "I jest. Nothing could make me happier to hear you had fun. My friend Lady Astley likes to carry tales, but in this case, she missed her mark."

Charis exhaled. *Thank goodness.*

Lady Hartley waved her away. "Now, enough about that. I promised your mother I would buy you a wardrobe. Please do not make me break my vow. I plan for you to be out with my son, so you must look elegant so other ladies think well of him."

Any sense of guilt about receiving a gift far exceeding the deed she was to perform slipped away. "In that case, if it will benefit you, you are welcome to buy me all the pretty gowns your heart desires." Charis smiled. "I hope I don't let you down. My unmarried state must tell you something about my own skills with flirting."

"Your spinsterhood directly results from your lack of dowry and the fact your father has been very ill. You may even find your own beau at my ball. A rich enough man would not care." As long as he was not her son.

They got back into the town carriage and wound their way around the streets until they reached the riot of Covent Garden. Horses jostled with wagons loaded with baskets of produce. It smelled like a bouquet of earthy vegetables, sweet flowers, and the usual horse smell all London streets had. Charis had just pulled her handkerchief from her reticule when their carriage turned off the piazza and down a side street.

They stopped outside a double shop front with a golden needle and thread as the only sign, painted on a black background and swaying in the icy January wind. There was a pretty black-and-white-striped canopy over the door, but when they entered, it felt like the dressmaker had only just set up shop.

The walls were whitewashed, with a counter placed at the back of the shop twenty feet away. There was nothing in between, just a wide expanse of space and floorboards with no carpet. Racks down the side of each wall held bolts of fabric and could not help but look messy.

Lady Hartley leaned in. "I know it looks to be in disarray, but I've heard she trained in Paris and is the best in London. We shall soon discover if it's true."

A tall, thin lady dressed entirely in black entered the room.

Lady Hartley leaned in again. "And here she is."

Madame Le Favre looked to be in her late twenties. Her eyes were dark but shining with intelligence.

"Ah, Lady Hartley, you have returned." Her bright gaze rested on Charis. "And you have brought a protégé. Please tell me I have the honor of dressing her." She curtsied. "I am Madame Le Favre, at your service."

It was likely something she said to every new client to make them feel valued and appreciated. Charis took it with a pinch of salt.

She knew the truth, because Mrs. Pritchard, her local dressmaker, told her often enough, "All arms and legs and not much between." If Charis could get a new dress and not end up looking like a giraffe at the Royal menagerie, she would count herself blessed.

"Dress her as though she had not a stitch to her name," Lady Hartley said with a laugh. "This is to be my gift to her for helping me, so I would like it to be lovely, but also practical for when she returns to her usual life in Kent. And perhaps snare her a beau."

Madame tilted her head to one side. "If my skills and her beauty cannot garner her a husband in her time here, I am doing something very ill."

"We shall see," was all Lady Hartley replied.

The next hour was a lesson in a very exalted sort of gown-making. A team of seamstresses entered, and Charis was measured, poked, and told to stand taller. Then swathes of fabric were pushed up against her face while Lady Hartley and Madame Le Favre made decisions without her opinion.

Madame thought she had seen just the right shade of yellow at a warehouse earlier that week, and Lady Hartley assured her she trusted her with every choice.

They probably figured her current dress, her very best walking ensemble, was reason enough not to trust Charis's own judgment. But it was hardly her gown's fault the white muslin had turned a little drab with age.

"The strong colors drain her of vibrancy," Madame said. "But the mint, soft yellows, and pinks are perfect."

Having never had dresses in any of those colors, Charis had no idea what "perfect" would look like. Would it make her feel smarter? Like she could climb the mountains and make things better for her family? Or would she be the same Charis, just with better gowns?

Eventually, it was all planned, and Madame Le Favre curtsied, sending her minions away with a flick of her wrist. "Come back in two weeks for a final fitting. It will be delightful, I assure you."

Charis left the modiste with precisely no idea what had been ordered.

"That was a great deal of fun," Lady Hartley said. "We had best be careful or we'll find you a husband before you've finished what I need you to do."

Charis laughed, but it was not particularly funny. "I think I have missed my chance, unfortunately." Father would not let men from a lower class court her, and those of a higher class had not been interested. It was frustrating.

They waited for the carriage, which was positioned farther down the street. Lady Hartley stilled. "Surely not, my dear. Why you cannot yet have reached your majority?"

"It makes no difference, when so many of our young men are at war, and I have no dowry." She kept her voice brisk, inviting no sympathy.

But Lady Hartley's face softened. "Then I am sorry to have made such a poor jest. It is difficult, I think, for your generation. These are terrible times."

"A generation of ladies who have to find our own way in the world. We cannot expect our parents to keep us forever."

Now she frowned. "No, I suppose not. But you are not a lost cause yet. It is silly to think so."

"Do not feel sorry for me, my lady. I have made peace with my circumstances. A contented spinster, you might say." Her heart railed against the lie.

"Hmph." Lady Hartley did not sound happy.

"In some regards, it has made my life easier. I used to be terribly shy around men, always tongue-tied because I wanted their regard. Now I don't care as much. It's liberating."

Both of Lady Hartley's eyebrows shot up. "Liberating! If you're not careful, you'll run with the bluestocking club."

She looked over Charis's shoulder at a young lady and her mother approaching them. "Why Lady Buxton, good afternoon. Have you heard of this wonderful new dressmaker too? Word travels fast."

Charis swung around to see an elegant lady with silver hair poking from beneath a very modish bonnet and dressed in a deep-blue cape. The younger lady wore white muslin that was too thin even with her pelisse. "Beatrix discovered her, but it looks as though you have too." She looked inquiringly at Charis. "But who have we here?"

"A charming young friend from Hartley Green who wanted to see my new interior remodeling."

Charis frowned. Was Lady Hartley embarrassed she was helping? Or did it just not look *de rigueur* to have someone so inexperienced assisting her?

Lady Buxton's head tilted to one side, her mouth pursing. "Indeed. You will have to visit and tell me all about it."

"And so we shall," Lady Hartley said. "But don't let us keep you."

The ladies continued toward the door, but Lady Buxton turned back just as they reached it. "Don't forget to bring your Ashcroft with you. Such a fine young man."

Lady Beatrix muffled a groan.

Lady Hartley waved, then turned to Charis as their carriage pulled up. "Did you hear that? Bring Ashcroft?" She closed her eyes as though in delight. "Lady Beatrix would be the ultimate match. Lively, vivacious, and with an impeccable pedigree. Not to mention the Buxton fortune behind her. She's their only child, you see. Nothing could be more perfect."

The footman lowered the carriage steps. Lady Hartley entered first, taking the forward-facing seat, leaving Charis to ride backward.

They rode home in silence, Lady Hartley likely planning the wedding and Charis unsettled, but with no good reason why. *Well. When at a loose end, think of your designs.* She spent a few minutes staring blankly out of the window, thinking of the library. The one room she was not allowed to touch.

"Lady Hartley?"

The lady in question snapped out of her reverie. "Yes, my dear?"

"With regard to the library, I have two requests."

"Brave girl. Do go on."

57

"Firstly, the window is too small for Lord Ashcroft to enjoy the garden. Could we replace it with something larger?"

She nodded thoughtfully. "A lovely idea. I will have Lambley contact the glazier and carpenter. And secondly?"

"I was thinking of adding a small area for evening drinks to the secretaire."

She shook her head vehemently. "No, no. The secretaire must not be touched."

"Really?"

She nodded. "I mean it. It is a masterpiece and has secret compartments and drawers all over the place. My husband would be most displeased. Although I think Ashcroft will enjoy a bigger window. Or perhaps some French doors leading out to the garden? I will organize the gardeners to put a birdbath in if you think it will make Ashcroft happy."

"That sounds lovely." So, a bigger window but don't touch that secretaire, because it was a precious magic place to hide things.

Drat it. How was she ever going to sit in the same room and not investigate its secrets?

CHAPTER 6

IN WHICH DIMPLES BECOME A GOOD EXCUSE
FOR ANYTHING

Under the guise of cleaning, Charis took a rag and spent the following afternoon prodding the drawers of the secretaire. The impressive piece of furniture was built into the bookshelf and made from mahogany with inlaid walnut decorations.

But where were those hidden compartments Lady Hartley spoke of?

Very well hidden. Charis knocked on the wood to see if it was hollow. It certainly sounded like there was something behind the wood, but she couldn't find a way to reveal it.

Why would one *need* hidden drawers? For the safe-keeping of precious items against thieves? Secret missives? Bills of collection one hoped would go away?

Daylight was fading, and a footman slipped in and out to light the candles.

"Pretty *and* vexing," she said to it. "Show me your secrets." She ran her hand along the inside of the drawers, thinking she might find a catch, but no.

"Show you *what* secrets?"

His voice sent a thrill of alarm through her. She whirled

around to see Ashcroft standing in the doorway, filling it admirably, his gaze part curiosity and part suspicion.

Her breath hitched, and her heart seemed to stop. *Caught.* "Good afternoon, Lord Ashcroft. You will want the library. I'll leave."

Escape, posthaste.

She took a step toward the door, but he was standing in it, holding up a hand. "No, no. Stay." He motioned to the chair. "Please be seated and tell me what you were doing." He walked into the room and leaned against the desk, waiting for her response.

Charis closed her eyes. This was a nightmare. Why must she be so curious? Now he thought she liked to pry into things that were not her concern. It was her besetting sin. And worse still, she *did* like to pry. Pulling and poking the secretaire had been enormous fun.

She exhaled. "Your mother told me this secretaire holds secret drawers and compartments. It sounded magical. I just wanted to find them." There. The truth was sometimes the quickest way out of a situation.

He said nothing, his gaze intense. The prick of perspiration burst under her arms.

"You wanted to find the secret drawers. Are you *looking* for secrets?" His tone was slow, almost torturous, as though he had all night to follow this line of questioning until she squirmed. His body was still, but his eyes were bright and alert. All focused on her. He held her in the room as surely as if he'd tied her to a chair.

"Of course not! But you must see, I love furniture, and this is something I have never encountered. I just want to understand it. Where are they? Do you know?" In for a penny, in for a pound, as her father would say. Perhaps she could brazen this out. "I have found plenty of drawers, but none of them are hidden. I promise you, if I had opened a drawer and found anything, I would have stopped. But the cabinet is empty."

He paused for the longest moment in the history of humankind.

She held her breath.

His face broke into a smile. "I will show you the secrets. In truth, I used to do the same thing myself when I was a boy. I was forever in this room tinkering with it. We'll probably find some tin soldiers wedged in there."

He stepped away from the desk and stood next to her. "Watch this." He crouched down to the lower section, where there was a small cabinet with two doors that opened out to a small cupboard.

"I've done that." They were so close, a waft of something citrus and clean drifted past her. She inhaled deeply, like his cologne was a sparkling glass of Champagne. It went to her head just as fast, relaxing her body, her stress evaporating.

He looked at her over his shoulder and winked. "Have you?"

Instead of opening the doors, he pulled, and the entire cabinet slid out.

"Oh!" She didn't know whether to be more shocked by the wink or the secret area revealed behind the cabinet.

"But wait, there's more." Then he slid what looked like the cabinet's back out to reveal a bank of four drawers. "There you are. Secret revealed. Well, one of them, at least."

"How marvelous!"

"There's nothing in here. Father moved everything back to Hartley Green." He pulled one of the drawers, but it was wedged in tight. He tugged harder, frowning.

"Don't break it." There was a piece of folded paper poking out. "There's something stuck there."

"Hmm." Ashcroft prized it out. "Must have fallen in between and got wedged." He unfolded it. "Most likely a bill of purchase for his boots or something."

He scanned the letter, then closed his eyes briefly, his eyebrows drawing together in distress. "This is not a bill of sale."

"What is it?" Charis whispered. He could ignore her if he wanted to; she'd asked so quietly.

He shook his head. "It is a letter from Monsieur Trellier to my father while he was still in France. Goodness."

"During the revolution?"

He stood and got a pair of spectacles from atop his desk, putting them on. "He was trying to get a young lady out of there. Listen. 'She should arrive in Margate by packet on the twenty-fifth of April. My *dearest* hope is that you will be there to meet her. She is my light and my love. Please treat her with kindness while she waits for me.'"

Charis drew in a shaky breath. "Poor Monsieur Trellier. I hate the fact we are at war at the moment, but it's not the same as having it right on your doorstep. They all went through so much, it's terrifying."

"We still lose too many of our countrymen." His hands tightened on the letter.

"True, but you're not trying to get innocent women and children away from the conflict. I do hope she made it."

"Considering he has never married, we can assume she did not." He folded the wafer-thin paper back into a crisp square.

"Oh, but how tragic."

"He goes on to instruct my father to go to the French Embassy to get the direction of a priest to marry them."

Tears sprang to her eyes. "In vain. Please, tell me no more. I was *not* looking for secrets, only secret compartments. Now I fear I know more about Monsieur Trellier than he would ever want me to."

Ashcroft shook his head, and Charis could swear his eyes were misty, too. "He's always so vibrant. It's easy to forget what he lived through, not very long ago."

"Did she even make it out of Paris? I choose to think maybe

she made it as far as Holland and decided not to risk the sea journey. Perhaps she married a Dutch man and is still living there, happily surrounded by her children."

His face fell. "We both know that's not how this tale ended."

"Until we know for certain, I prefer to think of her that way. Now put it back where it was."

He placed the letter in a hidden drawer and then pushed the compartment into place. "Yes, that is for the best. Let's forget we ever saw it."

How could she forget a letter like that? But his gaze held hers, asking for agreement. She nodded, and he put his big hand over hers and clasped it.

She inhaled sharply and he let go, but it still sent a thrill through her.

"Apologies."

"No, no." She rubbed up and down her arm. She really must get over this reaction she had to him. Looking for him in each room was bad enough, but when even the smallest touch set her alight, she definitely had a problem.

"Tell me what else you have been working on, other than prying my library apart." He walked over to her desk and the watercolor she had completed earlier. Did he know the effect he had on her?

Charis looked down along with him. Her breath hitched. This was the first design he had seen, but it was not one she would have chosen to show him.

"I *dearly* hope that is not my drawing room." His voice was an unimpressed drawl, so deep it felt like it vibrated within her.

She could normally listen to him all day, but not if he was going to malign her work. She lifted her chin a little, ready for combat. "What would you say if it was?"

He turned away, walking to the sideboard, where he poured himself a small amount of whatever dark liquid was in the decanter. "I would say I did not realize we were aiming to look like an opera house."

She smiled, knowing it would incense him, and he'd already had a long day. "Perfect. That's exactly what you should think upon entering this room. Do you also think it looks like the inside of a jewel box?"

He walked back and looked more closely. "Yes. I can see that. An expensive jewel box. Plush." He peered closer, making out the lettering she had placed in watery strokes on the window. "Madame Le Favre?"

"Your mother's dressmaker. She took me to visit the other day, and I knew I had to design her shop." In the end, the vision had come to her in that magic time just before sleep. Swathes of red velvet for drama, soft round sofas, thick rugs on the floor, and hothouse roses in vases.

Like an expensive boudoir woke up and found itself at the opera.

He made an exaggerated sigh of relief. "So, it is *not* my drawing room."

"No, it is not. Hopefully, it is a place where ladies will feel cherished and beautiful."

He nodded and lifted his hand to his chin. "I like the seating. I have never seen a round sofa."

"To be honest, I'm not sure they can make them. But I like it." She looked at her painting. It was close to finished, but the light had faded now, so any final touches with her ink could wait until morning.

He smiled. "They can make anything with enough encouragement. Which leads me to a question …"

"Yes?"

He motioned for her to sit and then sat himself in the leather chair that looked out through the small window to the garden. Birds were making nesting noises outside, and the sky was turning a deep gray that was almost purple.

"What is my mother's purpose? Because she never does anything without a point." He swirled the golden liquid around his glass. "When she built the folly at Friar Park, it was because she was having arguments with my father and wanted to escape. When she redid the servants' quarters, it was because they had been acting improperly, and she needed to separate them. So why is she here? This is a big undertaking. She doesn't do those things without a reason."

His stare was intense. Deep brown eyes willing her to answer him, almost as though, if he tried hard enough, the answers would just start tumbling out. Like he could pull them from her mind with a string if he tried.

He underestimated her.

"What has she told you?"

"She's being cagey." He blinked slowly. "So are you."

Charis very much did not want to be in the middle of this argument. It was not fair of either of them to put her there.

"I'm sure if you think hard enough, you'll come upon why a mother might try to make her son's residence more appealing and stylish when he is ... Is it rude to ask how old you are? It feels rude." She ended with a shrug. "Anyway, when he is a man in the prime of his life."

"Oh." He took a deep breath, as though her response had surprised him. "I thought I could take care of those matters myself. If you mean what I think you mean."

He was dancing around the subject just as much as she was. Her heart skittered as she tried to find the right route to take. Honesty or loyalty to Lady Hartley? "I do, I believe. And I will be the first to wish you happy when the lady of your choice falls in love with the new chaise lounge or whatever fribble we devise to trap her."

His gaze sharpened, but he also looked intrigued. "You disapprove?"

She instantly regretted her sour response. It was no concern of hers what the outcome of the refurbishment was. She was only there to enjoy the process. "Of luring someone into marriage? In truth, I have seen mothers do worse things than buy rugs and sofas."

She smiled. Her own mother might not have the money to devote to the cause, but she'd tried her very hardest. It was hardly her fault Charis never took. In retrospect, she had no idea whose fault it was at all.

He took a sip of his drink, his mouth twisting. "If she stops there, I agree. But I am concerned I am about to become embroiled in matchmaking when parliament will take every moment of my time."

Charis shook her head. "Then rest easy. Her plans are months away when the Season begins." When Charis would be well gone and would not have to witness Lord Ashcroft falling in love.

"Am I such a curmudgeon then, that she thinks she must sweeten me up by putting me in the middle of my own jewel box? And *what* plans?"

She answered the last question rather than the first. "A ball, I believe? I thought she would have told you."

He shuddered. "With me as the prize. Charming."

"You may wish to work on it if charm is the desired effect. Charm takes effort."

His eyes sparkled with roguishness. "Perhaps I'll practice on you. You can tell me when I'm getting close."

She drew in a shocked breath. Could it be he wanted to learn to be attractive to ladies just as much as his mother wanted it for him? If so, this would make her job so much easier and the burden of guilt over having an agenda he knew nothing about would be gone.

"An interesting prospect. I would be happy to help you *appear* to be less of a curmudgeon in any way I can."

His lips tipped up at the side, and before she knew it, he broke into a smile.

Sweet heavens, it was obvious she'd *never* seen him smile properly before. Dimples appeared, and he looked younger and less like a man who had the troubles of the world on his shoulders.

"Do you think you can do it? A gargantuan task."

"I think I should try, and, while I'm being totally honest, your mother said I should make you learn to flirt with me, to lighten your mood. I have obviously been dismal at it thus far."

His brows drew together. "And she was not concerned I might become attached to you? She isn't trying to—"

"Match us? Heavens, no. She actually said I was the perfect person for this task because you would never look at me that way, and I would never have the impertinence to look at you. She has visited me so often over the years, we probably feel like poor cousins."

"We are *nothing* like cousins," he said hotly. "By Jove, I want to serve this back to her."

"How?" A burst of excitement rose through her. Mama would be appalled at her behavior, but all this just put her in the mood for mischief.

"She needs to stop meddling in my life. I am a grown man. It will serve her right if ..."

"If what?" But she knew. Every time he looked at her and his gaze hitched on her lips, or he smiled into her eyes. He wanted to flirt with her, and he was finding himself an excuse to do it without consequences.

And she *definitely* was.

"If we do exactly as she has asked. It hasn't escaped my notice you have been nowhere and done nothing that constitutes relief from all your redecorating. Allow me to make this up to you."

Yes, please. "I thought you were too busy to entertain?"

"Sessions only start at four and are only on Mondays, Tuesdays, Thursdays, and Fridays. I have plenty of time around that.

Let me squire you around town. They'll say you breathed life into me."

"Were you dead?" She tilted her head to one side, unable to stop the excitement rising within her.

He blinked slowly. "I think maybe I was." He looked down at his drink. It was almost empty now. "Is it true you are the perfect person for this because you would never want to marry me? I am fast developing an aversion to being managed."

"I am perfect because I would never have expectations. She is right in that." Which was not answering the question, but with any luck, the liquor would have taken the edge off his shrewdness, and he wouldn't notice.

He nodded. "Then let's do it. Let me show you London. My next free day is Wednesday." He stood and came over to her, then held out his hand for her to shake, as he would to a man, as though they were sealing a bargain.

She stared at it for a long moment and then put hers in it. Her breath caught again. He was just so large, warm, and strong. So sure of himself and everything around him, and it was all in that one handclasp. No wonder the Scots called marriage a handfast. It felt like a bond, her reaction to it as sure as her own beating heart.

He smiled again, the proper one with the dimples and the devilry that she could become addicted to if she weren't very careful.

And her plan was formed. She couldn't care less about him marrying or living in an elegant house. She just wanted to make him smile like that every day she was in London.

No matter what it took.

CHAPTER 7

IN WHICH IT BECOMES APPARENT NEITHER OF THESE NUMBSKULLS HAS THE LEAST IDEA HOW TO FLIRT

"Where are we going?"

The carriage had wound its way along the streets until they were down by the river. The air seemed colder near the water. Charis rubbed her hands together, wishing she had those warm wool pelisses from the dressmaker.

"I've seen you staring for unnatural amounts of time at the paintings in the hall. I thought you might like some variety," Lord Ashcroft said.

The carriage stopped in front of Somerset House. He was taking her to the Royal Academy? She smiled to herself. "There is nothing unnatural about appreciating art."

"There is when it's a portrait of my grandfather, and he has nothing more than a giant nose to recommend him."

"He's a very distinguished man. I find him quite handsome."

He frowned. "Not an epitaph many would have given him."

Hopefully, he'd never been told how much like his grandfather he looked, or he'd realize she had inadvertently told him she thought *he* was handsome.

Nothing could be more mortifying. She could only pray her sensitivity to having him near her was wearing off, or this would be a very long and draining visit. The highly alert and yet increasingly languid effect he had on her was extremely annoying.

After all, she had work to do.

They entered from the Strand, under a tall arch and into a vestibule that would suit Ancient Greece more than modern London. "How very grand this is."

"Do you see the marble bust of Michelangelo over the door? That is the entrance to the Academy. The learned Societies have one of Isaac Newton. This way, nobody gets confused as to where they are going."

"What would happen if we swapped them around?"

"A cruel joke to play on the greatest minds of our time."

Their eyes met, a smile playing at the corners of his mouth. *I like it when you smile.*

When they entered the exhibition gallery, he stopped at the entrance and shot her a sidelong glance, obviously waiting for her response to the grandeur.

The huge room had walls that tapered up toward curved windows in the ceiling, letting in shafts of natural light. Each wall was filled with masterpieces, frame jammed against frame, climbing all the way up to the skylights.

There were a series of long benches covered in green fabric where she imagined crowds of people would mill around, looking at the paintings, lounging on the seats, and talking about everything before them. But it was barely ten o'clock.

The sky through the windows above was gray and ominous, casting a cool light across the room. It seemed they were the very first visitors to the gallery for the day, and the thought of all this just for them and no one else was astonishing. "Why, there's nobody else here. I would expect travelers or tourists might be amongst the first to line up."

He smiled in a superior fashion. "I think you'll find we have this room for at least thirty minutes before any company arrives."

She whirled around. "Did you buy all the tickets so nobody else can enter?"

He shook his head. "I had no need to do that. The Academy was kind enough to grant me this half hour. I always find it so annoying to have somebody in my line of sight."

"How *very* spoiled you are!" It should be enough to have all these masterpieces in one room without having to cast everybody else out. But even she knew it was a lie. Having the room to themselves, even if only for thirty minutes, was a priceless gift. She went to one of the long benches and sat, taking it all in.

He shrugged. "My father is a patron. So, this kind of thing is really no bother. Mr. West has offered to come here in a few minutes and tell you about some of his favorites. He is self-taught, but has produced some wonderful pieces." He led her across the room to a large canvas hung at eye level. "This is *The Death of Nelson*. A terrible topic, but incredible work."

She had not known it was possible to be physically moved by art, but the scene on the deck of Nelson's ship brought tears to her eyes. The face of every person in the painting added to the emotion of the moment. "It's like he has caught time on his paintbrush."

"He'll tell you himself it's a picture of what might have been, rather than fact. But still."

"It is magnificent and a true tribute to our heroes."

He turned, nodding. "Exactly." He looked around. "This … This is not too overbearing? We are supposed to be having fun and flirting, if I recall, and instead I've brought you to this serious place."

"Why, no. I love art. You know I do. This was almost at the top of my list of things to see in London."

"What is at the top?"

She looked back to Nelson. "Gunter's. I have always wanted to try an ice."

"I don't suppose I should remind you it is now February, not April, and you'll give your insides a chill?"

"It would do no good to point out such practicalities. I am above them. But why do you think this is dull? It is the finest art in the land."

He inspected his fingernails. "You see, I once brought a lady to this very place, thinking I had enough art education at Oxford that I could teach her something."

"You mean pontificate rather than *teach*, I gather?" She couldn't help smiling, because she could hear the humility in his voice. "And this did not go according to plan?"

He shrugged. "I don't know. She seemed interested at the time, but then ..."

She was left to fill in the rest of the sentence because, obviously, his modesty only went so far.

But did it mean he had not brought her here because of her interest in the arts, but rather to relive a scene of failed courtship?

Fascinating. She took a breath. "Let me see, did it go something like this?" She put a haughty look on her face, lifted her chin, and took a determined step around the room. "And here you will appreciate this composition in oils of the Madonna with the baby Jesus painted by Raphael himself. This painting was in my family for two hundred years, and we donated it to the Royal Academy in 1799. The Marquis of Hartley have been patrons of the Royal Academy since its inception in 1768."

She kept talking and walking, not looking back to see if he had followed her, much in the same way she assumed he must have treated this poor young lady, who had thought herself in for a treat of artistic pleasure for the afternoon.

She turned and looked at him only to see he had crossed his arms over his chest. "When you say it like that, I can see my error."

"You actually did that?" Laughter burst from her.

He nodded and looked up at the skylights. "I may have."

"Nobody likes a braggart." She took a step toward him. "Let's pretend we are back with that young lady and redo this scene, shall we? In the interests of the aforementioned flirting. Not everything needs to be serious. Even if the art around us takes itself very seriously indeed. Now, you be the young lady and I will be you."

"I could not begin to imagine what a lady might be thinking, feeling, or saying in this situation. Indeed, half my problem is the fact I have no idea." He looked away from her.

What must it take for a man like him to admit that? "Very well. I am going to do what *I* would do in this situation and ask you questions."

His gaze snapped to hers, and his head tilted slightly to one side. "Why is that?"

She exhaled. "Firstly, because it's much easier to ask questions and listen to the answer than it is to create an entire speech and thrust it onto an unsuspecting lady. Secondly, because it makes the other person feel important and everybody likes that."

"Show me your favorite painting in this room." She turned to him, gazing into his eyes as though he were the most important person in the room, rather than the only person in the room. That was her idea of flirting.

He stilled, searching her eyes, and then looked down to her mouth as though drawn to it against his will. The moment stretched out, and she thought he leaned toward her just a little before he took hold of himself.

He pointed to a large war composition. "I've seen them all so many times, however, this one always gets my attention." He walked over and stood before Zeus riding a white horse with a thunderbolt in his raised hand, pointed toward the earth.

Charis joined him, standing by his side. "What do you admire about it? Is it the action of the scene or is it the beautiful sky that looks like a storm come to life?"

He shook his head. "Actually, it's this little group of people down here. See how they cower before him like their entire lives are in his hands? But look at Zeus, he doesn't even notice them. He is so intent on his goal. He doesn't realize his very existence is a threat to others."

"Why does this make you feel so strongly? Does it strike you for a reason?"

He thought for a few moments, then turned to her, his eyes flaring. "You're right. It does. I feel our titans of parliament are like him. Off to war with their own goals and their own battles, not seeing how their actions inflicted pain on people with much less power than them. The theme of this piece is the essence of why I ran for parliament in the first place."

He frowned, as though surprised she had managed to pull that from him so easily.

"You are a man of principle, and I admire that," she said softly. "Now you ask me. It may take me a little longer because this is my very first impression of all of these paintings."

He held out his arm to her, and they took one slow circuit around the room. His arm was taut, and she wasn't sure if it was stress in him or just strength.

She moved a little closer, linking her arm in his. His taut muscles relaxed, and she smiled to herself. Why was she so sure he was an island of a man who longed for connection but just didn't quite know how to do it?

"Perhaps I will ask you which one holds your attention, because I'm sure your favorite will only come to you over a few viewings."

It was interesting he thought she would have the chance to see the gallery more than once when this was likely her first and last visit to the Academy. She had to use every second of her time there, and however long they spent, it would not be long enough.

But there was one painting that drew her eye and begged her to come closer.

She changed directions and walked across the room to stand before the landscape. It was large, easily nine feet wide and ten feet tall. It was slightly tilted down on the concave wall, and the light from the opposite skylight lit it beautifully, making the sunrise that was on the horizon seem real.

It was the English countryside, and the artist drew her eye up the hill toward a beautiful folly that had been built in classic Roman style. "I don't know who painted this, but I feel like I could step into it. I would walk up and sit on the steps with my back against one of those columns, and I would watch the sun come up."

Echoing her comments earlier, he said, "And why does this strike you so? Why does the thought of a peaceful morning walk in this world appeal to you?"

She nodded in appreciation. "You are a fast learner, my lord." She pulled away from him, missing his warm and solid strength as soon as she did. "There has not been a great deal of peace in my life lately. Our situation and my father's illness have meant our lives seem to be one scramble to the next with never quite enough money to make life comfortable. However, this makes me feel at peace. My favorite dream is to have a dilapidated country house with grounds like this and bring it back to life."

She stopped talking, just staring at it for a few moments as a well of emotion grew inside her. "And maybe a kitten." She took one deep, steadying breath and then another until she felt him take her hand and place it on his arm and put his other hand on top of it. As always, his touch brought her a calm more real than any painting. It was almost a tonic. Settling her. She closed her eyes.

"I understand. I'm sorry things have been so difficult for you. Is there anything I can do to help?"

She was instantly horrified that what was supposed to be a light-hearted flirtation had become something much deeper. She shook her head and pulled her hand from his, even though it hurt to do so. "No. My father is a proud man and will accept no charity. The only thing for me to do is to try to earn a living of my own so I can stop being a burden to them."

He turned to her and searched her face. "Or marry? But I'm sure with the amount of work you do, you are more of a blessing than a burden."

"That is what I tell myself," Charis said. They walked on in silence and then he led her back to the center of the room, and they took their seats and looked at the art in silence together.

"Asking questions is a powerful thing," he said.

She nodded. "I'm sure you would like to know the lady you marry, and the only way to understand her is to ask questions and see what the answers are."

"But sometimes ladies have very practiced answers that are not truly how they feel. For example, the lady in question told me she enjoyed politics and making our country better. I found out later that nothing bored her more. I don't understand why people misrepresent themselves."

"You of all people should understand why," she said. "There is too much at stake for these young ladies, and they will absolutely tell you what they think you want to hear. In the same way that I am looking to find a way to earn my living, you are their future. They cannot afford for you to take a dislike to them."

"Then how am I to know who actually wants to be with me, for pity's sake?

"I'm sure you had a glimmer she was lying at the time. It is your job to press on to ask more insightful questions to get to the real answer. It's not hard. People always want to talk about themselves, and the more they talk, the more they tell you. It's simply not enough to rely on a few balls and picnics to choose a partner. This is your future, too. This lady will be the mother of your children. It is much too important to leave to chance."

They both looked up as a middle-aged gentleman with a very loosely tied cravat and a shabby brown coat entered the room.

He opened his arms in welcome. "Ashcroft, what a pleasure to have you visit this morning. And I understand you have a young lady on her first trip to London?"

Ashcroft stood and bowed. "Thank you, Mr. West, you are most kind to come and show Miss Eastwood the paintings. She is a family friend from Hartley Green, and my inferior knowledge just won't cut it in this case."

Mr. West laughed, bowed to Charis, and then lifted her hand and kissed the air above her fingers. "Miss Eastwood, a pleasure." He lifted his arm, encouraging her to take it. "Now let me show you our most beautiful pieces and tell you about the rascals who painted them."

Charis smiled and took his arm, leaving Lord Ashcroft to trail behind them as Mr. West gave her a curated tour of the Royal Academy of Arts.

Whether Ashcroft had meant to bring her to the very place she longed to see she would never know, but in the end, it didn't matter. He'd given her a gift nobody could take away.

CHAPTER 8

IN WHICH DRIVING TURNS MISS EASTWOOD INTO A VERITABLE HOYDEN

Two mornings later, Charis had a pile of parchment with pencil marks measuring out each room's dimensions.

Lambley had given her a long wooden ruler to make her job easier, but it still took hours. Then the following day, she transferred the grand proportions of these rooms onto her watercolor paper in pencil.

It would be the basis of her redesign. It was a small beginning, but a beginning nonetheless. After making copies for each room, she stacked the papers on the floor beside her.

With money as scarce as it was, every cake of watercolor and every sheet of parchment was precious. So, the designs must be vibrant in her mind before she committed them to paper, or else she would run out before the end of the week. She didn't want to have to ask Lady Hartley for more.

The only problem was her newly acquired habit of doubting her work. Would Lady Hartley love it? Would Lord Ashcroft hate it?

In her feverish imagining, he looked down at her paintings and laughed, saying she had made their rooms look like the interior of the Theater Royal. Each time she had this daydream, a little part of her quailed. There was every reason to believe he *would* approve the designs. So why must she ruminate on potential disaster?

The mind was a tricky thing. She was forced to spend five minutes staring out the window and bolstering her confidence. Something she never had any issue with before.

As if hearing her thoughts, there was a knock at the door, and Ashcroft stood at the threshold. "Good morning, Miss Eastwood. You are hard at work already. I saw you measuring out the hall yesterday. That's quite a mathematical approach, don't you think?"

"I must be precise, your lordship. Your mother is ordering furniture, light fittings, and drapes based on my paintings. While I know they won't be perfectly measured, I intend to get them as close as possible so there are no rude surprises upon delivery. The only thing I can't measure is the ceiling."

"Fourteen feet," he said. "Every room is fourteen feet, except the attic rooms." He moved over to his desk and sat in his chair, leaning back and regarding her with his usual serious and steady gaze.

Was he working in the library? The thought made her break out in a small sweat despite the chilly morning.

"Thank you. That is very helpful." She turned back to her parchment but had completely lost her train of thought. What was she about to do? Was it the garden room or drafts of the dining room furniture?

He shuffled through papers behind her, and while not noisy, his presence filled the room like someone had lit a candelabra.

Before he entered, she had enjoyed one of those exalted work states whereby time flew by. But all that had ground to a halt. Now all she could do was inhale his clean, masculine smell. Soap, starch, and a sweet citrus scent that refused to be named.

"What are you working on today?" His deep voice made the

question seem more intimate than it actually was. Like he'd asked her deepest secrets. She shivered and rubbed her arms.

What am I working on? Probably nothing. Not now. "Just gathering my thoughts before I start preliminary sketches for the dining room."

"Do you have time to go for a drive later this morning? I have work to finish, but after that, we could take a tour around the London streets. There won't be many carts and wagons on the road on a Saturday. If we have rugs and enough hot bricks, we could take my curricle. Then you won't need to crane your neck through a small window. What say you? Fun and flirting are guaranteed."

She laughed because he said "fun and flirting" in the same monotone as "carts and wagons." It was hard to tell if he was being droll or serious.

She really should get some preliminary work done on the designs. But she couldn't work *all* day, and Lady Hartley *had* instructed her to spend time with her son.

"I say that sounds lovely. I have seen a little of Bond Street and around Covent Garden, but my knowledge of London is woeful. I will probably be a most annoying companion, delighted, excited, or horrified by everything I see."

"That is what I most look forward to," he said absently. He leaned back in his chair, his neck tilted to look out of the small window at the birds.

"Do you like innocent country ingenues, then?"

"I like anyone with the ability to get excited by anything. Too much fashionable ennui in this society and not enough engagement. So, yes, I like that you are passionate about your painting and how you see beyond the surface of people. It's a good trait."

He said all of this with the very lack of passion he was deriding, so it was impossible to take it as anything more than an offhand remark.

"Is Mr. Lark out there?"

He shook his head. "I'm too late for him. But I spread some breadcrumbs earlier, and a flock of sparrows is having a feast." He smiled at them, and it squeezed her heart that this enormous man, who every servant held in reverence, took his breakfast crumbs out for the sparrows. Probably daily.

"You could stand by the window and watch them, you know."

He raised an eyebrow. "No, I would only unnerve them. And then they wouldn't finish their breakfast."

Much the same way you unnerve me. This room felt entirely too small. Taking a deep breath, she pulled her focus back to her work. She must overcome this feeling, for if he worked in the library every day, she would get nothing done.

They concentrated on their separate projects in silence. Now and then, the area between her shoulder blades prickled. Was he watching her? It felt like it. But she couldn't turn around to check, so she continued on, each stroke of her pencil a self-conscious effort as she etched in her ideas.

After an exhausting half-hour, he rose from his desk. "It seems my state of mind is not conducive to coherent thought today," he said. "I'll go for a walk, but when I come back, will you be ready to go?"

Did she have the same effect on him? The thought of it was heady, like the Champagne at the theater last week.

"I would love to watch you drive. I might learn something."

"You are interested in handling the ribbons yourself?" He lifted a single eyebrow.

"We have a one-horse gig Father has not driven since his apoplexy. I am keen to learn, for Mother said she cannot and will not, and it does make market day difficult."

"I could teach you." He ground out the offer as though it were against his will. But now that it was said, he could not take it back.

"Would you?" She could barely believe her luck. From the

many times she had seen him driving around his estates, he was an accomplished whip. "I would be most grateful."

"I am a great believer in the independence of ladies. First driving, next suffrage."

"I couldn't agree more," Charis said.

"So perhaps instead of me driving you around London, I'll take you to the ring in Hyde Park. It's gravel, and the horses know it well. It's not as busy as Rotten Row, and any mistakes you make will be between you, me, and the ducks."

"If I can just learn to navigate my way from our house to the market, then I will consider myself quite accomplished." That was if she didn't return home and discover they had sold both Sally the horse, and the gig. Father had steadfastly refused to part with either, but circumstances could change rapidly.

He went to the door with his papers tucked under his arm and an air of resignation about him. Perhaps he got even less work done than she. It should not hearten her to think so.

"Until then, Miss Eastwood."

───────

In retrospect, teaching Miss Eastwood to drive was the worst outing he could have planned. If being in the same library had been distracting beyond belief, having her sit next to him in a pretty chip bonnet, her cheeks flushed, would be the death of him. There was no ignoring the excited glint in her eye or the answering joy he felt when he saw it.

He drove them through the gates of Hyde Park and then spent the next little while finding the safest place on the ring for her to start her lessons. He'd had the stable hitch up his most reliable pair, two chestnuts who were the opposite of flighty and loved nothing more than a solid trot.

Carriages on this frosty February morning were few and far between. The bench of the curricle was meant for two people, but he took up so much space he could feel her leg nestled up against his. It was both perfect and appalling at the same time.

He pulled the carriage to a stop. "First, let's teach you how to hold the ribbons, for if that is wrong, nothing can be right. Our motto when driving must always be 'slow and sure,' for the safety of both the horses and equipage."

"And my own good person," she added with a cheeky smile.

"That too," he agreed. What was it about her that put him at ease? He was normally tight-lipped around ladies, never knowing what to say, knowing he failed to amuse them. But she seemed so happy with life itself that he could say anything. She had no expectations of him.

It was liberating.

"Now, show me your hands, and I'll thread the ribbons correctly so you can see how it should look. These reins are an inch wide. They may be a little big for you, but ..."

He looked down at the hands she held out for his inspection.

"These gloves are a little big," she said. She had long elegant fingers. He could see that even in the too-big gloves. There was an inch of skin, the most delicate kind, as soft as a rose petal, between her sleeve and the start of the glove. His gaze was hooked and unable to move on. It happened often.

"You were saying?" She tilted her head to one side, politely encouraging him to continue.

Yes, he had been about to say something before he had lost all coherent thought. Over her wrist, for Pete's sake. *Get a hold of yourself, man.*

"Big gloves are all to the good. Your hands won't cramp." In the end, she threaded them through herself. "I read about this in a magazine once, and I have practiced a few times using hair ribbons rather than proper tack. Same theory, though." She nimbly traced the reins through her fingers. "There, is that correct?"

"No. Firstly, hold both reins in the left hand. Then it has to go

83

over the top of your index fingers and then through your hand." He clumsily tried to rearrange them correctly without touching her, which was altogether impossible. So, he just took a breath, pulled his own gloves off, and fixed it. He felt a blush creep up his neck and hoped she didn't notice.

"That feels uncomfortable," she said.

"You'll get used to it," he said, probably too briskly. "Now, make sure your reins are perfectly even or one of your horses will turn without you meaning him to. If you want your team to go to the right, slide the reins to the left. This puts pressure on the horse's right side. Opposite to go left."

"I understand." She looked at the horses with steely determination.

"Be kind and polite, but firm. Never use your whip, only in an absolute emergency, of which there should be none."

"Can we go now?"

"Impatient, aren't you? Slow and sure, remember. Keep your carriage upright and don't lean forward."

She set the team to with a *rar* that sounded very practiced, and they were off. She managed quite well and was soft on their bits, driving with a naturally light hand. She spoke to the horses in a gentle, reassuring way that suggested she had been around them often.

He breathed out and relaxed a little. Everything would be fine. There would be no runaway curricles at Hyde Park today.

"You like horses." He knew some ladies were scared of them, which was understandable. Some horses were huge and rather frightening. He also always wondered how it felt to ride sidesaddle and not have the same level of control riding astride could give. Not that it stopped most ladies from being incredibly accomplished riders.

He looked across at her and she was smiling broadly, her cheeks flushed with either excitement or the very cold wind. The tip of her nose was red, and the ribbons of her bonnet flapped in the wind. Luckily, the bonnet was secured under her chin with a large green bow.

"I think I have this now," she said and ratcheted up the speed by encouraging the team on. They immediately picked up to a trot, and she giggled in delight.

"Slow and sure, I believe I said."

"Come now, Ashcroft, let's get the wind in our hair."

He blinked. This was no demure country miss. This was someone else entirely.

He liked her calling him Ashcroft like they were old friends.

But no. "This is your first drive. Please show me you have the ability to slow them down.

"I pull on the reins, yes?"

"Draw them in. Gently, yes. Equally."

"Very well, but not yet. Let's drive to the Serpentine."

"Let's not," he ground out. "Slow down."

She turned to him, realizing he was serious and spoke to the horses before she pulled on the reins to slow them down, shooting him an annoyed look.

He was obviously dampening her fun.

"Watch your traces. They need to be in a straight line, but not too tight, otherwise, it will pull on their necks. Careful now. We're on a slope I never intended us to be on. You must always slow down well before you actually want to stop."

She ignored his strict tone. Probably because sunshine just kept on shining, whether you were in a bad mood or not. "Did you see me? I did it. I drove your team. Wait until I tell Father you let me drive your team in Hyde Park. He will not believe me." She shook her head. "I don't believe me."

His heart pounded, and every part of him itched to take the reins off her, but he wouldn't do that. Not when the learning had brought her such joy. Not when she glowed like this.

When was the last time he'd seen someone so incandescently happy? He couldn't remember. It pulled him like a moth to a candle. He wanted to reach out and touch her warmth, have it for himself.

She is not for you. He'd ruin her joy eventually, with his crusading.

They slowed to a stop, and she handed him the reins. "Thank you. It was so much better than I thought it would be. The feeling of control over such speed and strength. No wonder you all love driving so much."

"You will need many more hours of practice before you're ready to drive on your own. Perhaps your father will take you out when you return home."

She glanced up at him, so obviously crestfallen that it tugged at him.

"And I will take you out again, as often as we can."

"Oh good! Thank you." She leaned toward him and planted a kiss on his cheek. "You are the very best of men."

His heart thumped in his chest, and it was everything he could do not to pull the strings on the bonnet and kiss her, on the lips this time. Soundly. Taking her joy and happiness for himself.

He should say something, but it was moments before he could form words. She'd taken them all from him with a simple kiss on the cheek.

It was just unexpected, that was all. Ladies never did that kind of thing.

Not to him.

"Yes, well. Listen to me next time I tell you to stop," he said gruffly when all he could feel was a scorching brand on his cheek where her lips had just been.

The flirting had just officially gone too far.

CHAPTER 9

WHERE MISS EASTWOOD RECEIVES AN
UNDESERVED SCOLDING

The clock in the hall chimed eleven. *Drat it all, I should be finished with the grand drawing room design.* But every time she put pencil to parchment, she hesitated, trying to balance *I-Want-to-Impress-You* with *Can't-I-Just-Be-Cozy?* Like ladies wearing muslin in winter, it was the eternal struggle. She wanted it to be both.

Lady Hartley had gone to call on her bosom friend, Lady Astley, with not even the *pretense* of asking Charis to accompany her. She sighed. There was so much work to do before she gave the workmen their instructions that perhaps it was a blessing.

Lord Ashcroft had gone to his club before attending the Commons, which would also give her overactive imagination a rest. Her mind constantly heard his footsteps in the hall, making her turn to the door to see if he was coming to the library. Wanting him to be there. Knowing it would be entirely awkward after she'd been so forward on their drive.

She had *kissed* him! Without the slightest provocation.

His expression of wide-eyed shock mixed with a sprinkle of wonder after it would live with her forever. The way his gaze seemed to catch on her lips, and he appeared unable to look away.

Well, he should stop being so grumpy and kissable.

In fact, Lord Ashcroft was too distracting altogether. Striding around this house with his long legs in breeches, pushing his spectacles to the end of his nose at breakfast. Listening as though he were interested in her opinion. How dare he?

It seemed the moment she'd promised *not* to set her cap at him was the moment her heart decided it wanted nothing more.

So, the house was quiet and the library an oasis without his presence even as she agonized over the grand drawing room. It was a double room, currently a mix of elements from eighty years of habitation, and would benefit from the kind of clean sweep Lord Ashcroft would hate.

She smiled to herself. It might be fun to needle him. But no, she must have his best interests at heart.

There were pieces to keep, of course—the artwork, piano, and sofas, if she could get them reupholstered. But the drapes, papering, and carpets needed replacing, and if her current thoughts were correct, it would be more sumptuous than any room she had designed so far.

Something to show future clients. She must make a copy of it.

Lady Hartley had purchased a large chandelier for the room, which begged to have a small table directly beneath it. She imagined people playing cards or reading a book underneath. It would be a lovely centerpiece.

Lord Ashcroft would hate that it was in the center of the room.

Then, of course, she wanted to create Lady Hartley's boudoir, even though the lady in question had told her not to bother. And the nursery, with a mural that she intended to paint herself. So a room for Ashcroft's future wife, and then one for his future children. It gave her a pang of … What was that? Heartache or jealousy? *Who could tell?*

The deep tones of Lambley echoed down the hall as he welcomed a visitor to the house.

But she was the only one at home.

Whoever was calling had a loud, blustery voice that seemed to make the walls vibrate. "If he is not here, I shall await his return."

"But, sir, I have no idea when he will return." The unshakable Lambley sounded exasperated. "We will send a messenger, and you are welcome to wait in the drawing room. I know he will not want to miss you, Mr. Kinross."

"I should have brought a book with me."

The gentleman visitor must be of some stature, or Lambley would not show him into the drawing room to wait. She supposed he was a colleague from the Commons or someone wanting Lord Ashcroft's influence.

Charis went back to her painting, which was now coming along beautifully. She had sketched in the elements and was about to start the first wash of buttery yellow.

More than anything, she wanted to create serenity. It was sorely lacking in the London metropolis. Living in the city required a haven, after all the mud and dust and smoke.

Like her daily walks, which took her through the central parkland of Grosvenor Square, where the bustle got quieter and quieter the closer to the center she ventured. The house had to be like that. A place to escape.

She leafed through her copy of *Household Furniture* to find a picture of the sofa she had in mind for the main drawing room.

Ashcroft's visitor was still grumbling in the background, like a bad oboe recital.

Was he talking to himself, or did he still have Lambley with him? Unable to ignore it any longer, Charis rose from her seat and padded across the hall so she could listen at the door.

"Sends me five messages and then isn't home for my call? Butler says he's at the club I just left. Why didn't I see him there?

Put me in this room that looks like something King Louis spat out. How long am I supposed to wait?"

Charis smiled to herself because he sounded out of sorts with the entire world. He probably walked through his life like this. It reminded her of Father when he became so frustrated with his condition you couldn't look at him without having your head bitten off.

In some ways, that was when she loved him most. He was vulnerable and needed the love and support of those around him. Not that she let him berate her. But she knew the reason behind it.

This gentleman would likely scold her, too, but she would try. It was a small way she could help Ashcroft. Maybe he would be grateful and take her somewhere fun, or smile at her. With the dimple.

Decided on a course of action, she peered around the door. He was standing at the window, one hand holding back the drapes to look onto Grosvenor Square.

He was a short man and would likely only come up to her shoulders if she stood next to him. He wore his steely hair cropped extremely short á la Brutus, combed forward onto his forehead to hide a large bald pate.

There was no tea tray for him. She snuck away from the door and went to the kitchen, standing at the threshold. There were five maids, four of them standing at the bench while one stirred a pot on the range.

"Good morning. Is there a tea tray for the gentleman in the front drawing room?" The scullery maid's eyes darted over to the counter next to the range. There was no tray.

"It doesn't look like it, miss."

Charis nodded. "Very well. Could you please send tea with some of those lovely almond cakes to me in the drawing room? My thanks."

The scullery maid bobbed a curtsy, and Charis bobbed one in

return, not feeling far above the maid in station, and made her way back to the drawing room.

The euphoria of being in charge of a situation and doing the right thing put a lightness in her step as her heels clipped along the marble tiles.

She poked her head around the door, only to see the man had not moved and was *still* complaining. Heaven help her.

"Good morning?" She stepped into the room.

He whirled around, his eyebrows shooting up, most likely at the outrage of a young lady introducing herself to him.

That was not to be helped, for there was nobody around to introduce her.

She stepped forward with a welcoming smile and a curtsy, even though hers was not the place to welcome anyone into the house.

"I am Miss Eastwood. I hope you will not mind, but I have ordered a tea tray since I was ordering one for myself and thought you might appreciate something hot on such a cold, blustery day."

She went to the sofa, knowing his manners would not allow him to stand while she took a seat. "Will you take tea with me?"

He frowned but could not ignore the plea.

He bowed with a quick incline of his head. "I am Mr. Kinross. Pleased to make your acquaintance." He sat on the opposite sofa, his shoulders slumping a little. "I appreciate the tea. You are correct."

"I was painting in the library and heard you come in. t was as good a time as any to stop for tea. I do like to make a new acquaintance."

Especially such a grumpy one.

"Painting, hey? Young ladies do like their accomplishments." He shook his head ruefully. "Very well. Get them and show me. My daughter loves to show me each time she ends a line in her stitching."

Charis smiled. "I would never bore you thus. I'm sure you have much more important things on your mind."

He harrumphed. "Nothing I wouldn't appreciate distraction from."

"Are you in the Commons with Lord Ashcroft?" She smiled. "You'll find me most unknowledgeable. I have come here from Hartley Green as a guest of Lady Hartley."

He almost smiled. Almost. "Is this your first visit to the metropolis?"

"Not if you count the time when I was nine. I find seeing London through adult eyes very different from those of a child."

"I'm sure Lord Ashcroft doesn't have the time at the moment to squire you around."

"I would not expect it of him, but he has taken me to the Royal Academy and taken me driving in Hyde Park. He has a very busy schedule. The Commons is a harsh mistress."

"It is indeed."

"More so at the moment. He doesn't bring his work home, but I see him reading the newspapers, and I know you are all facing a sore trial in the coming weeks." She didn't have to school her face into sympathetic features, for it was already there. She felt sympathy for all the men dealing with the drama and the scandal of the Duke of York's behavior. Whether he allowed his mistress to sell commissions to the highest bidder or not, discovering the truth would be no easy feat.

He closed his eyes briefly. "If you must know, it is why I am waiting for Ashcroft."

The tea arrived, and Charis poured, noting the brew was strong, and gave Mr. Kinross the second cup so his brew was even stronger. She added sugar at his request and handed him the cup.

She sat back. "Then we shall wait with a nice strong cup of tea and hope he does not arrive too soon." She took a sip and sighed with pleasure. "I'm not too proud to tell you the tea Lady Hartley keeps is the best I have ever partaken of. What is it, do you think?"

He took his first sip. "I would say a mixture of Assam and Darjeeling. Just what I needed." He sank back into the sofa, resting the tea on his knee. "I was ready to put my fist through that pane of glass in my annoyance. Tea fixes everything, does it not?" He took another sip and exhaled.

Sensing he might like to talk about the reason for his visit, Charis probed gently. "And what *is* the house currently contemplating? It seems to me, from reading the newspapers, that you do not quite know how to proceed. I am quite in sympathy. It is such a messy scandal. Do you close the doors to the public and try to deal with it quietly or open them and create a fracas none of you want or need?"

He narrowed his eyes, likely due to her strongly stated opinion. Then he nodded. "You have hit the nail on the head. I shouldn't wonder at it. My wife also can see the wood from the trees in matters like this. I am of the opinion we need to close the doors, keep out the riffraff and protect the duke from all their scurrilous activities."

Charis felt her brows drawing together. "And how is keeping the doors closed going to stop the press? In some respects, I wonder if it will only give them greater license to invent their own story. Suddenly, rather than having the actual information, they have to rely on leaks and second-hand gossip from people who might have their own agendas."

"There seems to be no right answer."

"Perhaps if parliament is open and honest, you can get it over with quickly and move on to the real problems."

"Which are?" He smiled.

"Why, our troops in Spain and Portugal. The very army the duke is supposed to be leading."

"If he makes it through this to lead the army."

"For the sake of our troops, you must discover his culpability or innocence in the cleanest, quickest way. Does it protect him to close the doors and have the half-lies of the press run rampant?"

His mouth quirked, and he blinked a few times before nodding, taking one last sip of his tea, and putting his cup down. "Out of the mouths of babes, as they say. Well, I must be off. I don't think there's any reason for me to wait any longer for Ashcroft."

She put her cup down and rose, too. "Was I too outspoken? I apologize if I've been too forthcoming with my opinion."

His face broke into a smile, showing a set of crooked teeth. "No, quite the opposite, my dear. I find I do not need to speak to Lord Ashcroft now, as my opinion is set."

He bowed, and Charis curtsied. "It's been a pleasure to meet you. I do hope to introduce you to my daughter one day soon. I believe you might rub along well. Both strong-minded young ladies."

He left the drawing room and went down the hall, allowing Lambley to shrug him into his coat and hand him his walking cane.

As Lambley opened the front door, Ashcroft appeared in it, looking like he had just run from his club. He had a brown paper package in his hands that Lambley took from him.

"Ah, Kinross. Thank you for coming. I appreciate your time. Apologies for not being at home." Ashcroft brushed past Mr. Kinross and turned, sweeping his arm to welcome him into the room he had just left.

Mr. Kinross stayed at the door. "Apologies, Ashcroft, but I have waited too long and must go." His voice was brusque once again, and Charis wondered where the kindly man of a few moments ago had gone.

Then the doorway was empty. Lord Ashcroft looked from the door to her and blinked rapidly. "What happened?"

"We had tea. He got tired of waiting, I suppose." She grimaced because it did look bad.

"Is all well?"

Charis shrugged. "I have no reason to believe it's not."

He looked to the retreating form, then back to her, his brows knit together. "Then why did he leave? I've been sending messages to him all week. He finally visits and in five minutes you've chased him from the house." He closed his mouth in an angry straight line.

Charis felt her own temper mounting. "I did no such thing, and it was hardly five minutes. If you think it was wrong of me to offer him tea and company while he awaited you, I apologize. But I heard him getting angrier by the moment."

"Forget *him*. *I* am getting angrier by the moment. I worked on that man for weeks, and in the space of a cup of tea, it is all dashed."

"You are being very unjust. I was trying to help. I *did* help."

"I do not need or ask for your assistance. These negotiations are delicate. You can't bumble into them with a smile and good wishes. It's too important." There was a little tic pulsing in his jaw.

"And I could not possibly comprehend a delicate situation. I am just a girl from the country who wouldn't know a Tory from a Whig."

He blinked. "Well, you are young and from the country, and you've admitted yourself that you don't know anything. How could you?"

What was worse, the fact he hadn't waited to find out what had been said before he jumped to conclusions, or that he assumed she wasn't capable of having tea with someone?

"You're *infuriating*." It felt good to let go of her lady-like inhibitions and just tell him.

"It's hard to believe you've only just noticed." He strode past her and entered the library, closing the door with a firm click.

She looked at the closed door in consternation. *How dare he walk away?*

This flirting debacle was definitely over.

The numbers he had clawed together all week were slipping away one by one. Parliament would close the doors to the press to try to protect the duke, heaven knew why, and all hell would break loose in the newspapers.

The meeting at the club had gone for longer than expected, and he could not sway any members to his way of thinking. He'd left in a temper and walked the streets of Westminster.

And now Kinross had also slipped from his grasp, with Miss Eastwood having pushed him down the slope.

But it was always the way with parliament. The way you thought something should go seldom did.

There was a gentle knock at the door.

Ashcroft closed his eyes and took a breath. Obviously, she would not leave it alone.

This was a conversation he did not want to have. He liked Miss Eastwood, he respected her, and did not want to tell her to keep her nose out of things that did not concern her.

She would already have the shadow of hurt in her eyes when she entered the library.

Ladies were so incredibly fragile. She would beg his pardon and ask for forgiveness. That she should never have become involved and was deeply sorry.

He would accept, of course.

He stood. "Come in," he said with more than an ounce of regret.

She looked neither fragile nor hurt, arching an eyebrow like he was nothing more than an amusement. He wished he could look so effortlessly sardonic. It would come in handy in parliament. Although whether anyone would notice a single eyebrow amongst the riot that was the Commons was anyone's guess.

The package on his desk sat between them like a witness to the argument that was about to happen. Her eyes drifted down to it, taking in the brown paper wrapping, tied with string.

He motioned to the chair in front of his desk. "Won't you sit?"

"Thank you." She looked at him, her gaze even and unperturbed. She sat primly, hands folded in her lap but a slightly militant air about her. "Lord Ashcroft, I did nothing wrong, and request an apology."

He blinked as he waited for his mind to catch up. "*You* would like an apology from *me*?"

"I believe you have it the right way around, yes." There was a gleam in her eye that made him rethink. She was the daughter of a captain who had distinguished himself in battle. She had steel in her blood.

"I am more than capable of handling a touchy gentleman or two and bringing them around to my way of thinking. My father can be the most prickly man you could meet. I am also, in case you didn't notice, empathetic to the plight of other people. And this includes you."

He heard her say "unfortunately," under her breath. She looked out the window. "I spent a great deal of time this morning on your behalf. I think you'll find I have done you great service and to find you judging my abilities before seeing the outcome is beneath you. Perhaps I overstepped the mark. Maybe I should have stayed in the library and continued to paint when I heard him grumbling in the other room about how ungrateful you were. If I'm sorry for anything, it's that I can't listen without doing something. And so I did. I don't regret it, and I would most likely do it again."

Two splotches of red on her cheeks belied the evenness of her tone. She was politely telling him he was wrong and rather than admonishing her, he should thank her. Worse still, maybe she was right.

Was it really her fault? He was the one who was not there to receive Kinross.

He searched for the proper words, leaving a silent gap in the conversation. "Mr. Kinross is a very peevish creature, and the slightest thing can set him off. You were not to know, but I need his vote in the Commons this week to open up this ludicrous hearing to the public. We do not need furtive whispers and untruths told by the press. I've already lost three votes today and his was the fourth. I am fighting a losing battle. I let my anger at the situation be directed at you."

"Yes, you did. Please go on." She motioned with her hands for him to continue.

"If I'm honest, I'm angrier at myself. I allowed myself to be distracted, and was not actually at my club where the message of his arrival would find me." Why was he telling her this? A voice inside yelled, "Retreat, retreat."

"Distracted by what?"

"You." Now he'd gone and told her. *Damnation.* "As I have been all week. I have too much happening to be flirting. It was supposed to be lighthearted fun, but I'm afraid I can't even afford that right now."

Her eyes flared with shock. "But I have done nothing."

"It's hardly your fault I can't be around you and also concentrate. I wish the two things were compatible, but they are not." She did something to his brain. Turned it to pudding. One of those blancmanges that wobbled weakly when put down on the table.

She clenched her fists in her lap. "As you wish."

He looked away and then back. "That easy?"

She shrugged one shoulder. "Certainly. I promised I would not fall for your charms."

"Charms!" He barked out a laugh. "We are talking about yours, not mine. I'm sure I have none." But what did she think his allure was? How did she see him? No, he would not ask.

"You have enough." She still looked at her hands, as though she didn't trust herself to look up. "Although I am severely disappointed by your inability to admit I was right."

He had a flash of insight that she was changing the topic. "I don't normally have to admit I was wrong, because I invariably am not."

She still looked down at her hands. Waiting.

He waited for one breath and then two, but she held on, not looking at him, not speaking to him. Just looking down so her long eyelashes fanned over her cheeks. Demure, ladylike. Waiting for an apology.

To Jericho with it.

"Oh, very well. If you must have it, lending your company to Kinross was the right thing. I'm sure his vote will have no impact or bearing on what happens. I apologize, Miss Eastwood."

When she looked up, her eyes were sparkling with mischief. The vixen. "Apology accepted. I am surprised you did not argue more. Surely it is in your nature." And there was that sardonic eyebrow again, arching itself in a most opinionated way.

"I suggest you enjoy this rarified time." His eyes went down to the package. "That is for you."

Her eyes returned to the package, and he saw a definite flicker of interest overcome her frustration. He didn't want gratitude to stop her from being angry at him, for so few people really told him what they thought.

If he ever wondered if she was setting her cap at him, the answer was right there. She wasn't trying to impress him and didn't care if he thought her impulsive. She would do it again, no matter the consequences. She had shrugged one shoulder when he said they had to stop flirting, completely unconcerned. Was this an entirely one-sided infatuation? Was that what it was?

Her eyes brightened, as though she had never had a present, and his heart clenched. She was so lovely. And yes, it was infatuation, *damn it all*, whether he had time for it or not. She'd just annoyed him royally, and he still couldn't take his eyes off her.

She leaned forward, picking it up and turning it over in her hands. It was the reason he wasn't at his club when the footmen had come looking for him, but he dared not tell her.

She pulled the bow apart and then ripped off the brown paper like it was her birthday morning and raised the book out of the wrapping. *"The Picture of London for 1809,"* she said, flipping open the cover. *"Being a Correct Guide to All the Curiosities, Amusements, Exhibitions, Public Establishments, and Remarkable Objects, in and Near London.* How lovely."

"Mr. Hatchard said it was the one he recommends."

She looked up at him, her eyes wide, and then back down at the package. "It's beautiful, thank you. It could not be more perfect." She fingered through the pages. "Oh, look, it says the House of Commons is an attraction. Can I visit you?"

"It feels like a barnyard, more than a place of law sometimes. I would recommend almost *anything* else."

She drew her finger down the table of contents. "Let's see, page one hundred and eight." One moment later she was on the page and read for a minute. "Goodness, they spend a great deal of time talking about the wall decoration. How strange. Should I care if they are entirely wainscoted? I suppose I must." She read down a little farther. "Well, that puts paid to that idea. Ladies are not admitted during sittings."

"No member wants a lady to witness his bad behavior," he said dryly. "Choose something else."

"I will look at it. Although I am very busy finishing the designs and would be loath to leave them. I have completed some rooms and hope to show your mother tomorrow."

"I would like to see them, too. What time?"

She hesitated. "Midday." Her gaze slid away from his. She was such a bad liar. Would he arrive to find all the designs had been approved hours earlier? Probably. But nothing could happen without his approval. "I hope you won't change any of my ideas, for I loved each of them. Sometimes pulling one thread of a tapestry can ruin the whole thing."

"If your designs are everything we both discussed at the beginning, then you have nothing to worry about. I cannot be wrong about how I would like my home to look. In that, I must always be right. But I trust you. I had only to see the design of the dressmaker's shop to see how talented you are."

A blush of red appeared on her cheeks, which was endearing. "Now then, I didn't say it to make you blush. You know I only ever speak the truth."

"You do, don't you? You speak to me like an equal, not like you must spare my feelings or some such nonsense. We have had our first argument and come out the other side. Our friendship has officially been seasoned."

"Like a skillet?" It seemed friendship with Miss Eastwood meant putting himself up against the fire of her honesty and hoping he didn't get scorched. "I don't think the daughter of a captain of the queen's Dragoon Guards would want it any other way."

She nodded, and her smile was entirely proud. As she should be. "Then let's meet tomorrow and get this house underway. So we can have a ball and find you a wife."

"Heaven help me," he said with a roll of his eyes, just to amuse her.

It was a ball with him as the prize, and he had no way to stop it.

Unless he just refused to participate. Put a stop to all this nonsense right now. If he didn't have time to flirt, he most certainly did not have time to find a wife.

CHAPTER 10

IN WHICH LORD ASHCROFT NEEDS A LESSON IN APPROPRIATE COMPLIMENT GIVING

Charis cleared everything off the table in the garden room and opened the curtains to their fullest extent.

Still not enough light.

There were candelabras on the side benches, so she lit them too. She would not be judged on designs that were poorly lit. After carefully laying them out in the order she wanted them inspected, she stepped back and took a deep breath.

Done.

There was nothing more she could do but wait for Lady Hartley to arrive.

But not Lord Ashcroft. She did not need him in the room while she bared her soul with her designs. She smiled. He'd be an hour late and come when everything was decided.

That would teach him to interfere.

Lady Hartley entered. "Am I late? Apologies."

Charis waved the apology away. "I have been busy organising everything. Think nothing of it."

Lady Hartley's ensemble looked like she had stepped straight from the pages of *The Ladies Monthly Museum*. And Charis should know, as she'd read the January edition from cover to cover when she found it in the drawing room. The dress was of cornflower blue satin with white sleeves and a white fichu frothing at her neck. The crisp white point lace adorning the bodice would not come from her old dress, as Charis's had.

She looked ready to go out on her morning calls.

"Wilson must put my hair in braids today, of all days." She patted her silver-shot dark hair piled with elaborate plaits criss-crossing her head.

"It was worth it, they look lovely."

Knowing her maid, Wilson, would not have gone to this trouble without Lady Hartley's express directive, Charis took the apology in the spirit in which it was meant.

"Thank you. My dear, I know you will think I have abandoned you, but nothing could be further from the truth. I am grateful you are such a self-sufficient body and have gone about your business and created my designs. I know I will love them."

Her eyes lighted on each of the watercolors Charis had laid out.

It had been very late the previous evening when Charis finally finished the grand drawing room, giving her five finished, designs to present. The dining room, the front receiving room, the garden room, the upstairs grand drawing room, and the ballroom.

Each was designed to be a play on the same color palette of soft sage green with gold and white. All rooms were connected with cream ceilings and ornate plasterwork that tied into the hall design. There was nothing more jarring than walking from one brightly colored room to another. In her completely uneducated opinion.

It was, in some ways, simpler than Charis expected it to be, but it was still sumptuous. Once she decided on the plaster mold-ings, she felt free to continue these elements in big and small ways throughout the house, finding furniture from the catalogs that would work in harmony.

"What an achievement! While I have been catching up with friends, you have been toiling, my dear." She took her time, looking from one painting to the next. "And you have exceeded my expectations. The rooms belong together, don't they? Like parts of a puzzle."

"I must give credit to our days spent visiting the warehouses and the inspiration they provided. With such beautiful things to purchase, it was easy to create the rooms around them."

"Oh, Charis, it is so *pretty*. I cannot help but wish I lived here permanently. Tell me again why we're giving this to Ashcroft?"

"You mentioned enticing the young ladies to see his eligibility. Although how they could miss that I cannot fathom. Is he not young, handsome, hard-working, in possession of a substantial fortune, and heir to a title?" Charis shook her head. "They would flock to him if he would just deign to visit Almack's."

"When you phrase it that way," Lady Hartley said and shrugged. "However, it seems most young ladies like the brooding poetic kind who can recite sonnets about their eyes or some such nonsense. The rest of them like the dashing gentlemen to squire them around town. I spend a great deal of time at balls, and I see which gentlemen attract the cream of the crop. And I want that for Ashcroft. I want him to find his match and to find love. But if he spends entire balls standing with the gentlemen in the corner, posturing about this bill or that, trust me, no young lady would want to be courted by him. Or if she did, it would be at the behest of her parents and against her better judgment." She raised an eyebrow. "I find it encouraging that you think him handsome, though. I think he is beautiful, but then, he is my son."

Charis thought it was best not to wax eloquent about how attractive she found the fiery intelligence in his eyes. Or the way he commanded the attention of a room just by entering it. Or the way he looked at a person as if they were the most talented, important, and cherished being. So, yes, he was handsome, but it was more than that.

These thoughts made the heat of a blush rise up her cheeks, and she was both grateful and appalled when the object of their discussion strode into the room.

Charis sighed. So much for trying to separate mother and son for this meeting.

"Ah. Here we are. I would not miss this for the world." He stood behind his mother and looked at each of the pictures. "You have worked so hard, Miss Eastwood, to reach this point. Now, what have we?"

"A serene and beautiful home that will be an oasis for you." The knot of nerves in her stomach bloomed into something sicklier. It was one thing to spend every day getting excited by the designs in the rooms she created, and quite another to have people look at them.

Had she hit her target of both a sense of the picturesque *and* the prestige of being a marquis's eldest son? This had to be the home of a modern man at the very forefront of everything stylish and elegant. A house that would suit him for years to come and be a place he welcomed his family, friends, and colleagues.

No more sending Mr. Kinross into the front receiving room, only to have him met by baroque magnificence that would make anyone feel irritable.

"And you have succeeded admirably," Lady Hartley said. "There is nothing I would change. I even have that beautiful boudoir chaise lounge I admired so much in Hartley Green. It looks lovely, and I don't care what the cost is. I am to have it."

"You? Are you moving back to Grosvenor Square?"

"No … no," she stammered. "Although we could put it in my room. After all, I am going to a great deal of expense here for your benefit."

"A benefit I never asked for, if I remember correctly. I was quite happy with how things were. Anything you do is a ball off your own bat, Mama."

Lady Hartley frowned, but at the childlike moniker, her face softened, and she patted his cheek.

He scrutinized the grand drawing room painting and frowned. His gaze did not move past the round table under the chandelier that served as a centerpiece for the room. Just as she'd known he would. Charis ignored the impulse to wring her hands and pushed them behind her skirts.

His eyes narrowed. "I thought I specifically requested not to have furniture strewn about the room." He pointed to the drawing room. "And yet there is a table in the very center and chairs strewn everywhere. I won't be the only person who falls over something. Large pieces of furniture should be near a wall."

Dear heaven, he doesn't like it. All that work and she'd be back to the beginning. Worse still, this was the very best she could do. And she wasn't joking about the tapestry thread metaphor; changing entire elements would make the whole design worse.

She steeled herself for the second argument of their friendship. He would be apologizing by the end of it. "Yes, you did say that. However, you were wrong."

Every ounce of aristocratic arrogance he possessed was displayed in one lazy look. "How can I be wrong about what I would like in my own home?"

Lady Hartley watched her son through wide eyes. Then she shot a glance at Charis, waiting for her reaction. She opened her mouth to say something, but Charis held up a hand. She didn't need a defender.

"The furniture will not move every day. It will stay in these positions unless *you* move it. You will know exactly where everything is within a week, and you will *not* trip. After all, if you can dance about the ring at Gentleman Jackson's and not fall over your own feet, I trust you will not fall over a five-foot-long settee as large as a carriage."

Lady Hartley's trilled laughter filled the room, but she stopped when she realized her son wasn't laughing with her.

"You must admit the room would look silly if the furniture were just against the wall. I fully support Miss Eastwood in this matter. You must have an open mind, my dear. Because things have always been a certain way doesn't mean they should be. We must move with the times."

Charis felt him roll his eyes, although his gaze was direct and steady on her. "*I* must move with the times. I, the most progressive member of parliament, must muster myself along a little faster."

Charis nodded and smiled as though proud he'd caught on. "You'll be used to it in no time, and it is fetching, is it not? By putting furniture in this configuration, I created some lovely nooks for private conversation. Like these chairs by the window. Do you see?"

He peered closer. "Quite right."

"And if you look even closer, there is still a definite path through the room."

"True." He lifted his gaze from the painting to her. His eyes were almost mahogany in the mix of candle and daylight. They weren't dark and intense, but warm like the rarest wood. "I suppose I must once again admit I was wrong. And after I advised you not to make a habit of this."

"Oh." It was a small win, because when he looked at the dining room and saw her mix of classical elements from Greece, Rome, and maybe an Egyptian table leg in there somewhere, he would be annoyed all over again.

Sure enough, a few moments later, he pointed to her dining room design and politely cleared his throat. "Am I also wrong about the Greek influences I see in the plasterwork, the Chinese-inspired dining chairs sitting unhappily with a console table that most definitely looks like something from a Pharaoh's tomb? Could we not just stick to one thing?"

She straightened and pushed her shoulders back. "Actually, the dining chairs are the ones your grandmother purchased. The plasterwork is consistent throughout the rooms, and I found the console in Lady Hartley's upstairs bedroom. It is a beautiful piece and deserves to be in a more public place. Certainly, this constitutes a mixing of classical elements, however, they are all elements found currently in your home, just displayed slightly differently. You can't really argue with something that has been here for years, can you?"

His eyes widened, and she saw a spark of … Was it anger or just frustration? It was impossible to tell. "I cannot be wrong about this. It is my heartfelt opinion. Put the console back in my mother's room, I beg you."

He was not begging. It was a directive.

Charis shrugged and turned to Lady Hartley to see she had an equally ambivalent expression on her face. "I suppose we have taken him as far as we can," she said with a smile.

Charis looked at Lord Ashcroft, a question in her eyes. "Is that everything? Are you happy for us to move forward with these designs, except for removing the console from the dining room?"

His mouth closed as he contemplated the pictures. "Let me think on it."

Lady Hartley huffed, exactly what Charis would do if she were not the guest and using her best manners. "You will do no such thing. These pictures are beautiful and we're going ahead with them. I'm indulging you by removing the console, but that is all. Don't be a spoilsport, Theodore."

Charis blinked rapidly. His name was Theodore. It suited him perfectly, that mix of studiousness and boyish charm. It was not hers to use, but she tucked it away like a small treasure one could carry in a pocket.

"I am allowed to think about it. It is pretty, I agree, but is it too pretty? I don't want to live in a jewel box. It does not feel like I belong there."

Charis inhaled sharply. A lump formed in her throat and refused to budge.

To say he didn't belong in a home she designed … Her knees felt weak, and she steadied herself on the table, hoping no one would notice. He might not hate it, but he didn't want to live in it either.

Had she just made the greatest error of all and designed a house for herself rather than her client? What she and Lady Hartley liked carried no weight when faced with what the *actual* inhabitant of the house wanted. She'd spent so much energy trying to get him to see she knew more about decoration, that she'd conveniently forgotten to take his wishes seriously.

Oh dear. How could she possibly fix this? She would have to start again. Which was a shame, too, because it really was beautiful. Or at least she thought it was. How many hours had she spent imagining him living in it? Too many, it seemed.

"What you mean is that you are a serious man, and this refurbishment has levity. It is comforting and elegant. I have not reflected your gravity and reflected too much of my own levity." She blinked away the tears forming in her eyes, willing them to stay put. "You are right. It is all wrong. I'm sorry." She met his gaze and hoped he could see her genuine contrition there.

She had been ready to go to battle with him over her choices, but him telling her the house did not feel like his home was like a dagger to the heart. Not to be dramatic about it.

He was right. He literally could not be wrong. And so much money was being spent.

Lady Hartley frowned at her son, her mouth an unhappy pout. "Now look what you've done!"

"I will think on this," Charis said. What she really meant was that she was going to her bedroom to indulge in a good cry.

The rooms would never be ready in time for the ball if she had to start the designs all over again. So, she had let Lady Hartley down too.

She left the room to the dulcet tones of her host telling her son precisely what she thought. "There were so many things we could have done, but chose not to. Floral wall hangings and drapes in so many shades of crimson and purple it would make your head spin. Charis kept it classical and, dare I say, more masculine than it currently is. This is an *improvement*."

"I'm not saying it's not an improvement. You are both bent on misunderstanding me. I just want to think on this so I can give thoughtful feedback."

She turned on the stairs to see Lady Hartley shooing him out of the room. "That's enough from you, Ashcroft. You are no longer helpful in our project. You will love it and if you don't, I truly don't care. I have plans that hinge on these designs being finished by Easter, and you won't hold me up."

He knew those plans were a ball and a wife because she had told him. Charis could still hear her ladyship's voice echoing across the marble as she climbed the stairs.

She climbed faster, not wanting to encounter Ashcroft. It would be impossible to look at him.

Not when she'd pinned all her hopes on him reacting with wonder, awestruck by her talent and what she'd created.

Instead, he'd said he had to think about it, which suggested he had to convince himself of the merit of what she'd done.

It was hard to believe she thought she could make a profession with this skill.

She'd fallen at the first hurdle.

CHAPTER 11

IF IT LOOKS LIKE AN INSULT AND SOUNDS LIKE AN INSULT ...

He couldn't do it. Couldn't let her walk away feeling like she'd failed when there was nothing wrong with her designs. How could he explain that every day he put off his mother's matchmaking was another day he didn't have to face courting a virtual stranger? Hearing his mother say her 'plans' hinged on the designs had got his back up instantly.

If he were an army, he would about-face and march as fast as he could. But now he couldn't even remember what he didn't like about her designs, because in fact, they were beautiful. There was a lightness and elegance to them that would be a joy to live in. But how could he say that now?

All he knew was looking at them felt like looking at a future he wasn't ready to step into.

He'd said he needed time to think. He should have been more delicate.

Who would say that, when she looked at them with her heart and soul plainly visible?

Now she was climbing the stairs to her room, disappointment written in the way her shoulders slumped, and her hand trailed along the banister as she climbed.

"I do like them, Miss Eastwood." He climbed after her. "But you know I can't do anything without deliberation. It is my weakness. I have no impulsiveness."

Her manners were too good not to turn around, but he soon wished she had not. Her eyes were glassy with unshed tears. "Yes, of course. Please take all the time you need, and let me know how I can change the designs to suit you better …"

He reached out his hand to her, but her chin lifted, and there was a note of defiance in her eyes. "I do not need sympathy, Lord Ashcroft. If it needs changes, I will make them. It is perfectly fine, I promise you."

She turned away to continue up the stairs.

All he wanted to do was tell her that his argument was not with her, but with his mother, whom he could feel pushing him toward decisions.

He didn't want a woman who came to a ball and decided she'd like to stay because the house looked fetching. And he didn't want to marry someone he barely knew. If ever there was a decision made in haste to be repented at leisure, a quick marriage was at the top of the list.

"This is not about the designs," he said.

She turned around. "What is it about, then?" She was two steps above him now, and he had to look up at her. The light from the arched window behind her turned her dark gold hair into a halo. It was like staring up at an angel. Possibly the avenging kind.

"We both know why Mother is doing this and why she is throwing a ball when she hasn't thrown one outside of Hartley Green in ten years. I'm not ready to …" He searched for a way to say what he was feeling. The way she was steadily backing him into a corner. "I'm just …"

"Not ready to marry?" Charis kindly finished for him.

"Not that," he ground out. "I'm ready. But this—"

"Is too big to let someone else choose."

She understood him perfectly.

"So, you actually like it? And all this rumpus is just because you don't want to be pushed into anything?"

"Maybe … yes." He looked down at his toes and then up into her eyes. "I'm not proud to admit it."

She actually rolled her eyes at him, and despite everything, it was amusing. "Have you thought of just telling your mother you'll find your own bride?"

"That's the rub, you see. She's right, much as I hate it. I do need help to find a wife. I just hate the fact that I do." Tedious dancing at Almack's week after week was his idea of hell. Country house parties followed swiftly after. He'd tried that, and failed.

"Then take the new house, have the ball, but tell your mother under no circumstances will you be pressured into such a big decision."

Huh. That was a good idea.

"You have a wise head under all that fluffy hair."

She raised a hand to her head. "What do you mean, fluffy?" She patted it down. "My hair is not fluffy."

"Fluffy like a chick." Adorable, in fact. He'd like to touch it, just to see if it was as soft as it looked.

"I'm not sure that's a compliment."

"What, the wise head, or the fluffy hair?" As far as methods for changing the subject went, it worked rather well. She was no longer talking or thinking about the fact he was unable to find a bride for himself. He felt a spurt of irritation at the way she always stripped him down to the truth. Even when he was trying not to look too closely at it himself. Something about her forced him to be honest with himself, with her.

"I am not going to dignify that with an answer. Fluffy, indeed. Now, do I need to make any changes to those rooms?"

He exhaled and shook his head. "No, they are perfect. As I'm sure you well know."

"I had an inkling. But I must protest at being the object of your distemper. I will let it go this time. Are you off to your club?"

She even knew his daily schedule. Was he so predictable?

"I am. I'm still trying to convince people over to my way of thinking on the vote, so it's White's today."

"The lion's den." She smiled faintly. "Good luck. Give Mr. Kinross my regards."

Her tone was cool. Had he lost her good opinion with his thoughtless talk? The thought his actions could dim the sunshine she spread had him frowning.

"If by lion, you mean mangy old toothless thing with a penchant for Burgundy, then yes."

"Ha! I like it. We shall finalize the tradesmen while you are gone."

"If they're anything like the ones I usually get in, Mother won't get her ball until next year. I have my reprieve."

She nodded. "I am glad." They parted ways. He'd made her sad with his feedback on her designs, and his uncouth remarks about her hair made her self-conscious.

Excellent work, idiot.

The mile to White's was chewed up quite fast when he was mired in his own thoughts, and he arrived at the steps to the venerable club in a short space of time.

He stepped inside, having his coat taken from him, and wandered into the lounge. The only available seat was next to Kinross. Just his luck to sit next to the one man who had definitely made up his mind against him.

He gritted his teeth and steered toward the table, grabbing a newspaper and folding it under his arm. He stood next to his chair. "Good afternoon, Kinross. Would you mind if I joined you?"

"Ah, Ashcroft. Please do. I apologize for leaving so quickly the other day, but I had decided, so there was no point in talking to you."

Precisely what he *didn't* want to hear. That Kinross and all his cronies had closed the doors of parliament on the inquiry and made the entire problem so much the worse. He sat, but kept his newspaper folded. "I can guess the decision."

Kinross smiled jovially. "Yes, I suppose if you spoke to Miss Eastwood, you would be entirely sure of my direction."

"I had hoped to speak to you myself before you decided."

"I don't need a young fribble like you helping me make my decisions. I've been in the Commons decades longer than you've been alive. But Miss Eastwood had the right of it. I will reluctantly agree. She changed my mind."

So, she'd actually *changed* his mind. He'd come to Grosvenor Square to give his vote to Ashcroft and had his mind changed. How could one innocent young lady cause so much havoc? Mother was right. He needed a shrewd wife if this was what could happen. But because he'd flown off on his high horse, he did not know what they'd actually spoken of. Best to get the whole of it.

"Actually, Miss Eastwood did not tell me what you spoke of, so I am in the dark. What did she say, exactly?"

Kinross cleared his throat and continued to read his newspaper, not looking up at Ashcroft. "Only that the press would fabricate more if we close the doors, letting only half-truths leak out. This will be a mess either way. However, by getting the facts into the public domain, perhaps we can avert some of it. You were right. Now don't tell anyone I said that. Bailey, Williams, and Norfolk are with me, as well as their cronies, and I think you'll find you now have the numbers you are looking for."

Ashcroft sank in his chair, at a loss for words. "And Miss Eastwood influenced your decision?"

A bud of hope bloomed inside him. All was not lost.

But he had maligned Charis entirely.

"Out of the mouths of babes. Although she is not exactly a babe. But I digress. The ladies can gently say something to reach you in a way no headstrong, opinionated man can. They lead you rather than push, if you catch my meaning."

Ashcroft thought on it. She *did* do that. She challenged you, then backed away to let you think. Of course, she felt more comfortable with him, able to say "because you are wrong" in a way most ladies of his acquaintance would not.

He thought he was annoyed, but maybe what he actually felt was admiration.

She had done him an invaluable service, and he hadn't even trusted she could give the man tea without ruining it. He had written her off as not being raised in the right circles to be politically minded, but she had a very fine mind and had the empathy to lead people without browbeating them as he so often did.

In every respect, she was his perfect foil.

"Huh."

This deserved further investigation.

"What do you mean, 'huh'?" Kinross looked at him expectantly.

"I may have underestimated Miss Eastwood, that is all. She has a good head for thinking."

"Under all that glorious hair, you mean? I can see why it would be easy to be distracted from her mind."

"Huh."

It felt like a shaft of sunlight had opened up and was shining on him.

She was a gentleman's daughter, and he had enough blunt that her lack of dowry didn't matter a jot. Too bad for his mother's scheming for a dynastic union.

Charis was perfect.

CHAPTER 12

IN WHICH MISS EASTWOOD IS TEMPTED TO FALL OFF A LADDER AND INTO ASHCROFT'S ARMS

With the right monetary encouragement, Lambley had found a team of men to start early the following Monday morning. By the time the clock struck ten, Lady Hartley's voice echoed down the hall, demanding to know what "that infernal noise" was. It was workmen's banter, joviality and scaffolds being put up.

All the furniture had been commissioned or sent to the upholsterer for recovering. New drapery had been ordered, and the grand drawing room and dining room were cleared for the workmen to start.

The papers for the walls would arrive from Mr. Bromwich's manufactory by the end of the week. It was not a simple case of papering over the old ones, as the original flocked paper had to be removed; however, the men supplied by the manufacturer assured them removal would go smoothly.

Wearing her oldest dress and a pair of truly embarrassing sturdy shoes, Charis left her room to oversee proceedings. Perhaps today she would learn the correct method of removing paper hangings. Or the right brush to use when painting a ceiling.

For once she prayed Lord Ashcroft was out, so he would not see or distract her. She couldn't be worried about her hair when there was so much to learn.

Descending the stairs, with her head full of plans, she collided with Lady Hartley coming up. My lady was dressed to go out in a white robe with a grass-green coat made of the softest merino. Her shoes were maroon velvet with bows on the front.

Lady Hartley steadied them both on the stairs. "Did you hear that rumpus? I almost spilled my cocoa. They are apparently constructing a scaffold so they can reach the ceiling of the dining room. I ask you." She shook her head in disbelief. Then she inspected Charis's ensemble. "You look dressed to milk a cow."

"I was going to oversee the work, but shall I accompany you? I can change." It would be hard to leave, but they wouldn't be long, and it would be wonderful to see something outside of Grosvenor Square.

"And deprive you of all this excitement? No. Lady Astley and I are just visiting Sheridan at the theater to see the new set design for his upcoming play. Nothing could be more boring." She looked down into the hall where a team of workmen laid down drop cloths, and she shuddered.

Charis inhaled sharply. To meet professional painters creating landscapes? To learn how they tricked the eye to see depth where there was none? Nothing could be better. "I would love to go with you, please. I have a mural planned for the nursery and could use some inspiration." Lady Hartley's eyebrows drew together, and Charis paused. "If you want it, that is."

"Of course I want it. But some other time, perhaps." She put her hand under Charis's dropped chin and lifted it gently. "You will have fun today. But don't fall off a ladder. How would I explain to your mother?"

There would be no outing for her. Lady Hartley had glossed over it as though Charis had not just begged to go. Well, Charis would pretend she hadn't noticed and unwrap this all later in her room, like a sour bonbon. "She wouldn't be in the least surprised. We re-papered the dining room last year. She knows I enjoy the practical applications of my art. Although I expect these craftsmen will be on a level I have not yet encountered and will want me well clear." The thought deflated her. If she could not go out and about with Lady Hartley, and the craftsmen would not let her help, what would she do?

Lady Hartley put an arm around Charis's shoulder, which had drooped sadly. "They will do no such thing, and if they do, tell them I said you must take part. If your heart desires it, we will make it happen, no matter how it makes me shudder. I just want to see your paintings come to life exactly how you envisage them. Of course, you must be here. What if they do something wrong?"

It wasn't that Lady Hartley didn't want her company; she just knew how important this was. The show of support made tears gather in Charis's eyes. "Thank you. I'm so glad you understand. I could think of nothing worse than finding the workers had done entirely the wrong thing. I would cry."

"Having known you since you were a babe and determined to run before you could walk, I should have predicted you would be fixated on this project." She laughed, having amused herself. "But don't exhaust yourself, because this afternoon you will accompany me to Lady Buxton's."

"The lady we met outside the modiste?"

Lady Hartley nodded. "The one with the daughter I would love for Ashcroft."

Nothing awkward about the afternoon then, with both mamas angling their offspring together. "That sounds lovely. Do you think we can send a note around to Madame Le Favre to see if any of my dresses are ready?"

"Of course. I shall do it now. We can't have you visiting in that. I'm sure she will reply quickly, and we can have a footman fetch something for you." She continued down the stairs, showing the conversation was over.

"And did you secure Almack's vouchers, perchance?" Charis asked so softly that Lady Hartley could have ignored her and carried on. "If I have a gown, perhaps we could …"

But Lady Hartley stopped at the bottom, her gaze darting around the room before landing on Charis. "Not yet, but I doubt we would be successful. They are such dowdy sticklers. They might consider it if Ashcroft were to attend, but there's no getting that man to Almack's." She waved the idea away like it was smoke in her face. "Don't think on it."

"If you say so."

"I do say so."

With that, she sailed down the hall, and after a quick word to Lambley about the dressmaker, the door closed behind her.

Charis was still on the same step, brow knitted and a horrible tightness in her jaw that was turning into a headache. While working on the designs, she'd been happy enough to not be included, but she'd been in London almost a month now, and that interaction was … strange.

There were only two possible explanations. Firstly, Lady Hartley did not want to introduce Charis to her friends because she was not sophisticated enough; or, secondly, because she had not received her new dresses and looked dowdy.

She would give Lady Hartley the benefit of the doubt and wait until her gowns arrived to see what happened. Hopefully something, or she would have no stories at all to tell Father when she got home.

Charis made her way down to the drawing room, where the carpets had been removed and the floorboards were protected by a series of large, thick sheets. The men worked on four ladders, wetting the wallpaper, allowing the water to soak in, and then stripping the paper off with wedged spatulas.

She introduced herself to the foreman, Mr. Adams, and explained her place in the proceedings. He was a wiry man about a foot shorter than Charis, with thin hair and a receding chin. As expected, he looked mortified.

Charis pretended not to notice. "His lordship is a very busy man but would like me to keep abreast of your progress. If you keep me informed of what you have planned for the day, I can pass this information on. He is also interested in your methods, so please explain them to me, too."

After all, if she was to run her own enterprise, she needed practical knowledge of renovations.

He scratched his head, mussing his light brown hair. "If it pleases his lordship, we can do that. But everything will be right and tight. I've been running my team for five years now."

And it was true. The men worked quickly and efficiently and had the paper almost half-stripped by midday.

When they took their wrapped lunch to sit in the back garden, Charis seized the opportunity to examine their handiwork more closely.

She climbed the ladder, thinking to get a high view of the room that might influence her furniture placement. She turned, five or six rungs up, bracing herself on either side.

It was a splendid room, full of light pouring in from the street now the drapes were down. The cornices that had shrieked at the old wall paperings would sing with simple paint.

The door swung open, and Lord Ashcroft appeared at the threshold.

My, but you have a lovely head of dark, unruly hair. The sight of him, after so many days, made her breath catch. There was none of the annoyance she'd felt at their last meeting, no embarrassment at how she was dressed, just a strange relief at being in the same room as him. Like coming home after a long day out.

He looked around and spotted her on the ladder, his eyes lighting, one eyebrow arched. "What *are* you doing?"

"I am up a tower, surveying the kingdom I have pillaged."

He laughed. "You have certainly laid all before you to waste. I can't believe the speed this room has been cleared. It feels ..." He took a deep breath. "Light."

The simple comment warmed her. "We haven't done anything yet."

"I didn't realize how suffocating the wall paperings were."

"Indeed. Were you looking for me?" He seemed to be looking *at* her, rather than for her.

His gaze went from her slippers, up to her waist, then to her mouth, then to her eyes, and then slid away from her altogether. It was as though he didn't trust himself to linger on any one part of her for too long. It shouldn't be so thrilling to have that effect on him.

Perhaps she shouldn't have worn her oldest dress. It truly was bedraggled and in no way fit for a noble house. But she was *working*. "Are you, that is, is everything all right?"

He shook his head. "Yes, I suppose it is. I was thinking about having lunch and couldn't find Mother."

"She is with Sheridan at the theater."

He nodded. "Father invested in the building, so she is always interested." He looked around. "Then I heard the workmen go to lunch, so I thought I would see how things progressed."

"A welcome distraction from the woes of parliament?"

He grimaced, but it turned into a smile. "How astute you are. We will be interviewing these people forever. But please, come down from the ladder. Every moment you are up there, I imagine you tumbling. Then I would have to catch you and ..." He trailed off, seemingly unable to finish his sentence.

"That sounds very gallant. Perhaps I shall fall off." Charis smiled, but Ashcroft frowned.

"Is this flirting?" His eyes narrowed like he was contemplating a scholarly question. She could imagine him at Eton as a boy, deep in the library, spectacles perched on his nose.

"Do you want it to be flirting?" She lifted her foot off the rung and circled her ankle a few times.

His gaze caught on it. "If it was, what should I say?"

"Only your thoughts."

"That your ankle is pretty, but I really shouldn't be looking at it."

He thought she had nice ankles. A bloom of happiness spread from her heart outward. "*Far* too plain. To be proper flirting, you must dress it up a little. How about 'Miss Eastwood, please remove your incandescently beautiful ankle from my gaze.'"

He pulled his gaze to her face, looking much too serious. "Miss Eastwood, unless you want to fall and crack your head open, please proceed down the ladder posthaste."

She laughed. "That's the Lord Ashcroft I know."

Of course, she *could* step down, but whether she could do it gracefully was another matter. She needn't have worried. He saw her dilemma and held out his hand.

She looked at it for a moment before grasping it. She descended one slow step at a time, so aware of his ungloved hand under hers she nearly did stumble off the ladder. Then he really *would* have to catch her. What a shame.

"There you are, safe on firm ground again. Thank you. It's a relief not to have you teetering above me."

"You have enough to do without house guests throwing themselves at you."

"I always have time for that," he said, blinking at her seriously. "Much more interesting than the duke's scandal."

She looked down at her hand. He was still holding it, his fingers entwined in hers. She'd never thought of herself as a small person, but his hand looked so large against hers. It felt right.

Her mind bounced like a marble between thinking he was just flirting and hoping he meant every word.

Please mean every word. "Are we still flirting?" She heard the breathless whisper for what it was. Hope.

His gaze shifted to their hands, too, and he released her, his hand falling back to his side. He rubbed it on his coat.

"Of course," he replied.

Charis felt the blush rising up her cheeks. "Then I must tell you that mentioning the duke's political imbroglio will render all flirting moot. Nothing bores young ladies more quickly than talk of Whigs and Tories."

He smiled ruefully. "I will never master this."

"Maybe you just need to find someone equally interested in politics and stop looking elsewhere." She shrugged. "But tell me, would you say it's true that the more you learn about Mary Anne Clarke, the worse it is and the more likely the duke will lose his position and his standing?"

"Have you been reading the newspapers?" His eyes widened and he shook his head.

"Only the ones you leave behind after breakfast." Scanning the pages for any mention of him, reading about his exploits and questioning had been thrilling. Not that she would tell him.

"It feels like the scandal of the century, even though we are only nine years in." He inhaled deeply. "And it's all so sordid. Between you and me, the duke definitely compromised his integrity, but whether we will ever find the truth is up for debate."

"I have never met someone who was responsible for the nation's moral compass. I always thought politicians were a gaggle of geese until I met you."

His eyes narrowed. "Let me guess, still flirting?"

"In saying you are not a goose? No, not now. Truth in all its unvarnished glory. But back to your statement. Your only duty can be to gather information, verify it, and look beyond what anyone is telling you and hope the truth is there. Only then will you know you have done your duty by the country and yourself."

He blinked slowly and tilted his head slightly to the side. Had she gone too far with her opinion? It was not for her to tell him how to do his duty or what his duty was. *Foolish girl.*

"See, this is *my* kind of flirting. Hold the mirror up for me. Let me see myself how you see me. I find it enthralling in a way no flimsy talk of eyes like aquamarines ever could."

She had eyes roughly that color. Had he made poetry for her? "Are you saying any lady who can argue with you about politics all night would find a way into your heart?"

He opened his mouth, closed it, and stared at her with so much heat in his gaze that she looked away, to the window, to the street, anywhere not to see what she longed to see there. "Perhaps not just any lady."

Her breath caught in her throat. This sounded like something beyond their ordinary banter and more like the things a man said when he was serious about a lady. She must not read too much into it.

"You would tire of it. I have far too many opinions and think I can solve the woes of the world when really I can change none of it. It comes from too much breakfast talk with my father. He has opinions on everything."

When he spoke, his voice was rough. He cleared his throat. "I always welcome different points of view, although it may seem like I am very fixed in my beliefs."

"It's true," she agreed. "Look at the way you have changed your mind about the table in the middle of the drawing room."

His sudden smile was like the sun breaking through. "I did, didn't I?"

The silence drew out between them for a few long moments, and it was hard to tell if it was the comfortable kind or the kind where there was so much to say that nobody knew where to start.

He broke first. "Oh, Lambley said there was a note for you from the modiste."

So mundane, when it felt like her heart was bursting with wanting to hold his hand again.

"Excellent! Apparently, this dress will not do for our visit to the Buxton's. What time do we leave? I would like to go to the modiste rather than send a footman."

"Two o'clock. I am coming with you because there is no parliament today, and Mother thinks I should strengthen my friendship with Lord Buxton."

Or his daughter.

"A welcome reprieve, I'm sure." There would be no time for her own lunch now. It was definitely more important to have a new dress if she was to go calling on London society.

"Shall I take you there? I just asked Lambley to have my curricle hitched to visit my office. But I can just as easily escort you to Covent Garden."

Charis took a deep breath. Now, besides clasping hands for far too long, they were to embark on a trip to Covent Garden together. Certainly, in an open carriage. But it would be quite delicious to be squired around town again by the handsome Lord Ashcroft.

"Wonderful. I can't thank you enough. If I get changed, can you take me directly?"

He bowed. "But of course. Your servant."

When he bowed, it felt like more than a simple bow. It felt like he was giving her something.

My, but she had a vivid imagination.

Charis ran upstairs, pulled the bell for Mary, and once she arrived, changed into her best walking dress.

The maid picked pieces of wallpaper out of her hair, complaining as she brushed it. "If this is to be the state of your hair, miss, I suggest you wear some kind of cap and don't take it off."

"Excellent idea," Charis replied. "Thank you for your help. I would be lost without you."

She'd never had her own maid, and her hair was only attended to when she was going to an assembly or to a dinner. Even then, only by Bess, who had firm notions about what looked pretty, and only three different styles she knew how to achieve. All of which looked becoming on Mother, but not so much on Charis.

Mary, however, had a lovely touch, and Charis traipsed downstairs with a pretty knot of braids poking out from the sides of her bonnet.

She ran into the library and grabbed the watercolor she had created for Madame Le Favre, and then made her way to the front door, where Lord Ashcroft was waiting for her.

His curricle was out front, with a beautiful matching pair of gray horses with white socks. "These are different horses from our drive. They're so pretty," Charis said, unable to help herself. "Are they related? They look like twins."

He laughed and handed her up into the carriage. "No, not related, although they do share bloodlines. I was very lucky to find them. May I introduce you to Pepper and Rudolph?"

"I shall have to take apples to them this afternoon when we return." She settled onto the bench. "I must tell you I fully intend to enjoy this ride around to Covent Garden so I can watch you drive in real traffic. It's not every day a spinster like me gets to sit next to a noted Corinthian. I hope *many* people see us." She glanced at his astonished expression. "There, now I have embarrassed myself."

He laughed and jumped up beside her. "I am not a Corinthian. Indeed, if you were to ask anyone, they should say I am a noted boorish bear."

"Never say it." She laughed because he was most likely right.

He was very serious and took his responsibilities to heart. "I know who you are."

He launched them smoothly into the traffic. "And who is that?"

"A man who entered parliament far too early, and sometimes finds it overwhelming and silly. He ends up playing many games he would not normally endure, and wonders if he's making any difference, anyway. He is only just realizing he may be sacrificing the better part of his youth to this folly."

He threw her an amused glance. "I was looking for more 'handsome and intelligent.' Goodness me, Miss Eastwood. It's far too early in the day to look into my soul in such a way."

He didn't say she was wrong, though.

"Of course you are handsome. Any fool can see that."

"Can they?" His bemused expression suggested he thought otherwise.

"Oh, hush. I'm not going to sit here and list your features." But how could he not know how handsome he was? Just looking at him made her heart skip along a little faster.

"No, it would be entirely inappropriate. Instead, I will bask in the fact you find me irresistible." He shot her a quick look and then concentrated back on the traffic.

"Nobody said that."

"It was intimated."

"Well, you find my hair fluffy, but I'm not holding it against you."

He shook his head. "Can we please forget I said something so ill-advised?"

"No. If you are going to go around telling young ladies their head resembles that of a duckling, you shall never marry, and it will be entirely your own fault."

"I am duly chastened." But he did not look chastened at all. There was a lightness to him she wasn't used to.

She waited for him to correct what he'd said. To tell her she was beautiful in the same way she'd told him he was handsome.

But nothing was forthcoming. Was it because compliments from gentlemen to ladies could be misconstrued as an admission of intent, a promise of sorts?

There would be no compliments and no proposal.

And the sooner she realized that kind of promise could not and would not come from Lord Ashcroft, the better off she would be. She was to school him in flirting, lighten his mood, and make him appear more roguish to the ladies of society. She was not meant to want him for herself.

Dreaming of him was nothing but clouds in the sky. Well, it was time to get her head out of those clouds and back to the reality of her life.

She must not fall in love with him.

Please, don't fall in love with him.

They arrived at the dressmakers.

Ashcroft slowed the horses, pulled over, and the footman jumped off to stand at the horses' heads to keep them steady. "I will wait here. You won't be long?"

He exited the carriage and came around to her side, holding out his hand. She gave him one hand, clutching her rolled-up painting in the other.

"I will be but a moment." Charis allowed him to hand her down from the carriage, making eye contact all the way. He looked away first.

How silly of her to think he felt the same way. He was happy to enjoy the sparks between them and excuse it as flirting practice. She couldn't be angry with him; it was what they had agreed upon.

It was hardly his fault the highlight of her day was whatever conversation they had.

A small bell chirped as she pushed the door open.

One of the assistant dressmakers was pulling rolls of fabric off the shelves when she saw Charis. "Good morning, Miss Eastwood. We were expecting your footman. One moment, I will get madame."

The lady in question came into the main showroom with a trail of assistants behind her, carrying boxes. "Here you are. It was almost complete when we received Lady Hartley's message. We have worked our fingers to the bone to get this ready, but I trust you will find it sheer perfection."

Charis had not thought about how many boxes there would be; there was not enough room in Ashcroft's curricle to stow them.

"My goodness. I wonder if you could pull me out a pretty ensemble to wear this afternoon when we go calling on Lady Buxton, and then would you mind having the rest delivered?" Then Charis handed Madame Le Favre her painting. "And here is a small token of my appreciation for your efforts. I am staying with Lady Hartley to help her with the refurbishment of her Grosvenor Square house. But when I came to visit you, I couldn't stop thinking about all the beautiful things you could do with this interior. You may hate it or you may like it but, in any case, here is my vision for your shop. It is like the inside of a genie's bottle, for that's how I think of you, a genie working magic."

Madame took the painting from her and stared at it, transfixed. Her face was an impassive mask. Charis felt slightly ill, as she always did when anyone looked at her work. Perhaps she wasn't so talented.

Madame Le Favre looked up, her eyes watery with tears. "Why, this is exactly how it should look. It's wonderful." She reached forward and pulled Charis into an embrace. "I think *you* are wonderful. I hope you love your dresses." She called her assistants to come and look at the painting. "I will have to call in some favors to make this vision of yours a reality."

Madame tapped the side of her head. "You know, you should make an enterprise of these room creations. You could advertise in *La Belle Assemblée* or *Ackermann's Repository*, then have people send their room dimensions and whatever furniture they already have and their preferences. Then you could send them a painting as you did for this room. I'm sure you could charge enough to make a good living for yourself and your family. If you need to, that is. I do not know your circumstances."

Madame would have known her circumstances from the very dress she saw Charis in right now. But could she do it? "What a wonderful idea. I could be anonymous. Like a lady author using her initials. You are a genius, Madame Le Favre. Thank you."

She beamed. "You're welcome. I hope you enjoy your gowns." For just a moment, her accent sounded more Yorkshire and less French. But it was only for a moment.

Charis left the shop with her single box, the rest organized to follow. Ashcroft was waiting, patting Pepper on the neck.

"Well?" He inspected her. "No, don't answer. I can see it went very well indeed." He reached down and handed her into the carriage. "Nothing cheers a lady up like a new dress."

"Actually, I am happy because Madame Le Favre loved the design I did for her shop. I haven't even seen my dress yet."

He laughed. "I should've known."

"Known what?"

"That you would be fixed on furnishings and not fabrics."

"Is that a compliment or a veiled insult?" Was he proud of her passion, or did he see it as unladylike?

He threw her a lopsided grin. "Let's keep you guessing, shall we?"

CHAPTER 13

WHEN A MOTHER'S GAZE IS VEXINGLY SHARP

The intended morning visit took place well after lunch, unlike in Hartley Green, where a morning visit was undertaken in, well, the morning.

It was very confusing.

But Charis supposed the nobility led such busy social lives it was impossible to rouse oneself early enough to do anything before midday.

She descended the stairs, enjoying the feel of her new slippers, even if they were not yet worn to the shape of her feet.

The dress was, however, a perfect fit. Madame Le Favre was an artist.

With Charis's pale skin and dark blonde hair, it was often challenging to find colors that didn't wash her out. Fabrics that made other ladies glow made Charis look sallow. Which was difficult when she was a young lady and expected to wear plain white muslin most of the time.

Madame Le Favre had given a nod to white muslin but had used the powers of her talent to make her pelisse an exceptionally pretty lilac. It was trimmed in velvet ribbon of the same color and had a back full of intricate pin tucks she would never see, but others would enjoy.

The net effect of her ensemble was one of color. The looking glass told her it looked very well indeed and somehow made her appear less of a gawking giraffe and more of an elegant young lady.

Not an easy feat, but she would not embarrass Lady Hartley today. And maybe she might surprise Lord Ashcroft.

Ashcroft waited by the front door. He had changed into a deep gray cut-away tailcoat, buff trousers, and a cravat tied in an intricate knot. How difficult it was not to admire him when he looked so delicious.

"Watch yourselves in the hall, I just hit my head on a scaffold." He rubbed his head and Charis smiled. He may look elegant, but he was still entertaining.

"We are not all seven feet high, my dear. Do put a coat on," Lady Hartley said. "I feel cold just looking at you."

"We'll barely be outside." But his valet, as though waiting in the wings, appeared with a voluminous greatcoat he held up for his master to put on.

Lady Hartley reached out her hands as she spied Charis descending the stairs. "My dear, how enchanting you look. Doesn't she, Ashcroft?"

Ashcroft did not reply but bowed. His mother would not notice, but his gaze softened as though he *were* enchanted. His eyes went from the bonnet perched on her head to the slippers on her feet, and a small smile played across his lips. "Indeed, Mother, you will be surprised to hear she didn't even *try* the dress on at the modiste. Instead, she had it bundled into a box because she was too busy showing the dressmaker her designs for the new interior of the shop."

Charis had not shared her project with Lady Hartley, feeling guilty about spending Lady Hartley's time designing a room for someone else.

"You did? But why didn't you show me? Her shop is very boring, however, the quality of her dresses more than makes up for it."

Charis shrugged. "Now her surroundings will match her talent. I hope she follows through with it, although I'm afraid it will be quite an expensive endeavor. I used a lot of crimson velvet."

Lady Hartley looked Charis up and down, then frowned. "You need something extra. Wait here."

She dashed off and Charis looked questioningly at Ashcroft. "What do you think she is doing? I feel my toilette is, for once, perfect."

"At a guess, she will have something she would like you to put around your neck. She does not like bare necks."

"Oh, I could never accept. What she has done is already too much."

"If you listen to my advice, you will not refuse her generosity. It gives her a great deal of pleasure to share what she has with others. She has always been fond of you. I was forever hearing as a child she was going off to visit the Eastwoods. I'm sure no other inhabitant of Hartley Green ever had so many visits. You must have been an enchanting child."

"I was a dirty scamp who was always sitting in a puddle making mud pies. I was never enchanting. Ever."

Why did she say that? She could have painted herself as a veritable angel, and he would never have known any different. Instead, no, she must make him see her covered in mud.

This is why you have no beaus.

Ashcroft lifted an eyebrow as if trying to imagine it. "Now I can see it clearly, yes. Mother likely came over to make sure you washed occasionally."

She snorted. Hopefully not loud enough for him to hear.

But when she looked back at Ashcroft, he winked, actually

winked at her. What on earth did *that* mean? "Why did you just wink at me?"

He picked an imaginary piece of fluff off his sleeve. "You are mistaken. I did no such thing."

Lady Hartley skipped back down the stairs with a small box in her hand. "What did you not do, Ashcroft?"

He looked to Charis, his gaze heavy with something she couldn't interpret. "Nothing, Mother."

He flirted with me. But don't worry, he doesn't mean any of it.

Lady Hartley shrugged. "Very well. Wilson knew just where it was." She opened the box, then pulled out a gold chain hung with a small cross of amethysts. "You can keep this. I will never wear it."

She motioned for Charis to turn around, then frowned. "Ashcroft, you will have to do the honors. I always forget how tall Charis is. I hope the dressmaker hasn't given you heeled shoes. You'll be taller than any gentleman you meet."

Ashcroft briefly met her eyes, and there was an infinitesimal moment of connection. *Yes, you're going to put a necklace on me as though we do this every day. This isn't strange.*

He strode forward, took the necklace from his mother, and stood behind her.

His presence, so close, made her tremble.

No. This is *definitely* strange. Enthralling. Her pulse skipped along merrily.

It took a moment for him to unclasp the fastener, and then the cold of the metal touched her, and the brush of his fingertips kissed the soft skin of her neck.

She shuddered and heat rose up her cheeks.

Please don't notice, Lady Hartley. "I've never had something so beautiful. Thank you."

"There now, very good. Thank you, Ashcroft. Let us depart." They were brisk words, but the accompanying glance showed she had very much noticed Charis's embarrassment when Ashcroft had drawn so close.

There was nothing Charis could say that wouldn't make the situation worse, so she ignored it. But her skin still prickled where his fingers had brushed it, and even though neither of them had done anything wrong, it felt like they'd had a moment and, worse still, the moment had been in front of his mother.

They rode to Lord Buxton's house in complete silence. Lady Hartley stared out the window with a frown, and Ashcroft looked from his mother to her and back again, his brows drawn as though not quite understanding what had happened.

That made sense because he had not seen Charis blush or her shudder, and did not realize how his touch had affected her. He, in other words, had no idea she was fast developing an intense tendre for him.

She closed her eyes. If she was being honest, that was exactly what it was. It had crept up on her slowly. He'd been kind. That was all. He bought her a book when no gentleman had ever bought her anything before. He laughed with her and treated her like an equal. From his point of view, he treated her like a sister, but no gentleman had ever gone beyond jigging up and down with her at a country dance at the local assembly, muttering about the weather. Not for her the long country walks that led to a courtship that ended in a betrothal.

It was hard to understand why, and even harder not to look at oneself as somehow inferior to every other female.

But not with Ashcroft.

Ashcroft looked at her like she mattered.

Was it any wonder she never stopped thinking about him? *Drat it all.*

Lady Hartley still wasn't talking to anyone when they reached their destination, and Ashcroft presented his card to the Buxton's butler. They were ushered inside to an entry area even grander than the Hartley's Grosvenor Square townhouse. It was so large it had room for a staircase to wind up the right-hand side of the building, while the left-hand side had a small arrangement of sofas and chairs, for people waiting to be received by the family. They dutifully sat and waited.

Everything was of the latest fashion, and there were some pieces Charis and Lady Hartley had seen in showrooms and catalogs over the past few weeks.

Like a mother who always recognized her children from one hundred yards' distance, Charis knew without a doubt that the small folio under Lady Hartley's arm contained Charis's paintings.

Lady Hartley had not mentioned she would be bringing them along or showing anyone outside the family, but it did explain why she was finally included in a social outing.

"What have you there, my lady?"

Lady Hartley looked down at the folio as though she had forgotten it was there, which was highly unlikely. "Why, your paintings. I must have something to speak to Lady Buxton about while Ashcroft is politicking with her husband." She glanced over at her son. "You need as many numbers as you can get in the lower house. Is that correct? For the vote?"

Ashcroft nodded. "Buxton is very influential, even if he sits in the Lords. Although I'm sure you knew that when you decided to call here this morning."

Lady Hartley nodded with a satisfied smile. "You will think me a meddler, but until you have a wife capable of taking on these duties, it rests with me to help you, in the same way I do with your father."

Ashcroft winced. "I appreciate it. I do. And I would love to find the perfect partner to join me. But these things cannot be rushed."

Charis could do nothing but look at her toes poking out from under her white muslin gown. She couldn't look at either of them for fear the truth of how she felt about him would be written on her face.

"You relieve me. You are not like all these other neck-or-nothing young bloods rattling about town not knowing their duty."

Ashcroft's smile was a little stiff. He must hate this conversation. "It is not about knowing my duty. I want a wife. I need a wife. There is no point being coy about it. But I draw the line at you choosing her for me."

They were talking like she wasn't there. Or more to the point, it didn't matter she *was* there. As though she were a cushion or a travel blanket. It shouldn't hurt, really. But by goodness, it did.

No more could be said, blessedly, because and they were led upstairs to a double drawing room. Charis gasped and took a tentative step in. Imagine, she, Charis Eastwood from tiny Hartley Green, being received into such a room. The sheer height of the ceilings and the deep plaster work impressed upon a person the grandeur of the inhabitants. One wall was covered in glorious artwork, while the other had a bank of windows looking out onto the park. There were nooks where one could enjoy a quiet chat when privacy was required. The very kind she had designed for Lady Hartley's drawing room. *I must be on the right track.*

They were announced, and Lady Buxton rose from the sofa. She wore a frilly cap that seemed to be more lace than fabric. Charis could barely see her dress because she had wrapped herself in a voluminous mustard-colored shawl of the most beautiful cashmere. The tips of it had a thick paisley border that touched the floor as she walked.

She held out her hands to greet Lady Hartley. "My dear, I am so glad you have come today. Cook has made the most tremendous almond cakes. If you don't help me, I shall eat them all and then be reduced to potatoes for dinner, so I save this fine figure."

A young lady came forward and curtsied. Charis recognized her from outside the dressmakers on their first visit. She wore a white muslin gown that, like Charis, marked her as a young unmarried lady. Her blue eyes might be a little bulging for traditional beauty, but she had a sweet smile and rosy cheeks. Charis liked her instantly.

"As you can see, Lady Beatrix is here instead of haunting Bond Street, as she usually does."

"You seem to like the slippers I convinced you to purchase last week," Lady Beatrix said with a mischievous smile. Her light-brown hair had been coaxed toward golden tones, likely with a liberal amount of lemon juice, and sweet curls framed her face and gave her a very gentle look that likely fooled many people.

Introductions were made again, and Charis discovered Lady Beatrix was the youngest daughter of the couple's ten children. "Lord Buxton will be with us shortly," Lady Buxton said. Then she waved them both away. "Now you young ladies can go into the corner and giggle about whatever on-dit is doing the rounds. Lady Hartley, I can see you have brought along the paintings for your interiors. I would love to see them. Considering I have only just finished my remodeling here, I may have some insights for you."

Charis almost cast up her accounts. There would be no "insights." Work had already started, so there was no changing it now. And in no way did she want to be in the room when Lady Buxton tore it all apart.

With any luck, Lady Hartley had not told Lady Buxton that Charis was the artist of the designs. Otherwise, she would die of mortification. On her gravestone, it would read, *She Died as She Lived, in a State of Chagrin.* She would take Lady Beatrix and go as far away as possible.

Lady Beatrix had the same idea. "Quickly," she said, tugging on Charis's arm. "Let's make our escape before we get drawn into the vortex of which drape fabric is better and which design of carpet would be *just perfection*. I have endured years of this conversation and have had my fill."

"I fervently agree. How far away can we get? Lands' End would not be far enough."

Beatrix giggled and dragged Charis to a sofa in one of those little nooks, motioning for them to sit on deep-blue velvet cushions. Charis sank into them blissfully. Feather and down, no doubt.

Beatrix turned to Charis, lifting a hand to whisper in her ear. "Lady Hartley has brought Ashcroft here. That could mean two things. First, it could mean Ashcroft needs to speak to Father about boring parliamentary issues, or, it means the mothers are contemplating throwing us together on a more permanent basis. If you catch my meaning."

She couldn't exactly tell her it was Lady Hartley's dearest wish for that very thing. Or that it made perfect sense. Lord Buxton was influential. Lady Beatrix was lively and intelligent. Marrying into this family would be an astute move for the man who would one day be the Marquis of Hartley. A marriage of equals.

Charis took a breath and exhaled slowly. "What are your thoughts?" *Please say you're horrified and would never entertain the idea.*

Ashcroft loved nothing more than to be teased, and enjoyed companions with a lively imagination. Lady Beatrix fit that bill. But just the thought of Ashcroft marrying Lady Beatrix made her simmer, and as for them living happily ever after in the rooms she created? She suppressed a shudder.

"He's a little …" Beatrix looked around the room, as though she would find the right word painted on the ceiling. "Dull?" She fingered her necklace, a sapphire version of the one Charis wore. "Also, this sounds silly, but as well as being boring, he's *intense*."

She rolled her eyes. "About all the wrong things. He's not intense about romance, dancing, and love, but boring politics, law, and justice." She sighed. "I mean him no disrespect, I'm sure he will make some equally dull and virtuous lady the perfect mate."

There was only one thing Charis could say in all conscience. Because while this might be how Ashcroft appeared on the surface, he was so much more than that.

"I have been Lady Hartley's guest now for almost a month and in that time, my opinion of Lord Ashcroft has transformed. He may be quiet, but once he feels comfortable, he is quick-witted and entertaining. All that focus will be lavished on his wife. He will be a loyal husband and will change the world to make it a better place for their children. Any lady accepting his marriage offer would be very lucky indeed."

Conscious that she had exposed her true feelings, Charis felt a blush fire up her cheeks. "In my opinion."

Lady Beatrix blinked slowly, then turned to look at Lord Ashcroft, her head tilted to one side. "Surely you jest. I danced with him, and he barely spoke a word to me. I sat through supper with him where he brought me a *single* lobster patty like I had no appetite at all after hours of dancing. So, forgive me if I do not think he is perfect in *any* way, much less every way."

How dearly Charis wanted to prove her wrong. Everybody looked at Lord Ashcroft as the serious young man who'd entered parliament instead of kicking up his heels like every other dandy. She could only admire that kind of dedicated hard work.

Ashcroft chose that moment to look up from where he was speaking to his mother, seemingly stuck in the vortex of conversation they had escaped, because Lord Buxton had not arrived. Had he heard them talking about him? She took a deep breath. Of course not. He couldn't have.

"Come, let's save him from the endless talk of pelmets." Charis beckoned him over. "Lord Ashcroft, won't you come and sit with us for a few moments?"

Lady Hartley looked up and threw Charis a look that clearly said *thank you.*

Well, Charis would help, even as it pained her to do so.

"Please, Lord Ashcroft, sit with us. Tell us something exciting." There was an edge to Lady Beatrix's voice that suggested Lord Ashcroft would have nothing exciting to say. It made the hairs on Charis's arms stand on end. How dare she judge him so cruelly?

Ashcroft raised an eyebrow, as though he'd seen straight through her comments and knew what she was inferring. And could not care less. "Now then, Lady Beatrix. We both know I have nothing riveting to share. Why don't *you* tell *me* something exciting and enliven my day?"

This was not going well. They were already combative. Ashcroft was already defensive, and Charis got the feeling this was just one of many similar conversations he had with ladies.

"Very well," said Lady Beatrix. "I had the pleasure of attending Lady Fiona's wedding two weeks ago. That was exciting."

Her arched expression suggested this should mean something.

Charis's eyes flew to Ashcroft to find his cheeks had reddened, and there was a pulse in his jaw. "Indeed, how delightful." His tone suggested he thought the news was anything but delightful.

"Oh, yes. Sir Phillip bought her a high-perch phaeton with the softest Moroccan leather interior I have ever felt and two beautifully matched white horses to pull it. As a wedding gift. Can you imagine?" She pretended to swoon. "So romantic."

"I wish them both happy," he said in a tone that suggested he wished them both to Hades.

Charis was going to have to intervene.

"Lord Ashcroft, I have been meaning to ask you something. Next time you see him, could you ask Mr. Sheridan who makes the Theatre Royal curtaining? It will help my small project with Madame Le Favre."

His expression relaxed into a smile. For her. Beatrix made

him clench his jaw, but *she* made him grin. Charis squelched the little thrill of triumph.

"Of course. I am meeting him tomorrow at a coffeehouse near Drury Lane. Why don't you come along and ask him yourself? We'll see if he knows."

His dimple appeared, transforming him entirely, as it always did. His eyes sparkled, and Charis was hit anew by how attractive he was. A flutter took up in her stomach. *Be calm.*

She glanced at Lady Beatrix to see she was blinking quickly, too. Perhaps reassessing her opinion.

How could she not?

Lady Beatrix tilted her head to one side. "You are acquainted with Sheridan? I saw *The School for Scandal* once and greatly enjoyed it."

"Yes, he is an old family friend. Miss Eastwood and I joined him in his box a few weeks ago to see *Man and Wife*."

"There is nothing like watching a play with theater people. I've never been so diverted. Or drunk so much Champagne."

"I thought I was going to bring her home foxed on her very first London outing," Ashcroft added. "Mother would have been mortified."

Lady Beatrix's eyes widened still more, as though reassessing exactly how dull Lord Ashcroft really was.

Lord Buxton entered the room, and Ashcroft stood and bowed to the ladies. "I have bored you long enough." He left them.

Lady Beatrix did not look at Charis but put a hand on her knee, as though in shock. "I can honestly say I have never seen him smile. He is an Adonis when he smiles."

"I am never one so uncharitable as to say I told you so," said Charis. "Few are admitted to his inner circle. But once he trusts you, he is a great deal of fun. I'd rather have a man who only wants to write poetry for me than one who throws his sonnets around to any old thing in a gown."

What was worse, she was sure she spoke the entire truth, and she would never meet another like him.

This whole situation was not dissimilar to the rooms she painted. She might dream of living in them herself, indeed lie awake thinking about it. But that did not mean she ever would.

Worse still, she just wanted him to be happy.

Even if it made her desperately unhappy in the process.

CHAPTER 14

WHERE ASHCROFT SEES THE TRAP LAID
BEFORE HIM

Ashcroft left the ladies, regretfully, because he enjoyed watching Charis make a friend, and Lady Beatrix was surprisingly entertaining. Charis struck him as a solitary figure. In Hartley Green, she was seldom in the company of anyone but her mother.

He made his way over to Lord Buxton and bowed. "Good day, my lord."

Lord Buxton bowed in return. He wore a dark olive velvet coat and old-fashioned breeches, his silver hair cut short and his brown-blue eyes watery above some quite impressive bags.

But his smile was genuine. "Yes, well, no day feels like a good day at the moment with our current parliamentary debacle. I have coffee in my study. Will you join me?"

Perfect. A quiet opportunity to see what Lord Buxton thought of the interviews so far. "Sounds lovely."

He followed Buxton through to the library where two wing-back chairs sat on either side of a blazing fire. "February calls for fires in every room, in my opinion. These old bones need it."

Ashcroft estimated Buxton to be in his early sixties. "These slightly younger bones like it too. Bitter this morning, wasn't it?"

Buxton poured coffee into fine cups painted with blue pastoral scenes. "Sugar?"

Ashcroft shook his head. Buxton handed him a cup, and he took a sip before resting it on the table next to him.

Buxton took a gulp that almost drained his cup and refilled it. "I must tell you, I've been talking to Kinross."

"I see." His heart lightened. Perhaps Kinross had done the groundwork for this conversation.

"Yes, he told me he'd had an epiphany in your front drawing room without you ever being there. Rushed right over to tell me. We should never underestimate the ladies, my boy."

Ashcroft blinked. "Are we speaking of Miss Eastwood taking tea with him that day?" It seemed word spread fast.

"Yes. Brought him around apparently. He was quite amused. 'Bamboozled,' I believe, was the word he used."

"She bamboozles me occasionally, too." But now he most definitely owed her another apology. He had been wrong, not only about what she had done with Kinross, but worse, he had underestimated her intelligence, and she knew it.

Buxton laughed. "Don't they all. My daughter has taken to arguing with me over breakfast when I have not the wits to put up a defense. At least at the moment, she is only winning on increases in her pin money and whether she can have a new town horse."

"You are escaping lightly. Miss Eastwood and my mother have completely thrown the house over for remodeling. I can't walk into a room without tripping over a drop sheet or banging my head on a scaffold. I hope it will all be over soon."

Buxton groaned. "Ha! I feel like we only finish refurbishing here when it is time to start again because the entire process took so long. One day, my bedchamber will be moved to an entirely different floor without so much as a by-your-leave."

"They have already moved the water closets. No big renovations, said I. No turning the house on its head, said I."

"Said you to the breeze, I expect."

"I can't be angry if Miss Eastwood being here results in getting the numbers for this vote. She can shift my bedchamber to the scullery if she had that kind of impact. And something tells me if Kinross had met me instead, the outcome may have been very different."

"You have a certain intensity about you. You're brilliant, don't get me wrong, but you can put a man's back up. It's why you need a lady with the right breeding and social skills to act as your counterbalance. Miss Eastwood may have stumbled upon this, but someone, like my Beatrix, could do that for you every day. Smooth the way. It's a blessing in our line of work, and not to be underestimated."

"So my mother keeps telling me." He'd thought he'd escaped the matchmaking when he came in for coffee. Instead, he'd fallen straight into the trap. He pulled on his shirt collar, wishing he hadn't tied his blasted cravat so tight.

"And I don't need to tell you it has always been the dearest wish of your papa and I to ally our families. Nothing could make me happier. I hear the ladies think you are dull. But I see your passion, and I know you would make an admirable husband."

"Thank you, my lord." Nothing like it being well known he was a bore. The direction of this conversation must change before he showed Buxton that when it came to being pressured into marriage, he felt the *opposite* of dull. In fact, his anger felt incendiary. *I will choose my own wife, dammit.*

Buxton put his cup down, empty again. "Come, let us return to them and make sure they haven't divided and conquered my kingdom in the time we've been gone."

"You assume it was yours to start with," Ashcroft said.

Buxton clapped him on the back. "You've learned the truth at an early age. It will serve you well."

They entered the room to find all the ladies bent over the card table with Charis's paintings laid out before them.

Charis looked up, and their eyes met. Her brows were drawn together, and her mouth was an unhappy, straight line.

What on earth had happened?

Had Lady Buxton criticized her drawings? On top of his criticism the day before, it would be hard. Members of the aristocracy were very good at finding flaws in things. They had nothing much else to do.

He walked over to them with a little more purpose. "What is this?"

"I am just providing feedback for Lady Hartley to give to her designer."

Charis's eyes flew to his, warning him not to divulge her identity as the artist.

He looked over her shoulder. They were looking at the design of the dining room, which had the ceiling plasterwork painted in cream and gold, the walls a jade green, and a large Axminster carpet under the length of the long dining table.

"My favorite room. The way the carpet design reflects the original Greek fresco work in the plaster. I would never have thought of it, but it creates such simplicity and elegance. I refuse to change a thing in this design, so I hope you haven't, Mother."

The mother in question jerked her head back, her brow quirked. "Why yes, I agree with you."

"I think it is not nearly grand enough for a grand dining room. You should look to Carlton House. We are not supporters of the prince and his extravagance, but you cannot help but be impressed by that dining room."

"He may keep it," Ashcroft said, catching Charis's gaze and holding it. "And I will keep my green dining room that will make me feel tranquil whenever I am in it."

She smiled. For once, he had said the perfect thing. He wanted to tell her he wasn't lying. He really did like it. But she probably wouldn't believe him.

And in that moment, with the sun coming in from the

window and lighting her hair into a halo and with a smile on her face that was equal parts happiness and relief—she was the most perfect thing he had ever beheld.

Radiant.

Beautiful.

Why was she not his?

He didn't want her to leave, didn't want her not to paint at the desk in his study again.

He cleared his throat and looked around to see Mother staring at him through narrowed eyes.

His thoughts would not make her happy. Her dreams of a political dynasty through his marriage would be dashed. The person she herself brought to London was the reason for its undoing. He hated to thwart her. She was the best of mothers.

But how could he do anything less for himself?

If he could talk to her and convince her his future happiness was more important than the politics, more important than any dowry his wife might bring, perhaps she would come around.

"Ashcroft, I am thinking of bringing the date of the ball forward to the first of March. The workmen will have finished their plasterwork and painting. The carpets should have arrived by then, so all we need to concentrate on is the ballroom."

Or perhaps not.

Beatrix, who had never spoken to him in the past without a superior stab of sarcasm, sidled up to him like he was a long-lost beau. "That would be lovely. Town is so flat at the moment."

"If you think it can all be ready on time without the guests fainting from paint fumes, then do as you will." The small window of opportunity to cancel the ball altogether was firmly closed.

"Let's think of a theme," Lady Beatrix said. "Every good ball has a theme." She put a finger to her chin and pondered. "How about *Star Filled Night* where the ballroom is swathed in dark blue material with gold foil stars pinned to it?"

"I like it," Charis said. "Particularly since it's so cold we cannot go outside." Her brows drew together. "Or perhaps Ancient Rome? We could have plaster of Paris columns lining the ballroom joined by floral garlands."

Beatrix nodded. "The centerpiece could be a large empty clamshell that ladies could stand inside and be a Botticelli's Venus for a moment."

"Only if Ashcroft promises to stand in it, too," Charis said with a mischievous grin.

If his mother wanted it to be a bride-hunting ball ... she might as well go all the way and have him in the ridiculous clamshell.

Of course, Mother loved the idea, immediately clapping her hands. "Stop right there. Yes. I will hire a portrait painter for the night to do quick sketches of all the ladies."

"It does sound like fun," Charis agreed.

"Let's begin planning and purchasing. The painters can stay and help us with the ballroom. Parmentier's can cater. It will be wonderful," Lady Hartley said.

"We shall have to visit Madame Le Favre for new gowns," Lady Buxton said. "All of us."

Lady Beatrix put a hand on Ashcroft's arm. "Do you think a toga-inspired gown would be appropriate?"

"You will look becoming in whatever you wear," he said because what else could he say without being insulting?

The two mothers' gazes slid from Beatrix to himself, and their intent could not be clearer.

They made a lovely pair.

If Mother wanted him to find a bride at the ball, maybe he would.

But it wouldn't be Beatrix. Did she think he hadn't heard her tell Charis he was the most boring man imaginable? Or Charis's heartfelt defense of him, which caused Beatrix to look at him in a different light?

No. He didn't need her to discover he was worth pursuing.

He would use the evening to court Charis instead. Surely if she thought that well of him, he'd have a fighting chance on such a magical night. Finding a lady who didn't think he was a monumental bore was a miracle.

If she would marry him and take on the enormous task of being his wife, Mother could stop her machinations and life could go back to normal.

CHAPTER 15

WHERE ALL THE BEST STORIES START WITH 'NEVER TELL A SOUL' ...

A week later, the house was still in a renovation uproar. Teams of plasterers had standoffs with painters who had arguments with paperhangers until poor Lambley locked himself in the silver room. Ostensibly to polish things, but probably just for a moment's peace.

Lady Hartley had declared the house "a disaster of noise and smell," saying it gave her a constant megrim, and had decamped to Lady Astley's mansion until the dust cleared.

Ashcroft spent so much time in the Commons that at least she didn't have to deal with him complaining about it too.

Charis, of course, happily stayed in the house, up to her elbows in plaster, paint, and cleaning up the mess the renovation made. Each night, she picked paint from her hair and cleaned it from under her fingernails.

Today, her task was the nursery. The men had painted it pale blue and provided her with small buckets of wall paint so she could start her mural. It had to be something that would intrigue a baby with color and shape and yet spark the imagination of a young miss or master until they were ready to leave the nursery and go to school.

Researching the Hartley crest only revealed a lot of red, gold, and lions, which were not at all diverting.

But painting a sky with clouds with bright hot-air balloons drifting across it? Now that sounded like fun. Once she had done a preliminary sketch, she divided her drawing into a grid that she then mirrored on the wall to get the proportions just right.

Now would have been a good time to have information from those set designers that Lady Hartley visited. But never mind.

It took an hour to lay out the clouds and the balloons, using a ladder she borrowed from downstairs.

She picked a brush five times larger than she would use to paint a watercolor. "This is novel." Ten minutes into painting the wall, it became apparent she should have asked for assistance. This was going to take forever.

She was about to go downstairs and see who could be spared when she heard footsteps on the landing outside the nursery.

"You really do like to get your hands dirty, don't you?"

She whirled around to find Ashcroft in the doorway. He wore a dark gray coat, cut away to reveal form-fitting breeches. His hessians had been shined to within an inch of their lives. In all, it was a delectable view. She would only have a few more weeks in London, so why not enjoy it? "Why hello. I thought the Commons had eaten you alive."

"Yes, it did. Then it discovered I'm a tough piece of hide and spat me out. I am only due in at four, an entire morning and afternoon away." He inspected her equipment and then her drawing, and looked up, his expression confused. "You are painting a mural?"

"*We* are painting a mural." There was no point wasting such a golden opportunity for help.

"I?" His tone was confused, as though she'd asked him to stand on his head.

"Yes, you. A man as tall as you is always helpful. I was just thinking I underestimated how much work there was to cover such a large space."

He looked down at his beautiful attire and pulled on the light gray waistcoat that was embroidered with shot-silver thread.

"You may want to change."

"You really mean this." He ran a hand through his hair but a lock fell straight back in his face.

"Well, it is *your* nursery. For *your* children. Imagine being able to tell them you painted that balloon for them yourself with your very own hands?" The thought of his babies being in there was both beautiful and heartbreaking. He would grow a family, but it was unlikely she would be a part of it, no matter how hard she hoped she could.

"I see your point. Very well, I will return."

He returned just as she set him out his own brush and bucket of yellow paint for the silk balloon. Now he had on worn breeches, the kind he might muck out a stable in, and a linen shirt with a loosely tied cravat.

She nodded her approval. "Much more sensible."

"In my defense, this was not on my list of things to do today." The more relaxed style suited him. She could imagine him walking through fields at Hartley Green like this.

"What was on the list?"

He took up the paintbrush and bucket of paint, watched her for a few moments, and then climbed the ladder to start at the top of the balloon. He didn't answer until he had finished climbing and looped his bucket over the hook. "Apologizing to you."

Charis almost dropped her brush. "Whatever for?"

He made long, even strokes. "For assuming you hurt my cause with Kinross when, in fact, you made him change his mind and bring all his friends with him."

"Ah, that." She concentrated on applying the blue to the wall, instead of turning to look at him as her entire body seemed to want.

He took a deep breath. "I was wrong. I treated you badly afterward, and I cannot tell you how sorry I am. Even if you had scared him away, you ... you deserved better."

"Apology accepted." In truth, she'd barely thought of it since.

They painted in silence for a few minutes. "That's it?"

"Does it need to be more complicated?" If there was one thing growing up with a wise army captain for a father had done for her, it was the ability to discern true remorse and forgive quickly. And in any case, she'd forgiven him days ago. Possibly when he came to her rescue at the Buxton's, but more likely just the next time he'd smiled at her.

"I suppose not, but I usually find it is. Mother, in particular, has a way of punishing one for days when she's put out. She won't actually tell you what the problem is. You're left to figure it out for yourself."

"Sounds like torture."

"Quiet, ladylike torture."

It was amusing, so Charis laughed and looked up to see him smiling down at her. The winter sun shone through the window, and the moment formed like a painting in her mind. Him on the ladder, her looking up at him. Forever captured to look back on in the future, when she once again cleaned the mold from the skirting boards.

Then it passed. She shrugged. "Sometimes we ladies are often not very good at voicing our true thoughts and feelings."

"I have discovered this to my cost," he muttered.

"Indeed? When has it cost you that a lady was not forthcoming with her true feelings?"

"Never tell a soul ..."

"All the best stories start like that." She was about to discover something new about him. A secret she should not know. Was there anything more delicious?

"Don't sound so enthused." He shot her an amused glance, dipped his paintbrush in the bucket, and continued on the large square of gold he was painting. "As I was saying, never tell a soul, but last Season I set my sights on a young lady of my acquaintance. The perfect bride for me." He came down the ladder so he could move it along a few feet, but leaned against it instead. "Intelligent, beautiful but most importantly, of a political family that it would be *very* beneficial to marry into. Here, I thought, is my future. Her parents encouraged my suit, and so I spent the summer months trailing after her from house party to house party, thinking I was courting her in a way that would end quite swiftly in our betrothal." He took a deep breath and exhaled. "Imagine my surprise when she threw me over for a second son who fancied himself a poet. You may have heard Lady Beatrix mention their wedding the other day."

So, Lady Beatrix truly had teased him in the cruelest way. She'd wondered why his face had reddened. Knowing how awkward he felt with the opposite sex only made it crueler. She laid a hand on his arm. The white linen of his shirt was rolled up so her fingers actually touched his skin. Shock made her pull her hand back. "I'm so sorry, Ashcroft. And a poet? How tiresome."

His gaze sharpened. "What do you mean, tiresome? My understanding is that a romantic attachment to a poet is the pinnacle of a young lady's aspirations."

How could she make him see all that meant nothing? It was just words and hot air. "No, tiresome is the correct word. They are so abstracted by their own genius that they spare no thought for what your wants or needs might be. The muse is their mistress, and if you are unlucky enough to be that muse, they will place wings on your back like an angel, and wax lyrical about your eyes being as the reflection of the moon or some such idiocy. I pity your young lady if this is the man she married."

He paused for a moment, then let out a noise that sounded

like "huh." "I saw her a few weeks back at a dinner, and she did not look happy. Perhaps you are right."

"Give me a gentleman devoted to me in more practical ways, and I'll show you true love."

He blinked, tilting his head to the side as though allowing her words to sink in. "Practical, you say? How refreshing you are."

———

He'd spent many nights turning the courtship over in his mind, wondering where he'd gone wrong and if the kind of partnership he wanted was beyond his reach. He didn't want a loveless marriage. He wanted one like his parents had, only better again.

She raised both eyebrows as though offended he doubted her. "I know I am right and, what's more, poets are most often not wealthy and spend most of their life unheralded only to be appreciated after their death. But, if she needed that kind of adoration, perhaps you were not the gentleman for her after all, Lord Ashcroft." She picked up her paintbrush and continued with the rolling green hills she painted at the bottom of the wall.

Look at her painting a beautiful mural. She was so talented and hard-working. One day there would be a crib up against this wall, and his babies would imagine flying in one of her balloons. An image of her looking down at their child filled his mind. *Yes. So right.* The rightness shook him to his core.

The use of his title was annoying. Surely they were beyond formality now. "Now that I have shared my courtship failures," he said. "I think we should call each other by our given names, at least in our own private company. What do you think?"

She held out her hand to shake his. "Agreed. I can't be your influential wife or perfect bride, but I can be your friend. My name is Charissa, but all who love me call me Charis."

She couldn't be his wife? *Why ever not?* And here he'd been, painting the wall of this nursery, imagining her telling their children the story of the day they painted it together. So many happy times to be had under its clouds and balloons.

And he couldn't ask her why. His pride wouldn't let him. He'd just rather keep investigating until he had his answer without embarrassing himself.

He held out his hand. "Pleased to meet you, Charis. My name is Theodore, but all who love me call me Ash." His heart clenched. Would she figure out he just told her he loved her? Because he called her Charis? Unlikely. Lord above, he hoped not. He hadn't even meant to.

"Or Ashcroft," she said, musingly. "After all, your mother loves you, but calls you Ashcroft."

"You may call me whatever you wish."

And she could do whatever she wished with him if only she knew it.

She smiled, her eyes sparkling with mischief. "Can I call you Ted, then, since your name is Theodore?"

He took himself up the ladder. "Not if you want me to take you to Gunter's this afternoon."

"I would love to see Gunter's. You know I would." She started to paint a little quicker. "I had hoped to finish the balloons today."

"I think I should call some help from downstairs so you can get ready. Is that a good idea?"

"The very best!" She put her paintbrush down and ran from the room so fast he did not have time to come down from the ladder himself.

"Excellent," he called after her. "We can leave whenever you're ready." Let this be a lesson that the quickest way to a lady's heart was through Gunter's.

She popped her head back around the door. "Am I showing a gauche amount of excitement?"

"Just the right amount," he replied.

He called for his valet, then spoke to Mr. Adams who sent two men for her to instruct on how to finish painting her hills and the balloons.

He had often waited for his mother when accompanying her to balls or card parties, and her toilette took forever. But when he came downstairs, he'd hardly been in the foyer a few minutes before there was rustling on the stairs.

She descended tentatively and with a shy smile that suggested she was wearing one of her new dresses.

She looked beautiful.

The dress was white and looked woolen rather than muslin, with a dusky blue short spencer that was made of heavier fabric to keep her warm. The ensemble was a confection that had him looking from bonnet to reticule, to the high neck sewn into small frills. From each shoulder, swathes of blue fabric met just beneath her bust in a large floppy bow, the tales of which hung down to her waist. After seeing her in practical working clothes, it was a shock to see her dressed like a marchioness. A good shock. He would have her always wear such beautiful things if she wanted them.

Her eyes sparkled. She was obviously determined to have fun. "I am ready for my adventure."

"You look ready for an adventure. Your dress is very fetching." There. He had commented on it and didn't even stammer at how beautiful she looked. But when he looked up, she was blushing tiny spots of pink on her cheek, hidden when she turned to include her maid. "Shall I bring Mary?"

It was a tactful way to ask him if she needed to be chaperoned where he was taking her.

"No. Gunter's is perfectly respectable for me to squire you to."

"Oh, good!"

The maid at the top of the stairs looked unhappy. Likely she had been looking forward to an outing. "Next time, Mary, I promise," he said.

Although if he had the chance to be alone with Charis, Mary would be left behind again and again.

They took the short carriage trip to the Strand with Charis's attention completely taken up by the streets outside the window. He couldn't help but smile. "Your excitement is refreshing."

"I don't have to pretend otherwise with you or your mother. Although it was hard to feign indifference when Lady Buxton pulled my designs apart just for the fun of it. I wanted to clock her on the side of the head."

"I would have paid money to see that. I should have warned you she has a penchant for disagreement for the sake of it." He steered the carriage toward the Strand. "We have one short stop before Gunter's. But I think you will like it."

"I am happy to go anywhere."

He'd watched her paint and draw for weeks now, running out of supplies she would never have used if not for his mother. And they weren't inexpensive.

They pulled up in front of number 101 The Strand, and the footman jumped off the back of the carriage and opened the door. Ashcroft exited first and then held his hand for Charis.

She took his hand absently, looking instead at the banner above the shop. "Ackermann's," she breathed, as though the word were magical.

"But not for the prints or the periodicals." He only hoped what he had seen there some time ago was of the best quality and something she would use.

She shot a quick glance at him, then down at the hand he still clasped.

He let go, but offered her his arm instead.

It felt strange to take a lady out. They weren't courting, but his nerves jangled as if they were. Hopefully, she would allow him to purchase everything she wanted and not be missish about it.

The shop was double-fronted, with large, mullioned windows

displaying a vast number of prints and people milling around inside. It was a fashionable place to be seen.

"Your mother showed me her copy of the *Ackermann's Repository* on the way to London. We have not visited the shop because she has no need of prints."

How very like his mother not to take Miss Eastwood anywhere but where *she* needed things. All and sundry thought her to be the epitome of generosity, but he had always had the feeling she was only generous where she expected a return.

"They have more than prints. I have brought you here to replace the art stock I know you have used in Mother's service. I can't have you returning to Hartley Green with less than you arrived with."

Her mouth formed a perfect *O* of surprise and, he hoped, delight. "Why, how thoughtful."

"So, you will allow me to purchase replacements?"

She nodded. "Most definitely."

"Excellent." They entered the shop and wandered around the print section until she spotted the wooden sign showing the "colors and requisite for drawing" department in the distance. It pulled her like a magnet, and he could imagine all around her was blurring out as the watercolor cakes came into full focus. It made him smile.

And Ackermann did not scrimp on the watercolors.

The display, stacked onto the table and the shelves behind, was a gorgeous thing. But it was the mahogany desktop easel that captured her attention.

She went to it, inspecting how the tilting mechanism worked, and whispered, "Wonderful." Then she focused her attention on the travel paint box next to it, picking up the small porcelain pallet, then putting that down to pick up the fat, sable watercolor brushes, then putting *that* down to inspect the watercolor cakes themselves. It was as though she didn't think she had enough time to take it all in and was rushing from one thing to the next.

He reached in and picked up a cake of paint, too. It was deep yellow. On one side, it had an embossed lion, and on the other *Ackermann's Chrome No. 1.*

"What happens when you rub the name of the color off and then can't remember what you ordered? There have to be sixty colors here."

She put her own blue cake of watercolor back on the stack. "Well, firstly, if you love color, you probably know your favorites off by heart, and secondly, there is absolutely no need for sixty colors."

She laughed as though the whole thing was absurd. "If you pick the correct ten or so, you have the rest through mixing correctly." She shrugged. "I suppose if people really want to spend their money, they could buy them all ..."

He picked up a book, written by the man himself called *A Treatise on Ackermann's Superfine Water Colour.* Why on earth did colors need a treatise? "I am thankful I did not have the presumption to buy these for you. I would have bought all sixty just to avoid having to choose." He put the book back on the stand.

The sales assistant came into view. "Did I hear correctly you would like to purchase the entire sixty-seven colors, sir?"

"Apparently not," Ashcroft replied. "Please be guided by my friend here, who will dictate my purchase."

Miss Eastwood beamed as though all her birthdays had come at once. "Well!" She eyed the display and picked up cakes of yellow, blue, green, and red, then a couple of brownish-yellow cakes of watercolor with the speed of a practiced eye. "These." She placed them on the counter.

"Not more?" He should have known she would be miserly with her gift.

"Perhaps some paper for miss?" The shop assistant saw his huge sale wither away.

Miss Eastwood turned to him with a question in her eye. "Their papers will be pre-stretched ..."

He had no idea why that was superior. "Say twenty sheets?"

Her eyes widened, so twenty was obviously enough. Good. "Thank you!"

"Shall I have those packaged, sir?"

Goodness, the assistant had capitulated far too early. "Yes, please. But also add a brush in every size and one of the desktop easels."

She gasped. "Too much, Ash."

His heart stuttered. She called him Ash, not Lord Ashcroft, or my lord. It warmed him. Made them feel like the friends they were fast becoming. All those times he'd visited Hartley Green, and he could've been on friendly terms with her, and he'd completely missed his opportunity. Now he would wait all day outside the pie shop if there was a chance to see her.

"Oh, and triple the cakes ordered." That should do it.

"You *must* stop." She laughed, but her mouth was a stern line.

"Very well. That will do … for now. Although what about that pot there? Perfect to wash your brushes in. There's a good chap, put it in, too, and have the goods and the account sent to me." He handed the shop assistant his card.

"Thank you"—he looked down—"Lord Ashcroft." He smiled happily to himself.

It made him happy to watch her shop. Her habit of touching surfaces, as though committing them to memory, was endearing as she trailed her hand along anything and everything. From the smooth marble busts to the leather spine of a book, nothing was safe.

He had an image, fleeting, of her running her fingers down his cheek. Feeling the contours of his face, learning him by touch. He lifted his hand to his cheek as though she had. But she was over at the print rack, flicking through folders.

"I would like to create a print room." She stopped on a lovely view, not unlike the one she'd chosen at the gallery. "Paste them all on the wall and then draw frames around them."

"Then let's buy you some to start, shall we?"

But he'd gone too far, for she held up her hand. "No, no. That's enough now. I can make my own if I truly want to. I can see I won't be able to look at anything without you wanting to buy it for me."

He shrugged. "It was my only aim in bringing you here, so yes."

"Incorrigible. But in that case, take me to Gunter's, and I'll allow you to buy me as many treats as I can eat."

"Your servant, Miss Eastwood, in all things confectionary."

Delighted, she made directly for the door, as though Ackermann and his illustrious depository held no more interest compared to an ice.

They drew some glances with their quick exit. He didn't care.

His coachman, Hicks, saw them and brought the carriage forward.

"I like that you know I would prefer watercolors to a bonnet." She was looking at the oncoming carriage and not at him, so he had no idea of the real emotion behind her statement. Was it just like, or "admire and adore"?

"We can buy bonnets if it pleases you." It was astonishing how happy just buying her things made him. Who would have thought it?

"No, this is more than enough. I shall go home to Hartley Green much enriched."

He thought he heard some sadness in her voice, but since she turned and smiled at him, it was impossible to be sure. She was adept at holding her true feelings just under the surface. Not unlike him.

The carriage took them the short distance to Berkeley Square and the famous confectioner.

"What will we eat, do you think? Will they have candied plums, or is summer too long ago?" She had read of so many wonderful things being sold at Gunter's. Surely winter would hold its own delights? She would dine out for weeks back in Hartley Green on this story. Being taken to Gunter's by Lord Ashcroft himself. So, she had better make it worth the retelling.

"They tend to change the menu depending on the season." It was hard not to notice the gentle happiness radiating off him when he purchased her painting supplies. The part of her that wanted to limit his purchases did not have the heart to deny him the pleasure. There were enough supplies to last her years and perhaps even establish the business she was only just beginning to think might come to fruition.

Twenty sheets of watercolor paper might be twenty new clients.

They alighted from the carriage, and she stood in front of the shop. A golden pineapple hung on a sign out the front, and the window was designed to showcase the confectioner's skills with cakes, marzipans, and all varieties of sugar art. And in the center of it all, a pineapple on a crystal platter. "Why, it almost glitters."

"Delicious, is it not? Wait until you see the inside, marble-top tables, and beautiful chairs. You will love it." He took her arm, smiling down at her.

This day was a dream. From painting the mural in the nursery to this very moment. She would remember it forever, etched in her memory like the most perfect of things.

They entered and were ushered to a small round table, where Ash gave her the seat facing into the shop so she could take everything in.

"Goodness," she said in a whisper. "How am I going to choose what to eat?"

"February may be too cold for an ice—"

"Do not blaspheme in my company, Lord Ashcroft." She

surveyed the menu and sat back with a small smile. "I will have the chocolate ice."

The waiter arrived in his long apron and fashionable short coat. Ashcroft ordered her chocolate ice as well as a raspberry jelly and some Savoy biscuits.

"Your mother has often regaled us with stories of all the dessert courses she ordered from here in minute detail. I did not realize a shop could be so elegant." She patted the green velvet of the seat next to her, letting her fingers fall through the gold fringing. It felt like luxury and fun.

"Mother has a great fondness for Gunter's. I suggest we bring her home some sweetmeats. Otherwise, she may not forgive us for visiting without her."

Her eyes widened, but then she darted him a mischievous look. "I cannot be sorry. A country mouse like me must take every opportunity she's offered."

He frowned. "I wish you wouldn't refer to yourself like that. The last thing you look or sound like is a country mouse. I can assure you no one in London could create more elegant rooms than you did for our house. It matters not where we come from, but who we are. And who we are is not where we come from."

If only that were true. "I think there are some instances where who we are and where we come from is *all* other people see," she said with a small sigh. "I attended many assemblies and balls where ladies who had little claim on intelligence or looks, had all the gentlemen's attention just because of who their mother or father was, or how big their dowry was. So you see, it is lovely to think it doesn't matter, but in this age, it unfortunately does."

"I have had my fair share of failures, too, and I have both birth and fortune to recommend me." He laughed. "No one is immune from the disaster that is love."

"Is it always a disaster?" Their gazes met and the noise of Gunter's faded away. His eyes were mahogany today, warmed by the lamp on the wall and looking at her tenderly. Two patches of red appeared on his cheeks. He wasn't unmoved, either.

The moment stretched out, and it seemed like he was about to say something when she looked past him, feeling her eyes widen and her mouth drop open.

"Your mother is *here*. She just arrived." Disappointment weighed her words down.

Ashcroft swung around. "So she is. With Lady Astley."

"The lady from the theater who glared at me?" Lady Astley wore a mauve pelisse and a large white muff she hid her hands in.

"She was glaring at me, not you," Ashcroft said, looking around the room for a table big enough for four.

A passing waiter, being very quick on the uptake, ushered Lady Hartley and her friend to a table that would accommodate them, so she could invite them if she wanted to.

She did not. Instead, she waved at him and told the waiter she would like a smaller table.

"This is bad, isn't it?" Charis said quietly. The idea that Lady Hartley did not want to be seen in public with her suddenly became a hard fact instead of a vague feeling. She looked down at her ice, stirring her spoon in the goblet and not lifting her eyes. This was terrible. She should never have come out.

Ashcroft turned back to her. "Don't fret. They likely have secrets they need to trade, and having us at the table would ruin their fun. Did Mother scold you for the theater? I got a lovely lecture. But I did not repent, you'll be pleased to know."

Ashcroft tried to catch his mother's eye, but she had her back to him, and Lady Astley was staring at Charis herself in a way bordering on rude.

"Is she still staring at me?" Charis asked. "I dare not look up."

"I have turned away. I don't know." It was said with the briskness of a man determined to ignore a problem.

She shuffled her chair so that Ashcroft was directly in front of her. "I feel like we've done something wrong. But we haven't, have we?"

"We have not. I can only put this down to Mother being surprised to see us."

"Your mother's friend looks familiar to me. Do I know her from Hartley Green?" She was attractive, with high cheekbones and a fineness to her features that struck a chord in Charis. The lady looked at her, and Charis slid her glance away. Her skin prickled, and it had nothing to do with the ices.

He nodded. "She has visited us in the country many times. Perhaps you do."

Did she? She searched her memory but couldn't remember ever seeing her. How strange it all was. Every time she felt someone's gaze on her, she looked up in time to see Lady Astley or Lady Hartley glance away. They were just as awkward. It was all so strange.

They finished their treats with none of the joy with which they started them.

She offered him a weak smile. "I'm sorry. It's hard to sit here with them so close." The visit was ruined, and no amount of biscuits or sweets could change that now.

Ashcroft seemed to know it too. "Let's go home, shall we?"

Charis rose from the table. "I need to buy my parents a jar of the lemon drops." She made her way to the counter, knowing it took her away from Lady Hartley. She had reached her limit of this discomfort.

Ashcroft left her and walked to his mother, bowing over her hand. Charis was not so far away that she couldn't hear them. "Good day, Mother. It is lovely to see you."

"Yes, yes, Ashcroft. I wish you had waited for me to bring Miss Eastwood here. I very much wanted the treat of doing so. It's vexing."

"My apologies. But you have had weeks to do so." He bowed his head at Lady Astley. "A pleasure to see you, as always."

Charis watched surreptitiously. A fiery blush burned up Lady Astley's cheeks as though Ashcroft had embarrassed her. Charis bought her gifts and waited for him by the door. He had best hurry before the tears gathering in her eyes started to fall. Nobody was looking at her, but it felt like everyone was.

He joined her, a frown on his face. "This has all confused me greatly."

Charis lifted her chin. She refused to cry. "Your mother obviously wants me to stay home. So, I shall stay home. Or maybe I'll just *go* home. To Hartley Green. The work is well on its way to being done. There's nothing more for me to do."

"Don't even think about it," he ground out, as though the very thought of it offended him.

This friendship was the last thing she expected of her time in London, and the very best thing that had ever happened to her. She smiled and took his arm. "Surely you see I cannot stay if I am not welcome?"

"That's not the case. She just told me she is upset I stole her thunder, bringing you here."

"We both know it's not about that. It's something else. Something I don't know."

"Do you think so? Well, you are not leaving. You have yet to decorate the ballroom for the 'find a bride for Ashcroft' ball." He handed her up into the carriage, looking as confused as she felt.

How could everything be so perfect and then so horrible in such a short space of time? If she didn't know what the problem was, there was certainly nothing she could do to fix it.

"I will drive you home, but I am due at the Commons in just over an hour. Will you be fine?"

"I will have a tray sent up and spend a quiet evening. I doubt your mother will be home."

"Likely not," he replied, but the grim line of his mouth said he was none too happy with it.

169

CHAPTER 16

WHERE HEAVEN IS FOUND AFTER A HELLISH NIGHT

Not only was Lady Hartley home for dinner, but she also expressly asked Charis to dine with her.

Now, of all the nights when dining with her would feel like torture.

"I was planning to take a tray in my room," Charis replied. "I have quite the headache after such a big day." Any other day, that would have been enough for Lady Hartley to skip away to one of her friends for dinner. But not today.

"Poo. You don't have a headache. You just don't want to face me after what happened at Gunter's, and I don't blame you. But we must speak. I see that now. So change for dinner, and I will see you shortly. Don't disappoint me."

It was amazing just how little choice one had when my lady used that voice. She would be at dinner, or insult her host. The choice was hers.

At least going to dinner might elicit some answers. It was better to know why the scene at Gunter's had happened than to go home to Hartley Green and wonder forever. The guessing would be at an end. She exhaled.

Charis arrived a half hour later to find the footmen gone from the room and a single course of dinner laid out on the table on platters. So, no observers, then.

Goodness. Nerves flared inside her like crackers at Vauxhall.

Lady Hartley sailed in. "Ah, very good. We shall serve ourselves. How delicious it all looks." She picked up her plate and placed some vegetables and a portion of rolled beef with sauce.

Charis followed suit, although her appetite had fled.

They sat, and Lady Hartley took a few bites, chewing thoughtfully. When she stopped and put her fork down, Charis did, too.

"Firstly, I must apologize. But when you hear the story, you will agree that staying at home and not venturing out into London really was for the best."

For the best? What could she have done? Unless Lady Hartley was having problems of her own that had nothing to do with Charis. "Please, do tell me. If I have done something wrong ..."

Lady Hartley held up a hand, closing her eyes briefly. "That was my fear, that you would think I did not approve of you. Nothing could be further from the truth."

The doors to the dining room flung open, and Lambley entered, his eyes darting about until they landed on his mistress. "Madam, the Theatre Royal is on fire! The whole thing is going up in smoke."

Lady Hartley threw down her napkin, not even bothering to fold it. "Oh no, how dreadful. Poor Sheridan. I hope everybody is out of the building?"

The butler nodded. "Apparently they had rehearsals and some workmen there this afternoon, but everyone is hoping it was empty."

"Let's pray that is the case," Lady Hartley said.

Charis's heart clenched as she recalled what Lady Hartley had said the previous day at the Buxton's. "Does Sheridan own the entire theater?"

Lady Hartley nodded. "Yes. Although we invested too. He

spent his fortune rebuilding the inside and making it beautiful. This is so sad."

Charis watched in horror as tears slid down Lady Hartley's cheeks.

Charis put a hand over hers. "Perhaps it can be saved," Charis said. "Doesn't it have special water tanks on the ceiling and an iron curtain to stop just this kind of thing? Everything will be fine, you'll see. I'm sure his insurance company has fire engines in attendance and thousands of people helping."

Then she remembered Ashcroft saying he would be visiting Sheridan. "You don't think Ashcroft is with him, too?"

Despite the emergency, Lady Hartley narrowed her eyes at Charis. "*Lord* Ashcroft, you mean?"

"Surely he would still be in the Commons?"

"He is, but so is Sheridan. I hardly think Ashcroft would leave his friend to face this alone. Indeed, if he is not already there, I shall be very surprised." Her eyes flared in alarm. "He'll throw himself in there, nothing surer. Dear Lord, no!" Her eyes darted around the room, as if she would see her son at the door.

Charis's heart picked up and started thumping in her chest. Fires were unpredictable and deadly. If Ashcroft found himself in the wrong place, he would be lost forever. "The walls might fall in. You don't mean he would actually try to fight the fire himself, do you? We should go to him, directly."

Lady Hartley clenched Charis's hand. "We will do no such thing. The site of such a tragedy is not the place for either you or me. Is it? Perhaps we might help." She stood, then her shoulders slumped and she sat again. "How could I possibly help? I am entirely useless."

"We could tend to the injured? My father made sure I know how to treat all manner of injuries." They had to do something; she itched to move and be useful.

"I can't abide blood. No." Lady Hartley blotted her lips with her napkin, folded it crisply, and placed it by the side of her plate.

"I believe I'll send Hicks with a carriage for him. If I know them, they will be close to the fire and not hard to find." She rose from the table once more and left the room to set her task in motion.

Charis looked down at her plate. The rolled side of beef was even more unappetizing than before.

After a minute or two, she went to find Lady Hartley. She wasn't in her bedroom or the drawing room. In fact, she was nowhere to be found.

Charis made her way to the front door. "Lambley, has Lady Hartley left us for the evening?"

"Yes, Miss."

She'd left, the wretch, and without a goodbye. So much for saying the fire was no place for them. A falsehood, obviously. Charis had keener eyesight and would be able to spot Ashcroft in a crowd and yet she was left to molder home alone. She was fast starting to think Lady Hartley had a vast talent for lies and half-truths.

Her heels clipped on the marble floor as she made her way to the front door, where Lambley sat at his post.

He cleared his throat. "You won't be leaving, I trust, miss?"

She wanted to leave. To run down the streets until she saw Ashcroft was safe. To make sure he wasn't being brave and heroic and diving into that death trap.

"I just want to see if we can see the fire from here." She walked down the steps, onto the pavement, and turned to the east, toward Drury Lane. Her own impotence choked her as she looked up.

It was past seven, and the sky was already dark. Even if she did not know which direction Drury Lane was, the sky was as good as an arrow. It had taken on an unnatural orange hue, like the fire lit the clouds themselves.

How big the fire must be to make its reflection on the tiles of the houses just off in the distance—how bright and ferocious.

And Ashcroft was probably in there somewhere.

She shuddered. What was he doing right now? Running into the building? Her legs were heavy with dread. Charis rubbed her arms up and down against the cold. A February evening was still bone-chilling, even with such a tragic bonfire in the distance. Then she turned and went back inside, not sure what to do with herself.

The brightness of the fire had made the sky glow with orange that turned to purple and then the indigo of the cloudless night. It begged her to paint it, just to do something, anything, to fill in the time while she waited for everyone to return.

She went to the library and lit an entire branch of candelabra. It wasn't the best time to paint, but it could be done.

Must be done, to stop her going mad. She cleared her small painting desk and grabbed her palette and a fresh sheet of thick preshrunk watercolor paper. Then, armed with fresh water from the pitcher and her brushes, she painted the fiery night sky.

It was not the souvenir one wanted from a trip, but it was an important night in London's history and one that she was living. Her strokes were furious, like the fire itself, lighting up the page in bright bold strokes.

Faster than she'd ever painted before, liberated from what she thought someone wanted to see. It was all her worry and longing for Ash on a parchment. Would he ever see it? People died in fires in London every other day.

She couldn't bear it.

The front door opened, and she heard the light clip of Lady Hartley's tread down the hall and the murmurings of Lambley.

Charis got up and poked her head into the hall. "My lady?"

Lady Hartley kept walking. "No, my dear, no news. There was no way we could get anywhere near the blaze. The roads are blocked by thousands of people. We turned around and came right back. I didn't find Ashcroft. I didn't see Sheridan either. They both might be gone for all I know." This last pronouncement was uttered with a hitch.

Charis clasped her hands, all annoyance at the frustrating evening gone. "I expect you will not be going to your evening's entertainment now."

Lady Hartley shook her head. "I will most definitely be going. I will leave my direction with Lambley. If Ashcroft arrives home, please send word to me immediately, otherwise I would much rather not sit and wait in the gloom for him to return. I will get more information at the party than I would otherwise get here. I will change now and leave directly."

Leaving Charis in the very gloom she herself escaped.

But it didn't matter. Charis couldn't move an inch from the house until she knew Ash was safe, and all was well. Thank goodness Lady Hartley did not want her company. "Perhaps they can still save it. No theater has ever had such modern measures in place."

But she was talking to the air.

Lady Hartley was gone, leaving Charis alone in the house with nothing but her own thoughts and her paintbrush to keep her company. And a mind that asked "what if" over and over. What if that perfect afternoon was the last one she was to have? What if she never got to see him smile again? Never got to tell him how he made every day exciting. How looking at the way his hair curled on his cravat was like inspecting a work of art. Or that the way his spectacles sat on his nose as he read the newspaper was entirely adorable.

And now it might be too late. But then her more rational self argued that he would not be so silly as to enter a burning building, and he was perfectly fine.

What a mess.

She continued on with her painting, working her way down to the London rooftops as she'd seen them, glowing with the reflection of the fire in the distance. She drew the houses and then when the painting was finished, she waited for it to dry by the fireplace.

Then she took her ink and quill and finished it with the inclines that would give the buildings their definition. It was by far the best and worst painting she had ever done.

The clock chimed eleven, but she wasn't going to bed. She would sit there until the candles gutted, and then she'd sit in the dark if she had to. She closed her eyes and sent as many missives to as many angels as would take them.

It was probably a busy night.

The front door opened. There was grumbling and a heavy footfall that was not Lady Hartley.

"Ash?" She stopped with her hand on the candelabra, her eyes wide, waiting for the footsteps to pass the door of the library.

He stood in the doorway, filling it, his brows drawn together in a frown.

He was safe.

Her heart sang with it. *He was safe.*

Relief took the strength from her legs, but she took a tremulous step toward him.

"You look …" She wanted to say "terrible," but that would only add insult to injury. He was pale, his normally groomed hair disheveled, and there were dark smudges under his eyes. His cravat was untied, and his normally pristine shoes were scuffed.

"Like death, I know." He ran a hand through his hair and came into the library properly. "It's gone. The whole thing is gone."

"But the iron curtain? The water tanks?"

He shook his head. "Ineffectual. I don't know what happened, but I suspect foul play. The whole thing is ablaze. I tried to run in, but it was already lost. The only saving grace is that the building stands alone, so with any luck, it will be the only thing that burns down. But burn down it will. Sheridan has lost everything. I can only pray no lives have been lost."

Charis took a step toward him, holding out one hand. "I'm so sorry. What a terrible thing."

"It's devastating. Where's Mother?" He took her hand and

176

squeezed it, then sat back against his desk, still holding her hand, threading his fingers through hers. His hands were dirty, and her fingers had paint on them. It was strangely captivating.

"She went to a party, hoping to get news. Earlier, she took the carriage out to find you. I'm sure someone is on their way to fetch her right now."

He nodded and rubbed his eyes, which were ringed in red, suggesting he'd been closer to the smoke than she'd first thought.

"How is Sheridan?"

"He was completely composed and even made a joke about getting a glass of wine so he could sit by his own fireside. The fireside being the blaze of his entire fortune." He shook his head. "I'd like to think I'd have the same level of sangfroid in that situation, but I doubt it."

"Sometimes drowning your sorrows is the only way to respond."

"They offered to adjourn parliament when we first heard the news of the fire at around four. But he wouldn't hear of it. Said we should take care of our issues first. As if we could do that while lives might be at stake."

She wanted to open her arms to him and pull him tight. Even though there was nothing in the offer but comfort from one person to another, she kept her arms by her sides.

He looked over her shoulder at the painting, and his eyes widened. He stepped closer to inspect it. "You did this tonight?"

"I didn't know what else to do. Your mother had gone, so I decided to paint." *I was beside myself with worry for you.*

"It's beautiful. I only wish it didn't make me so sad."

"I know. It's not the kind of painting one would put a frame around. But this does feel like a historic day for all the wrong reasons."

His eyes met hers, and all the restraint and all the seriousness and intensity were stripped away from him. He was not Ashcroft the politician or the reformer or the impossible-to-reach man.

He was standing in front of her, raw and devastated. Tears formed in his eyes. "I know it is just a building, but it was beautiful, and it was the livelihood and source of joy for so many people. Now it is gone. It's such a waste."

Charis did what she promised herself she would not do. She stood on her toes, opened her arms, and wrapped them around him. He stiffened, and for the briefest moment, she thought he would not respond. Her heart fell somewhere around her ankles.

But then he lifted his arms and let them hang gently over her shoulders as if unwilling or unable to do any more. "The good news is we think nobody perished. Buildings can be rebuilt, new jobs can be found, but hopefully, nobody has lost their mother, father, brother, or sister tonight."

He pulled her a little tighter, and she felt the pressure of his lips on the top of her head. "I want …" he murmured into her hair.

"You want what?" She may have leaned against him a little harder.

"This." He pulled the pins from her hair, and she felt it tumble down her back. He ran his fingers through it from her temples through to the back of her head.

Oh. It felt divine. How had she never been touched like this? Something so simple felt entirely decadent.

"And maybe this …" With a thumb under her chin, he lifted her face, a question in his eyes. *Can I kiss you?*

Yes, you can. She should object, but she wanted him to kiss her more than anything. And to kiss him back. Well, if she figured out how to, that was. "I've never kissed anyone before." Behind that statement, there was a wealth of loneliness and hurt. Nobody had wanted to kiss her. Ever.

"I must remedy that." He leaned down and gently pressed his lips to hers. After the briefest of moments, he pulled back, searching her face. "There. Now you have. I hope I have not shocked you."

"Not yet, but I do hope you'll keep trying." How could her heart hammer so loud after his lips had barely touched hers? It was like her entire body was tuned to his, the slightest touch enough to push her into a dreamy haze.

He laughed, and the low vibration thrummed down to her toes. It was suddenly easy to see how ladies swooned.

"I missed it entirely. Please, again." She took a step toward him, tilting her head up. "If that is to be my only kiss, I feel very shortchanged."

He smiled, as though he knew. "My apologies. I shall try harder this time."

And so would she. He sat on the edge of the desk, and she wrapped her arms around his neck and leaned into him. She kissed him as he'd kissed her, but he deepened it instantly, showing her slowly, one dreamlike moment to the next, how to taste and how to feel.

There had never been anything like it.

If she melted into a puddle on the floor of the library, she would not be surprised. This was eating strawberries fresh from the patch on a hot summer day or walking through a field at sunrise. It was life in the most beautiful and delectable way possible.

His fingers ran through her hair, and he pulled back to murmur something in her ear that sounded like "so beautiful." Not wanting it to end, she drew him to her so he would kiss her again.

He complied, and they lost themselves for a few minutes more, until they caught their breath, leaning their foreheads together.

"We probably shouldn't have done that," he said. "But I can't say I'm sorry. I've been longing to kiss you since the day you got out of the carriage and told me my dining room was an atrocity."

"And if I'd known how much fun it was going to be, I would have kissed you right back." She touched his cheek, tracing her finger down it. "Please don't feel guilty. Think of it as a wonderful gift for me to take home. But perhaps we had best not do it again."

Part of her grieved.

He arched an eyebrow, letting her know what he thought of that idea. "Let's see, shall we? I'm not sure I'm willing to give you up so quickly."

Her breath caught. A man like him would never suggest anything underhand. Did he mean he wanted to marry her? Then they could kiss all afternoon, and she could live in this magnificent house she had created herself and watch Lark with him each day.

She could see that beautiful life so clearly it felt real. But she wouldn't believe it until it happened. And marriage proposals from earls didn't happen on the spur of the moment. They happened after both families had deliberated and brought their best offers to the table. A merging of dynasties to secure the wealth of both families.

"You shall have to give me up when I return to Hartley Green. Unless you have forgotten what happened at Gunter's earlier today."

The sound of the front door opening and his mother's voice forced them apart. Footsteps sounded down the hall.

"I have not forgotten. And I don't kiss a young lady lightly, Miss Eastwood."

"That's Charis to you," she whispered. Because that was what everyone who loved her called her.

"Yes, that's Charis to me." He left the room, but the warm feeling of being loved stayed with her.

CHAPTER 17

IN WHICH LADY HARTLEY IS HELD TO ACCOUNT

The following morning, Ashcroft climbed the stairs in search of his mother.

The fire had brought home to him just how tenuous life and possessions were, how close each of them teetered on the edge of oblivion. That was his frame of mind when he'd stumbled upon Charis in the library last night.

He wanted to hold her, keep her, and not waste a moment more. The feeling was so powerful it made him question his sanity. It was scary but thrilling. Like he was finally alive.

When he needed comfort, the pull to her was magnetic. He didn't want anyone else to discuss the events of the night with. No one else he wanted to kiss and keep kissing until they both forgot where they were.

But a gentleman never kissed a lady he had no intention of courting. And the thought of courting her set him aflame too. But before the horror of the fire, his mother had thrown a tiny tantrum at seeing him with Charis at Gunter's, and he needed to know why.

If it was just her wanting to control his marriage choice, he would have no qualms setting her straight, but there was more there. His curiosity was piqued.

He intercepted the maid as she was climbing up the stairs with a breakfast tray.

"Allow me to take that to Lady Hartley," he said. "I am seeking her out, in any case."

Eliza looked uncertain, as though him taking the tea tray from her would somehow get her into trouble.

He took it anyway. "You may follow me up the stairs and open the door if it pleases you. You won't be in trouble."

She nodded and climbed the stairs in front of him, then opened the door to his mother's boudoir and bobbed a curtsy at his mother before departing.

He entered with the tray and set it down on the large table beside the chaise lounge, where she was reclining.

She was in her morning robe, with a frilly cap on her head and a cashmere shawl draped around her shoulders. She looked up from the book propped on her lap. Her mouth pursed. "I am glad you came. I would like a word with you."

"I had the same thought."

"Is Eliza bringing you a cup?"

He shook his head. "No, I don't feel like taking tea."

"And you are quite well after last night's escapade? Such a terrible thing. I was so worried for you, and it made me realize I can't put this conversation off a moment longer."

He sat on the chair across from her lounge. "Is it about Gunter's yesterday? I would love to know why my taking Miss Eastwood there put you in a temper. For it was temper. Do not deny it. Miss Eastwood thinks she needs to use her last shilling to take the stagecoach home."

She stiffened. "How silly. She has nothing to be upset about. I told her as much over dinner."

Ashcroft waited for her to explain, but she poured herself a cup of tea, taking an extra-long time about it.

He sat back in his chair and watched her steadily, waiting for her reply. She took a sip and then glanced at him. "Don't look at me like that. You remind me of your father when he discovered the extent of my gambling habit."

"I await your explanation on why you purposefully hurt a young lady who did nothing wrong and was thoroughly enjoying her first, I might add, visit to Gunter's. A joy that you extinguished in record time. If you could have seen the happiness vanish from her face. It was like kicking a puppy."

"You think too much about Miss Eastwood's sensibilities. Why is that?"

He shook his head. "No, don't do that. This was not the right way to repay her for creating the most beautiful rooms for you."

She put the teacup down and looked at him sternly. "I will not be lectured by my own son."

"Unfortunately, you will." When he wanted answers, he generally got them, no matter who he was asking. He crossed one leg over the other, ready for a long innings.

"You are pushing me to reveal secrets that are not mine to reveal."

What an entirely confusing statement. "And why would you be angry about someone else's secret in a way that makes you rude to Miss Eastwood? You're not making any sense. You know I am a trustworthy receptacle for any secret."

Her eyes softened. "Indeed. This stubbornness may annoy me, but your honor and integrity are what I love most about you. You take after your father with that, too."

With a slight shake of her head, she put her book down, finally committing to the conversation. "I should have reacted better yesterday, but I did not expect to see you there while I was in the company of Lady Astley." She paused and searched around the room as though she would find the right words on the ceiling.

"She has had a difficult time. You know Jeremy died at Salamanca. And Lord Astley died some years ago. All she has is that dreadful daughter of hers, Arabella. So, I brought Charis to London, hoping to reunite them. The house decoration was just a happy excuse."

This was even more baffling. "And why would Lady Astley want a reunion?" But even as he finished his sentence, the truth of the matter hit him. There was a reason Charis found Lady Astley familiar, and it had nothing to do with her crossing paths in Hartley Green. Lady Astley was familiar because they resembled one another.

Like family.

"Are you saying Lady Astley is related to the Eastwoods? Why didn't you just say so? Surely there's no harm in the connection? They are entirely respectable."

Mother shook her head sadly. "It is not a respectable connection, I'm afraid. Charis's parents in Hartley Green are adoptive parents, and her natural mother is Lady Astley." She pursed her mouth. "There I have said it. It has been a secret for all these years and now it is out."

Ashcroft stopped breathing and tried to understand. Charis was born out of wedlock. Did she know? If he had to be the one to tell her, oh, what a horrible thing to have to do.

"If you brought her to London to introduce her to her mother, why did you never do so?"

"I was so sure that Althea would be thrilled. Then I probed her gently about the baby and whether she would be interested in seeing her grown, and imagine my surprise when she flew into a rage with me. I had the entire situation wrong. If it were my baby, I would adore the connection, however tenuous it might be. But I must admit, not having seen Charis and Lady Astley in the same room, I did not realize their resemblance was as close as it is. I couldn't see past the fact that Charis has dark-blonde hair and Althea has red."

From not wanting to tell her secret, now his mother was unburdening herself at a clipping rate.

"Therefore, you have not been taking Charis out because Lady Astley would be on the lookout for her daughter and know you'd brought her to London without her approval."

"The encounter at Gunter's was the very circumstance I was trying to avoid. I felt terrible leaving Charis at home, but I know Althea is leaving London soon, so I thought I could just wait until she left."

It was very like his mother to do something rashly, and have to reverse course.

"When Lady Astley saw Charis with you at the theater, she immediately knew who she was and was *furious* with me. Since then, I've kept things quiet. Until you took her to Gunter's."

"I see. Now it is making much more sense. I didn't think you would bring a young lady to London and then not take her out and about. Poor Charis thinks she is not good enough to be seen in society with you. I fear you have almost done more harm than good."

It made more sense, but it was an entirely new basket of snakes to subdue. How was Charis to live in London with Lady Astley throwing deathly stares at her whenever they met? It was untenable.

Mother closed her eyes. "I hoped she had not noticed, being so busy with her painting and the refurbishment. But she did. As little as I like to be lectured, I fear in this instance you are right." She put her hand on her brow, dramatically. "I have made a mull of things. I don't know what to do."

"You do know what to do," said Ashcroft. "You have been visiting the Eastwoods since Charis was born. Your first responsibility is to Charis, not Lady Astley."

"You rush to her defense." She narrowed her eyes. "Is there something I should know?"

"I have grown fond of her. But it is more than that." He took a

185

deep breath, committing to the course. "She is essential to my future happiness. I ... can't imagine my life without her in it."

They were words he never thought he'd utter. Especially after such a short period of time. Indeed, he never thought his wife would be someone he couldn't live without, but just someone who sat on the periphery of his life, making things easier.

This wasn't like that.

He couldn't care less if Charis did nothing to help him, just as long as she wanted to stay with him, always.

Mother blinked rapidly, as though rifling through replies.

Finally, she spoke. "After a few scant weeks? You need to give this some time. With respect, Charis is the exact opposite of what you need for your future happiness. And I say this being very fond of her myself. People in your position, with a title and a political career, do not marry people with no pedigree. And worse, her background may actually hamper you some time in the future."

All of that was true. He also didn't care.

"I can see by the mulish set of your mouth that you don't care. And maybe you don't right now, but in the future you will. She will be out somewhere, standing next to Lady Astley and looking every inch her daughter. Somebody will put it together. You can't expect Althea to leave London altogether."

"Of course not. Who is her father?"

She turned away. "You have had enough secrets out of me today. Just stay away from Miss Eastwood. For your own good."

She rarely gave him bad counsel. But he wanted to go in the opposite direction, no matter what it meant for their relationship or his relationship with his father.

How had Charis become so vital in such a short time? How did his heart know this was the only right direction? That if he was just with her, he was on the right path. He only had to find a way around all the problems she outlined. It started with honesty.

186

"You must tell her."

"Must I?" Every inch of aristocratic marchioness was on display, eyebrow raised, posture ramrod straight. "I was about to last night at dinner, but now I think I will leave well enough alone. She is perfectly happy as she is. If you drop your idea of marrying her, there is no reason for her to be any the wiser." She smoothed her skirts over her knees. "Would it help if I gave her a dowry? Made sure she was taken care of and happily married?"

He gritted his teeth. "How would marrying her off to someone else help, when I have just told you she is essential to *my* happiness? And why did you not do that *before* rather than let her languish unwed? Surely you owed her more than a basket from the estate every season. Surely Lady Astley did."

Her eyes sparked, showing he'd just crossed a line. He'd blaze the line if he had to. "There is no talking to you today, Ashcroft. Let's discuss this tomorrow after you've had the chance to think about it. We can undo none of this just because we would like to."

She stood, showing it was time for him to leave.

"I shall start taking her out with me, warning Lady Astley of my plans."

Ashcroft made his way to the door, and he stopped with his hand on the knob. She was right; they *were* talking at cross purposes, and they would find no conclusions doing that. What he wanted was for his mother to support his marriage to Charis, not work against it. "Don't bother. I would rather do it myself."

She shrugged one shoulder. "As you wish. Now off to the Commons with you. I hear the interviews have been eye-opening?"

"They have indeed. I am bracing myself already." And just like that, she shifted the conversation back to mundane issues. He put his heart on his sleeve for her to ignore it and carry on a moment later.

Like she assumed he'd toe her line. He tamped down a spurt of irritation. Let her think it.

"I thought your father might come up to town for it, but I have not seen him."

"You may yet." Lord Hartley was notorious for turning up when one least expected. How many times had he thought a footman would pick him up from Eton only to have his father land on the doorstep in all his sartorial glory. Frills and laces, midnight black horses and devil-may-care riding. He was so seldom home that the word *father* didn't hold as much weight as it should. He wanted it to. Felt the need of it now, when his head hurt with decisions that should not be his to make.

He walked down the stairs slowly. He hated the thought of turning Charis's world upside down with this news. Hated to break the implicit promise of secrecy he'd just made to his mother. He was honor bound to keep the secret, but where was his honor toward Charis? In all conscience, how could he not tell her?

He must try to distance himself from her while he thought this through.

Ethical dilemmas were the very worst.

CHAPTER 18

IN WHICH CHARIS BUILDS ASHCROFT A DOOR
TO HIS FUTURE

"Is that what you had in mind, miss?"

Mr. Adams stood behind Charis as she inspected the newly finished French doors installed in the library. The smell of fresh paint hung in the air, and the fire was stoked high to dry it as quickly as possible.

"Let me see." Charis walked around the desk and sat in Ashcroft's chair. There was no need to lean back or tilt one's head to view the tree or the birds. The outdoors spread before her like a painting that would change with the seasons. "So much nicer than that tiny window. Perfection, Mr. Adams."

As she settled into the chair, Lambley came to the door. His eyes widened, and he seemed to teeter on his long, thin legs. "Oh, Miss Eastwood."

"I hope that's a good 'Oh, Miss Eastwood.' I'm not in trouble, am I?" She tapped out her apprehension on the desktop. Wasn't it always the case that when things were going beautifully, something would set her down?

He took a step into the room. "No. No, Miss. He feeds the birds every morning. And when he's not here, I do it for him. Now he can see them properly from his desk."

"So, you know the new door is just for the birds?"

"As soon as I saw it. I've been here a few years now. In my mind's eye, I can see him as a lad with his lordship, watching the chicks in springtime."

It was hard to imagine Lord Hartley being a caring and indulgent father, much less Ashcroft in leading strings. "That's a lovely memory."

He nodded. "And that's a nice thing to have put in. Well done, miss."

Charis swallowed. The kind words of the family retainer meant more than any effusive praise Lady Hartley could heap on her. "I only hope his lordship likes it."

The butler smiled kindly. "There now, I'm sure he will. How could he not? You need not worry about being sent off without a reference."

He laughed as though he'd made a good joke. But is that how everyone saw her? As a servant? Surely that wasn't how Ashcroft saw her? Not when he'd kissed her.

A kiss she hoped meant the start of a courtship.

Could they marry? She was a gentleman's daughter. Surely they could.

She didn't care about his title or those grand estates. She quirked her lips in a wry smile. *Well, not so very much.* She just wanted to keep sharing her life with him, just as she was now.

And kiss him again.

If she didn't imagine the entire thing.

But if none of that happened, and she left London with a thorough knowledge of how to redecorate a house, then she would learn to be content with that. What difference did her happiness make if she could make a difference in the lives of the people she loved?

Lady Hartley was out visiting. It appeared she had no intention of finishing the discussion they started at the dinner table. But after the kiss, Charis couldn't even find it in herself to care.

What was it to her if Lady Hartley did not want to take her around, if Ashcroft did?

She spent the rest of the day on the nursery mural, with a spare bucket and brush out in case Ashcroft returned.

He did not.

It would be easy to think he was avoiding her, but the truth was more likely that he was sitting bored in parliament.

Hopefully thinking of her. She groaned. The longing for him was worse than anything. It almost felt like a sickness.

After dinner on a tray in her room, Charis slipped down to the library for a novel. She was delighted to find *The Mysteries of Udolpho* on the shelf and curled into Ashcroft's armchair, the one worn in by countless generations of Ashcroft behinds.

He wasn't home yet. The Commons was running into the night with the hearings. But if he came home before she went to bed, she would show him the changes she'd made to his library.

Would he love it as she did? She was torn between wanting to show him immediately and keeping the door locked until she left for Hartley Green, in case he hated it.

Her book lay open on her lap. She had stopped at the end of chapter two, where Emily had left St. Aubert to his private sorrows, and stared at the candle as though it contained the answers to all her questions. Like why Ashcroft had seen her in the garden room at breakfast and ducked straight back out.

No, she wouldn't think about it.

A footfall in the hall made her leap from her chair, knocking the book to the ground. She peeked around the door to see Lambley taking Ashcroft's coat.

He had the look of someone worn down by the day's events, shoulders slumped, eyes blinking slowly at her as though she were an apparition. It was like the night of the fire, but with less dirt and soot.

"Welcome home. I hope the day was not too bad?"

He shook himself as though ridding himself of it. "It was just as I expected it to be. Speech after speech on the Duke of York from every angle known to mathematics. I am so weary of it all and wish he had never had a mistress at all."

He *must* be tired, to mention the word *mistress* in her hearing. "Reasonable. Let me show you something that will hopefully cheer you up."

He tilted his head to one side. "Is a room finished?"

"Yes, although not a room you saw a design for."

"Oh?" And because there was only one room he had told her not to touch, his eyebrows drew together, and he eyed her skeptically. "What have you done, Mischief?"

His tone was teasing. He trusted her.

"I know you told me not to change anything here, but I have been painting in this room for almost a month and, like you, I enjoy watching the birds. Each time they flit beyond that tiny window, I feel sad. So, I took matters into my own hands."

She walked toward the drapes and reached to the side to pull the cord. "With your mother's permission, of course. I was sure you would love it, and I wanted it to be a surprise."

Charis pulled, revealing the new set of shining glass doors. Since it was dark outside, all they could see in the glass were their own reflections in the candlelight.

She looked at him anxiously. "So you see, you can close the drapes if you don't want the sunshine."

"Hmmm."

"I also had a bird bath installed, and a seed holder hanging from the tree. The gardeners have planted gardenia and verbena so if you open the door in spring, the fragrance will enter the library. I hope you are not angry." She held her hand out to him.

Take my hand.

He shook his head and smiled, but instead of taking her hand, stroked his chin thoughtfully. "How could I be angry about such an improvement? Lark and his family have been a source of joy to me for many years. My father taught me to watch for them."

"Lambley told me." She dropped her hand back to her side, trying not to feel hurt. Good, he liked it. This moment was why she loved to improve things. Because future generations would enjoy this small space a little more.

She twisted away. "You can't see it now, but the hollow the starlings use for their nest is in full view. Come spring, there will be eggs, and you can watch the chicks as they grow. You must draw me a picture of how sweet they are."

Because she would not be there.

He blinked and looked down, as though he wanted to say something but decided against it. "Yes, I will send you a picture, although I don't draw as prettily as you."

Was it silly to hope he would say *"no letters will be necessary"* and give her that small secret smile she loved so much?

Carry on.

"Thank you for all your work. It's perfect."

It was perfect, but he didn't try to kiss her again. Or hold her hand. Or pull her into the embrace she so dearly wanted. Although this was the smallest room she had changed, it was the closest to her heart because she knew how he loved his library. But he'd already turned away and was decanting papers from his bag to the desk.

He was withdrawing. There was a distance between them that couldn't be seen, but could definitely be felt. Was she dismissed? Should she leave?

Like a servant.

Her heart squeezed, and she willed those stupid tears to stay right where they were. *Do not cry. Do not.*

It looked like *get yourself home to Hartley Green* was the correct choice after all.

"Thank you, your lordship. If there's nothing else?"

He shook his head, and she left.

CHAPTER 19

IN WHICH IT ALL STARTS TO MAKE SENSE

With one week left until the ball, all the tradesmen converged on the Grosvenor Square house to finish their work, each of them given hefty rush fees by Lady Hartley. Drapes went up in all the rooms, furniture arrived from Mr. Chippendale, and carpets from Axminster were laid in each room and down the halls.

Having been immersed in the project every step of the way, Charis could barely watch. What if it looked silly when it was all done? What if she'd made mistakes? *There's nothing that can't be fixed*, became a mantra of sorts, but seeing the dining room take form made her a little giddy. The blossom wallpapering and elegant dining setting, re-covered in silk from China, looked as fresh as a spring day.

She was about to go for a walk when Lady Hartley found her.

"Get ready, my dear!" she said as she swept into the room. "Ashcroft will drive us around the park, and then we'll stop at Fortnum & Mason. I must order pineapples for the supper table. Everyone has accepted. Everyone! I vow I never expected such success."

At least with Lady Hartley joining them, there would be no

awkward conversation. Ashcroft had been absent for the entire week, in and out of parliament, taking most meals at his club. Her heart broke with every glimpse of him. He was polite, but distant, as though he hadn't kissed her at all.

Like mother like son, it seemed. She had done something wrong, but nobody was telling her what it was. Well, they could all go to Hades.

"I refuse to be sullen about it," she said as she opened her bedroom door.

Mary followed her into the room to change her out of her working clothes. "Sullen about what, miss? Lord Ashcroft?"

Charis stilled. Servants knew *everything*. "Your insight should not surprise me."

"We don't gossip, miss. But Eliza is my friend, so I find things out. Apparently, her ladyship had an argument with him when Eliza brought a tray to her, and it was about you."

They'd had an argument and now he was avoiding her. Because he was obeying his mother's wishes not to court her. Charis exhaled. Just as she thought. But it would have been good, so good, if he had made his own decision.

"Eliza didn't know details, but Peter the footman told me he saw you and his lordship in the library after the fire, and you and he were … ahem."

"Kissing," Charis finished.

A fiery blush lit the maid's cheeks. "Just so." But her eyes sparkled. "Was it wonderful, miss? Or is it the thing you 'refuse to be sullen' about?"

Mary was very quick. Perhaps a little *too* quick. "Both."

"How could you not fall in love with him, miss?"

Charis just smiled. "I know, but I understand why it cannot be. It was obviously just a mistake in judgment." She looked down at her toes. "He knows he cannot marry me."

Mary frowned. "I don't see why not. Lords marry *actresses*.

Why shouldn't he marry a lovely lady like you? I bet he will ask you. Be prepared."

But the silence following the proclamation spoke volumes. "Thank you for the show of support. While it might be naughty, at least I have a kiss to remember him by."

"If I did that with a footman, I'd be shown the door without a reference."

"But perhaps it would be worth it." They shared a grin.

Dressed in her warmest wool cloak supplied by Madame Le Favre, as well as her muff and shawl, Charis waited in the entrance hall. It always felt better to be present and organized than to have them waiting for her. That would never do. She stifled a sigh. Oh, to be back in the early days of her visit when she and Ashcroft made a pact to flirt and have fun together. Far from having brought fun into his life, he was back to looking so serious and intimidating that she wondered if she knew him at all.

Lady Hartley walked sedately toward her. She was not dressed for the brisk morning, and instead wore a pretty dress of cream wool with a high ruched collar.

She lifted her hand as Charis was about to speak. "No, no, my dear. There is too much to do preparing for the ball. I must get my order into Gunter's by midday, or they won't have the time to make the delicacies I need for my dessert board. And then the painters will want direction in the ballroom, and the plaster columns are being delivered. I can't think why I agreed to come in the first place. You two go to Fortnum & Mason in my stead. I have a list." She held out a piece of parchment with her writing scrawled all over it.

"I should stay and help you," Charis said.

Lady Hartley shook her head. "I won't hear of it. Go with Ashcroft. You will be back soon enough and can help me then. I trust Ashcroft to show you the sights of Hyde Park. Indeed, it would be better to see it in a few weeks when the blooms are fully out, and the trees have more than buds on their branches."

Charis stood. "I will take Hyde Park however she comes, although I am sad you won't be joining us." *Drat*. Now she would be alone with him, and it would be entirely awkward. At least on her part. He was probably perfectly fine.

Ashcroft approached from behind, his deep-olive, many-caped coat and shiny black hessians a sight to behold. He held his hat in one hand and a walking cane in the other. Her heart flipped as though he commanded it.

"Not coming, Mother?"

Lady Hartley shook her head. "You two go ahead." She turned to Charis. "Don't let him bore you with the goings-on in parliament."

"He never could," she whispered.

Ashcroft smiled slightly and motioned for her to walk before him. It was friendly, but there was nothing special in his smile, no sparkle in his eye. No dimples.

She nodded. *Very well. But I should like to see you try to rebuff my friendship.*

The carriage was waiting to take them down Upper Grosvenor Street, which led them onto Park Lane and then into Hyde Park itself.

It was the early days of March, which technically meant the season had turned to spring, but the London weather had yet to comply. The air was so icy it created clouds of steam around the footman as he stood at the horses' heads.

"It's cold, but the sky is so blue that I cannot mind." Charis put a hand to her cheek. Ashcroft had ordered the open carriage since the day was clear, but she figured it was more for propriety's sake than to keep them warm. She did, however, have two blankets on her lap and a hot brick at her feet, so apart from her cheeks, she was entirely snug.

"Me either. I took Sirius for a ride in the park earlier, so to me, this feels much warmer than it did a few hours ago." There was a pensiveness to him this morning she could not like.

Then he was silent, and the horses' footfalls bridged the gap in their conversation.

It was so obvious he regretted their closeness. Which was the opposite of the joy she felt whenever she thought on it. Well, she wouldn't let him see her devastation. Nobody would see it. Ignoring the tears threatening to spill down her cheeks, she took a deep breath.

"This is a lovely barouche. The ride is so smooth I barely feel like I'm in a carriage at all. I might as well be floating on a cloud. Although perhaps that is your talent with the ribbons."

He smiled slightly, but kept his eyes on the road as they passed under the gates to Hyde Park. "No, it is not my skill with the ribbons. The carriage has wonderful suspension. I could ride it to Brighton and not feel a bump."

Imagine having the freedom to take your horse and carriage and take off on the Brighton Road. Doing whatever you wanted, whenever you wanted.

Upon reaching Rotten Row, Ashcroft slowed the horses to an amble. They complied immediately and joined the small procession of people out to take the morning air. The Season had not yet begun, but as parliament was sitting, there were more families in London than there would normally be. It seemed the scandal of the Duke of York brought them all to town.

"How often do people promenade like this?" She frowned at the slow pace. "It seems a somewhat boring ride, if I might be honest."

"You're always honest," he said. It was hard to tell if it was a compliment or not. Just a week ago, she would have assumed it was. "Rotten Row is not for the ride, but to show off your newest promenade dress or to be seen in the right company."

Charis brightened. "In that case, can we go somewhere more

exciting?" She didn't ask if she could drive again. He didn't seem in the mood for it.

"As you wish." He directed the horses away from the track as soon as there was a branching path and took them on a much more exciting trip.

Once his team were in an easy rhythm, and the ribbons held firmly in his grasp, he turned to her. "I am glad my mother is not here. First, because she would stop each coach we passed to talk and the brick under your feet would grow cold. Secondly, because I have something important to share with you."

Charis drew in a startled breath. Mary was right. He was going to ask her to marry him! A little "oh" escaped from her mouth, and she looked at him with rapt attention.

He guided the horses around a bend. "You need to know that in doing this, I break a promise. Something I cannot remember doing. Ever."

Or perhaps not. Her joy collapsed like a house of cards. "Please don't tell me if you don't want to. I have no need for new information."

He nodded. "Mother said the same thing. That you would return to Hartley Green none the wiser and be happier for it."

This must have been what the argument Mary told her was about. Charis shoved her trembling hands farther into her muff.

Ashcroft didn't notice, and continued to drive, although he slowed the horses to a walk. "But I can't ..." He exhaled a puff of air, creating a small cloud, and started again. "It should come as no surprise I look upon you most fondly. Indeed, as fondly as a man can look at the lady he hopes will become his wife." He darted a quick look at her.

"You what?" she blurted.

He turned to her, his expression solemn. "Would it make you happy?"

"The happiest creature alive, but ..." None of this made sense. Brows pulled together, she turned to him. "I don't understand. I was sure you regretted our closeness last week." She thought for a moment. "Or maybe you did, but feel obliged to offer for me. In which case, no thank you."

She could stand with him against a world decrying their match, but not if she was just an obligation to him.

"You misunderstand me. But I suppose my actions this past week have been hard to fathom."

"I thought I fathomed them quite well."

"I cannot dissemble, so I would rather keep my distance until I know my direction. My honor is my life. And while I did not promise to keep this secret, I believe it was expected of me. But I must tell you. I cannot marry you knowing something you should know."

"Very well. Tell me this deep, dark secret. Then ask me to marry you."

He flashed her a quick grin. "Very well. When you met Lady Astley at Gunter's, there was a reason she looked familiar to you, and it had nothing to do with seeing her in Hartley Green."

Why was he talking about Lady Astley? "Oh?"

"There is no easy way to say this." Ashcroft took a deep breath. "Mother confided in me that twenty years ago, Lady Astley, who was then Miss Laurent, had relations that resulted in her giving birth to a daughter. She did so in Hartley Green, where my mother could care for her. That baby was then adopted by a local couple."

Charis went entirely still. What was this? How could it be? She clenched her hands together inside the muff to keep them from trembling. "I don't understand."

She searched back into her past for some kind of clue it could be true, but it must have been a most well-kept secret. Nobody had ever intimated that she wasn't an Eastwood through and through. For pity's sake, they told her she had her grandmother's hair.

"You are sure it was me?" The green of Hyde Park blurred as

she leaned back in the seat of his barouche. It explained why she felt different to everyone else in the family. She'd thought she was special, but no, she just wasn't related to them.

"There can be no question of it." His voice was soft, like an apology.

"So I am illegitimate?" What a strange thing to ask on a ride in Hyde Park.

Ash nodded. "A stupid distinction made by men. It means nothing to me."

She ignored him. "Who is my father?"

"I don't know yet, but we will find out." Ash frowned. "All I know is if you are to be in society around Lady Astley, you need to be in possession of the facts. That's the only reason I am telling you. It bears no weight on my feelings for you. Thus, I have broken my trust with Mother when she told me. Marry me, and you will have the protection of my name."

She shook her head, a deluge of sadness draining her will. "How can I marry you, with this hanging over our heads? Society has a long memory and a fierce joy in discovering other people's secrets."

"You will have my protection if anyone should try to discover something buried for twenty years. Your past was not your fault and should not blight our future. But I refuse to start this relationship with anything but total honesty between us."

There would be no relationship. Didn't he see? For a smart man, he was being awfully thick-headed.

"Does she want to meet me? Is that why I was brought to London?"

"My understanding is Mother *hoped* Lady Astley would like to meet you, because she has recently lost a son at Salamanca. However, Lady Astley found facing her past too painful and would rather not acknowledge the relationship."

"That explains her reactions at both the opera and Gunter's." Pieces of a puzzle she did not know she was playing with fell into place. "How terrible this is." It was so very cold in the park. The tears on her cheeks had turned to little darts of ice. She dashed them away with her muff. "How dare they bring me into their silly games? I have feelings. I have a choice. I do not want to meet her either."

"It is a lot to take in." The sympathy in his eyes was almost her undoing. "But how we feel about each other is no part of this. Say you will marry me."

Charis closed her eyes, hoping for clarity, but none was to be found. "As much as I would love to accept, it would be prudent for me not to. Given the circumstances, I must think on it."

Listen to her talking about *prudence* and *thinking* when her head was a seething mess of confusion.

One thing she knew, though. She wouldn't jeopardize his political career. And how could marrying an illegitimate lady, albeit raised by perfectly respectable people, be anything but a disaster for him? The truth of it would come out at the worst possible time and something he had worked terribly hard for would fall to pieces. All because of her.

And she loved him too much for that. There. She had said it. She loved him. It was more than her heart rushing each time he entered the room, or hanging off his every word. It was wanting only the best for him. And this was the true test of it, being able to let him go.

He correctly interpreted the look on her face. "If you plan to be a martyr to this, you can think again. I will not let you go easily, my love. Not now I have found you. I refuse to allow anything that happened so long ago come between us. Say you will be mine."

She rolled her eyes, trying to make light of the situation. "I will say nothing of the sort." She needed to get out of the carriage. "Could you please put me down?"

His brows drew together. "Here?" They were quite a distance into the park, and there was nobody in sight.

"Yes, please. I will find my way home."

"Charis, surely you see I cannot leave you here alone." His voice was even and soft, as though speaking to a spooked horse. "I would only end up following you at a discreet distance, and you'd be aware of me the entire time, quite ruining your solitude."

She closed her eyes, knowing he spoke the truth. He would never leave her alone, and it would be impossible to think, knowing he waited for her. But she couldn't contain the swell of emotions whirling around inside her and didn't want him to see her let them go.

"Everything I've ever believed is true, is not. I cannot bear it. I don't know if I want to cry or scream or fly into a rage." Life had been hard enough before this. Lady Astley had been dripped with pearls and jewels at the opera, while her real mother darned socks thrice over while raising a daughter who was not her own. How was that fair?

"Any of those things would be understandable. But you are wrong. Only a tiny amount of what you believed is true is not. Mrs. Eastwood is still your mother, still the one who loved and raised you. The Eastwood family is still your family, and the Astleys …" He shook his head. "Are not. This does not change who you are."

Then why did it feel like it did?

"How could you ask me to marry you like none of this is important? Like it was just a piece of information I should listen to and then discard. I am illegitimate. It changes *everything*."

His gaze was strong, resolute. "Not to me. Never to me."

She closed her eyes. "Thank you. You are a good friend."

"I would be more." He placed a gloved hand on her arm.

"No, I thank you."

She would not be marrying now. The reason Lady Hartley disapproved of her being at Gunter's with Ashcroft was only partly because of Lady Astley. The rest of it was not wanting to see her son in love with her. She was to stay in her little box, where the lady of the estate shared her bounty of fruits and dairy. Not, under any circumstances, her son.

The thought of going back to Grosvenor Square felt like torture. Riding on with Ashcroft felt the same. Was there nowhere she could go to think and have a few moments to herself? What did a person do when their entire world disappeared from beneath their feet, leaving a chasm?

No, as much as she wanted to hide away until these feelings passed, she must make plans for her future. She could think of only one place that would help her. Madame Le Favre had been nothing but supportive of Charis's talent and had said she had ideas. "Could you please take me to the dressmaker?"

He pulled back, causing his horses to falter, and looked at her. "Did you say *dressmaker*?" As though that were the last place in the world she could want to be. "I thought we were bound for Fortnum's?"

"You may go there and fill your mother's list. But drop me at the modiste's first. If you would like to send someone back for me, I would appreciate it, otherwise I shall walk." It was only thirty minutes, and she was sure she could remember the way.

"I feel you are not listening to me. I have told Mother you are essential to my happiness, and that was *after* she told me. You said not a half-hour ago marrying me would make you the happiest creature alive, so nothing I just told you should change that." He stared straight ahead, his jaw clenched. "Don't go off like a half-cocked pistol. There's no need."

"Of course not. You know how I feel about you." Which is precisely why she could not marry him.

He turned to her, his head tilted, eyebrow arched. She wasn't playing along the way he wanted her to and he didn't like it. "How *do* you feel? Because right now I'm not sure."

"I would do anything for your happiness."

His face broke out in a smile, and he reached over and

clenched her hand. "That is how I feel about you and your happiness. Thank goodness." He heaved a sigh of relief and rode on with a small smile on his face. "We will work this out."

As a politician, he really should pay more attention to people who evaded questions.

CHAPTER 20

IN WHICH MADAME LE FAVRE REVEALS HERSELF TO BE A FAIRY GODMOTHER

Charis stepped into the dressmaker's workshop. Ceiling-to-floor red drapes encompassed the large workroom, and tall gilt-framed looking glasses were strategically placed around the room. Madame Le Favre had even managed the circular sofa that now graced the center of the salon and was covered in deep purple velvet that spoke of luxury and royalty. Charis's heart swelled, and her spirits lifted just a little.

Madame Le Favre had faithfully reproduced Charis's painting and then embellished upon it. Fragrance drifted on the air, even though there were no flowers in sight. It was exquisite.

Charis clasped her hands in front of her, allowing the door to swing shut behind her. "It's perfect."

Madame Le Favre entered the room, her face breaking into a smile. "It is, isn't it? I am thrilled and cannot thank you enough. Indeed, word is getting around town, and we only finished this room three days ago. I will have to turn people away unless I can employ more seamstresses."

"It may be prudent to employ more."

"Too true. Everyone is in town for the sitting of parliament, and the ladies have turned their minds to the Season and to me."

Charis nodded. "Yes, Lady Hartley has a ball next week. She planned a small affair; however, I envisage a sad crush. I am looking forward to it greatly."

Madame Le Favre narrowed her eyes, inspecting Charis's face. "I'm not sure I believe you. Although I know I supplied a beautiful ball gown."

Charis pursed her mouth. "I have suffered a slight disappointment." What a polite way to say it. She shrugged, as though such things happened every day.

Madame Le Favre's glance went outside to the barouche where Ashcroft sat, the pale March sunshine hitting his face. "I gather *he* has something to do with it?" She quirked an eyebrow.

Charis took a deep breath and let it out slowly. "Perhaps. But it matters not. I will turn my dreams toward my own enterprise now."

Madame nodded, looking happy with herself. "Good news. But I don't see why we shouldn't make Lord Ashcroft regret his decision. Wait here." She walked from the room and returned a few minutes later with a box.

"I plan to offer it to a lady visiting from Boston. She has a slightly more voluptuous figure, but a few darts will fix that. We will give you a new underdress to wear, but please be careful. If it's damaged, I can't sell it."

She opened the box and lifted the dress out, watching Charis's expression with avid curiosity.

"Behold this marvel."

Charis gasped in delight.

The simple white underdress was overlaid with golden fabric that sparkled and shimmered. The skirt was spangled with seed pearls and crystals, while the bodice and sleeves were of a diaphanous silk, pleated in places and held together by golden flowers and more seed pearls.

Madame Le Favre turned the dress around to show Charis the

small train attached to the bodice in the same sheer fabric that would float when one danced.

"Quickly, put it on, and I will make the necessary adjustments."

Charis ducked behind the curtain, and an assistant came to help her into the dress. It fit better than she could have dreamed, only a little big in the bust. She returned to the modiste. "It's glorious. I must admit, I would love to wear it."

"She is a great heiress. This is the most expensive gown I have ever made, and I hope to garner many new clients from Boston and New York with it. Having said that, she has not seen the dress, much less purchased it. So, at the moment it is still mine. I want to loan it to you for the ball."

"How could I not feel beautiful wearing it? But you must know, none of this is Ashcroft's fault. He tried as hard as he could."

Madame got her needle and thread and tacked some darts into the bodice. "Bah, the menfolk should always try harder. This will encourage him. Or at least make him *extremely* sorry."

Ashcroft did not deserve to feel bad, although making him feel a little sorry was tempting.

Charis took the dress off, and Madame Le Favre folded it back into the box. "And don't forget, if Ashcroft is not your future, you could still have a very profitable enterprise with your designs. You have exceptional talent, and I would hate to see it go to waste. A few advertisements in Ackermann's and you would be on your way, I'm sure of it."

This was just the thing she'd wanted to talk to madame about. "How would that work? For you are right, my family needs whatever profit I can make."

"Look in the magazine. There are all kinds of endorsements. The fact you have worked for Lady Hartley will have commissions flooding in."

"But I could not visit the clients." Why was it that all she saw were hurdles and reasons it couldn't work? Maybe it could.

Madame Le Favre shrugged. "I can make a dress if I have the correct measurements. Why would you not be able to paint a room with the same? You would not be asking for a vast fortune for each painting, so people would have nothing to lose."

True. She had done paintings for her cousin's home without ever seeing the rooms.

A small bud of hope bloomed that made rejecting Ash's offer of marriage a little less painful. For now, at least. She thanked madame and left the shop.

Ashcroft straightened when he saw Charis coming toward the door, followed by a footman with a large box. "This is going to be challenging to get home. Do you mind if I strap it to the rear?"

His jovial tone suggested he still thought she would marry him. She shook her head. "Of course not."

He handed her into the barouche, then fixed the box on the back and jumped up beside her, a worried expression in his eyes. It took Charis a moment to remember that when she left him, she was distraught. "She has followed my instructions precisely, and her shop looks like a dream. I am most gratified."

He pulled out into the traffic with practiced ease. She watched him handle the ribbons with the same surety and confidence he brought to everything. Her heart ached. He would never be hers.

But it would not be right to marry him.

He was just vulnerable from having been in close quarters with a young lady for the first time and likely felt sorry for her circumstances now that he knew her better. He had a strong protective instinct, and she was just the target. Leaving was the correct plan. To give him some space, to realize he had been about to make a grave mistake.

And perhaps her life could be rewarding and maybe exciting with the ideas Madame Le Favre had given her.

"Madame suggested I advertise in a periodical for work redoing rooms. She thinks perhaps someone like Mr. Ackermann might showcase my services, if, of course, I don't mark myself as a female from the outset. I could go by my initials, CA Eastwood, that should solve it."

He kept a steady hand on the reins but shot her a surprised look. Probably not what he wanted to hear when he had proposed marriage to her not an hour before, but she had to show him she truly meant what she said, no matter how callous it felt. "Perhaps if I make enough money, we can move out of our current house, and Father's health will improve."

Ashcroft frowned, bringing the horses to a halt so he could turn into Piccadilly. "Can I take this as a rejection of my suit? For if you marry me, your parents will live somewhere healthy and beautiful."

"Ashcroft, you know the high esteem in which I hold you, and I would never insult you, but surely you must see that we cannot marry. Our friendship is destined to stay just that, friendship."

"Esteem?" He looked like he would like to argue. Heatedly.

She shook her head. "Please."

He nodded. "Very well. I will not argue with you. But I also won't stop trying to make you see there is nothing to stop us."

"You will only make this harder on me than it needs to be. Indeed, I think I should go back home the morning after the ball. Can you take me to book a ticket on the stage? I think it goes from the White Hart in Southwark."

He huffed. "You are not taking the stage, Charis. If you go at all, you will go in our traveling coach." He chewed on his lip, obviously fighting not to say more. "I will have it prepared for you, since you clearly can't wait to get out of here."

She forced herself to smile brightly at him. "What can a lady say? Looking at your pretty face brings me pain. I do not want to prolong my torture."

He did not smile back. "Looking at your pretty face brings me pain, too, now, but I would gladly endure it if I thought one day you would be mine."

"You promised to say no more on that front."

"I did no such thing. If I thought you did not care for me, I would never speak of it again. But you care for me, don't you? You enjoy me as much as I enjoy you. You should not be made to suffer due to an accident of your birth that you have not even come to terms with yourself yet."

She looked directly at the road ahead. "That is life, though, is it not? We are each given our station according to our birth. It is best not to fight it."

"I disagree." It was annoying how his deep and gravelly voice shot a thrill through her, even when they were arguing.

"I will go home. You will forget about me and continue on with your life as planned. This was never supposed to happen. I promised your mother at the outset it would not."

"I will remember you each time I see that window in my study, or sit in the dining room, or stub my toe on that wretched table in the drawing room. I will not forget."

"You will forget. Just as you should."

He frowned and made an exaggerated display of concentrating on the traffic and his horses the rest of the way home. She thought she heard him say "what the deuce" under his breath, but might have been mistaken.

CHAPTER 21

COULD THEY NOT ALLOW A YOUNG LADY ONE NIGHT OF BLISS?

Lady Hartley took a piece of pink voile and tied it around a column in a bow. Both she and Charis had an armful of it to bedeck the decorative plaster columns that lined the room.

It was the day of the ball, and so far the setup of the ballroom had been a good way not to think about her own problems. That was, until Lady Hartley engaged her in conversation.

"My dear, did anything happen between you and Ashcroft I should know about? He seems distracted." She tied the bow and stepped back to admire her handiwork.

Charis's hands stilled on the pillar, a surge of very unladylike anger making her tremble. "Like him proposing marriage to me? That kind of happening?"

Lady Hartley dropped the fabric. It floated to the floor. "I see. Is that all?"

Was that all? She said it as though she was not in the least surprised. Was she more concerned about protecting the secret of Lady Astley being her mother? Checking to see if Ashcroft had kept his promise.

"You wanted more? He took me to the dressmakers and the new store looks lovely." She scratched her brow, as though concentrating. "He said he would dance with me only twice tonight, unless I accept his proposal." He didn't say that, but it felt satisfying to drop it in front of Lady Hartley like a handkerchief.

The footmen and maids stopped their work, straining to hear the conversation.

"You have not accepted him. Good girl." The note of disbelief in her voice was hard to miss. "You can see what a bad thing it would be."

She, Charis, was a *bad* thing? "I could never be a bad thing for Lord Ashcroft, as I only have his happiness at heart. But you said I was the perfect person to flirt with him because I would not look to marry him, did you not?"

Lady Hartley nodded slowly. "I did."

"And perhaps we flirted a little too well." And it had been so much fun. "But I held my promise."

"You reward my faith in you."

I don't want to. It hurts to.

Charis curtsied and went back to check on the giant plaster clamshell she'd painted earlier in the day. Lady Hartley had seen Botticelli's painting *The Birth of Venus* when she was in Italy years ago, and had instructed her to use pink, cream, and beige for the interior.

She ran a finger over the interior and came away with a swish of paint on her finger. Still wet. She moved the candelabra nearer, to lend it more heat. The last thing she needed was ladies getting a smudge of paint on their gowns.

The plan was to have them step inside and have their picture drawn by an artist who had been employed to do nothing else for the entire evening.

Lady Hartley had followed her. "I'm grateful, you know. You may be the wife he wants with his heart, but it would never do."

"I thank you. Rest assured; you need say no more." It was horrible how this trip to London had tarnished the glow that had always surrounded Lady Hartley.

Her ladyship hovered, as though she would like to say a great deal more and was only diverted when there was a commotion by the door. Charis looked up to see Lord Hartley himself, filling the doorway in much the same way his son would, but in a much more colorful ensemble than his son would ever don.

Saved.

"Sink me, but we're having a ball." He threw his arms open and walked into the room. "And m'whole house has been completely redecorated, what what? I adore it."

He walked to his wife and then kissed her on both cheeks. "You've worked marvels in a month and a bit, m'dear, marvels."

Then he spied Charis. "And who is this Venus rising from a clamshell? Why it's Miss Eastwood. I see she has you earning your keep. A harsh mistress, is my wife?"

"The harshest," Charis replied with a smile. She had always liked him, his stubborn clinging to the silks and satins of his generation. The way his hair was tied in a long silver cue with a velvet ribbon. He was himself and made no apologies. But did he know her secret, too? Of course he did. She was surrounded by people who claimed to like or even love her, but had kept the truth from her for her entire life.

Except Ash. He'd told her almost as soon as he knew.

"Well then, what can I do to help?" he said, looking around. "At home, I would be told to go to my library and not come out until it was time to greet the guests."

"Find your son. I think he needs your direction more than we do."

His head snapped around to attention. "Ash needs my help? Sink me, he hasn't needed that since he learned to vault onto his pony. I'm off!"

He left them, and all the footmen and maids were smiling. Lord Hartley lifted the spirits of any room he was in. He had greeted the Eastwoods at the yearly ball like they were the oldest of friends. Father was always pleased. Charis would always be grateful.

After a few hours, all the deliveries had arrived from Gunter's, and claret and Champagne from Berry Brothers. The eight Doric columns that lined the ballroom had ropes of silk flowers and bows draping between them in a most fetching way, and the enormous clamshell was finally dry.

All of which meant that it must be time for Charis to ready her toilette for the ball. It was a pity she was exhausted before the dancing even started.

Mary appeared by her side as she took one last look at the room. "It's perfect, Miss Eastwood, but you won't be if you don't come and get ready. Mrs. Douglas can only spare me for a little while longer. Please come."

Her eyes were almost wild, so Charis took pity on her and followed her up the stairs. It wouldn't do to tell her it didn't matter what Charis wore or how she looked. She would go home tomorrow as early as she could get herself out of bed.

But Mary outdid herself, fluttering the dress over Charis's head with ease by standing on the bed. She threaded pearls through Charis's hair and used her finger to make a few curls fall in ringlets to her shoulders.

"This dress is fit for a princess." She looked slyly at Charis. "Or a countess." We all heard what the mistress said to you earlier. That his lordship wants to marry you. You said no?"

"How could I say yes, Mary? He is way above me." Now everybody knew. Ashcroft would be so embarrassed.

"If he doesn't care, why should you? Like I said before, the newspapers are full of lords who marry actresses. Why shouldn't a captain's daughter get a look in?" Luckily, Mary wasn't looking for an answer. "There," she said, stepping back and surveying her work. "All the gentlemen will want to dance with you."

"Do you think so? I would love to dance tonight." With Ashcroft and as many others as would dance with her. All night long. She wanted to limp to the carriage in the morning and spend a week recovering. She ran a hand up to her neck. It was bare and Lady Hartley wouldn't like that. "Can you get my necklace off the vanity?"

Mary picked it up and secured the cross around her neck. "Now you're perfect."

Lady Hartley was waiting in the ballroom when Charis entered, not appearing to have even a sliver of the nerves that were alight in Charis's stomach. Dozens of staff buzzed around lighting candles, bringing trays filled with beverages. It was still a hive of activity, even though they had been working on it all day.

Her ladyship wore a white dress, but not as a debutante would. Her dress was Romanesque, draped across her shoulders and tied under her bust with an elaborate belt encrusted with jewels. They must be paste jewels, for otherwise it would be worth a king's ransom.

Ironically, she wore nothing around her neck, allowing all eyes to be drawn to the elaborate belt.

"How wonderful you look, my lady," Charis said, taking in all the magnificence and dropping into a curtsy.

"Why thank you. Our modiste has outdone herself." She looked at Charis and her brow creased. "I don't remember ordering that dress. Far too regal for Hartley Green. What was I thinking?"

It was the closest she had ever heard Lady Hartley come to being outwardly annoyed with her. Charis had broken the unspoken contract of the impoverished spinster.

"It is a model dress Madame Le Favre was working on to show a new client her skills. She has allowed me to wear it, as thanks for the design I did for her shop. I love it, but I will not be keeping it."

Lord Hartley smiled approvingly at her. "Nothing is too regal for the ballroom of Lady Hartley, what?"

"I agree," Charis replied. "I may only be here for one more night, but it would be nice to feel like I fit in."

Lady Hartley's face lightened. "I had quite forgotten you wish to return home tomorrow. Part of me thinks you just live with us now; it has been such a pleasure to have you here." She looked closely at Charis as though waiting for a reaction to the lie of it being a pleasure.

She would get none. Charis schooled her features into an expression so peaceful she threatened to float away. "It has been my honor. You have always been so generous with my family. I hope you understand how grateful I am." Wanting to end the conversation, Charis curtsied. "I should check the confectionery centerpiece. I hear it has been delivered."

Walking toward the kitchen, she met Ashcroft coming in the opposite direction. His eyes widened, and he stopped in his tracks, seeming to drink her in from head to toe. She bit her lip, making his eyes fly to her mouth and become stuck there for a few moments.

Heat flew up her cheeks.

He bowed, and by the time he straightened, he seemed to have a better hold of himself. "How beautiful you look, my Charis. I hope you will save me a dance tonight."

"Any dance," she said. *Every dance.*

He thought about it for a moment, then smiled. "The country dance?"

She nodded, and he lifted her hand in a courtly manner, bringing it to his lips. He pressed a kiss onto the back of her gloved hand.

She held her breath for one beat, then two. The musicians tuned their instruments and played a few bars of a reel. Maids and footmen rushed past them, taking no notice. Time suspended as he looked up. His gaze was enigmatic, dark, and asking something of her she couldn't understand. But she wanted to. Like a book unread, she wanted to open it.

The magic of a ball hit her with the light of a thousand fireflies.

Oh.

Finally, he released her hand, and it dropped to her side feeling heavy and limp.

He was striking in his evening clothes, severe black only relieved by a snow-white cravat and dove-gray waistcoat. His dark hair brushed his shoulders in waves that could only be termed poetic. But it was the smile he leveled at her, part heat and part mischief, that made her short of breath. "Until the country dance and whatever other dance I can steal you for."

He bowed and left her, going in the direction of the ballroom.

After watching him walk the length of the hall, Charis continued toward the kitchen, hoping to see the confectionery creation that Gunter's had made for the ball. When she arrived, it was being transferred to a trolley. It was a faithful copy of the Parthenon, complete with crumbling columns and steps. Miniature figures of Ancient Greece dotted the area surrounding the temple and were detailed down to the ropes tying their togas and the laurel wreaths in their hair.

"Exquisite," she whispered, moving out of the way as the trolley and four trustworthy footmen ushered it toward the drawing room, which was to act as the supper room.

Before she knew it, guests arrived and music filled the house, transforming nerves to joy. She entered the ballroom, hoping to see someone she knew. Maybe Mr. Sheridan or Monsieur Trellier. She was certain she had seen their names on the guest list.

But everyone was a stranger, except for fleeting sightings of Ashcroft as he danced with a young lady.

But then, that was the aim of the ball, wasn't it? Find a bride for the heir.

Gentlemen cast glances her way but they could not ask her to dance because she had not been introduced to anyone. Etiquette dictated the introduction come first.

Lady Hartley was overseeing the ladies hop in and out of the giant clamshell.

She looked down at her dancing slippers and swallowed a sigh. The dance ended, and she looked up to see Lady Beatrix steering Ashcroft toward her.

Her new friend took her hands. "Why aren't you dancing? You look a vision." She turned to Ashcroft. "You have not introduced anyone to her, have you? Because if you had, she would be wearing holes in her slippers." She hit him on the arm with her unfurled fan. "For shame, Lord Ashcroft."

Ashcroft grimaced. "Let me rectify this terrible mistake. I'm so sorry, Charis." He bowed and left them.

Lady Beatrix threw her an amused look. "Charis, is it? Interesting. You will have more partners than you know what to do with now. He may prefer to spend his time with aging politicians, but he went to school with every rogue in this room." She chuckled to herself, flipped open her fan, and delicately fanned her face, which was red from dancing.

"I have much to thank you for. I see Ashcroft in a new light now and am half in love with him. The other half will follow suit if he visits tomorrow. Can you believe I had this Adonis under my nose this entire time? He is quiet, so you don't see it. In any case, thank you, dear Miss Eastwood."

True to his word, Ashcroft returned with three gentlemen in tow and introduced Charis so quickly she immediately forgot their names.

But she danced, and suddenly the night looked a little brighter. Mr. Peterborough was attentive, Lord Beaufort was flirtatious, and Sir Peter Fernshaw introduced her to another group of ladies and gentlemen that would see her dancing for the entire night if she wanted to. Indeed, it would be *rude* not to. She managed to forget about Ashcroft for an entire hour. If you didn't count scanning the room for him at every opportunity, that was.

The musicians struck up a Sir Roger de Coverley for the country dance, and couples swiftly lined up across from each other down the length of the ballroom.

Ashcroft returned to claim her hand. He led her onto the dance floor, his gloved hand in hers, glancing at her sideways, his expression solemn. He'd been cheerful and smiling the whole evening until now.

The dance brought them together for a few brief moments. "No smiles for me, my lord?"

"Mother just told me you are definitely leaving tomorrow. Can't I convince you to stay?"

The dance separated them, and she had to wait an eternity before they were joined again. In all that time, he never looked away from her, his eyes locked on hers, mesmerizing and intense.

All this while, she skipped and bounced through the country dance, feeling like the most awkward creature ever to grace a ballroom.

She had never felt so much the object of someone's regard.

"Just promise me you will not call for the carriage until we have had the chance to discuss this in the morning."

Luckily, the dance separated them again, and she did not have to reply. The dance ended. Her heart was thumping, and the noise of the room seemed to swirl around her.

"Perhaps a drink?"

She shook her head. "I will let you go and sit here quietly for a few moments. Too much excitement."

"Then I will sit with you." He led her to a seat, but within a few agonizing minutes of his leg brushing up against hers, people milled around him, asking questions, begging his attention. Finally, an elderly gentleman tried to pull him away altogether to talk about something urgent.

"Go. I will be fine," she said.

His mouth twisted, but he went.

A lady in a pink dress sat next to her, and Charis turned to see

Lady Astley. Her … mother? No, to call her that felt wrong. Her chest tightened, and the fabric of her bodice prickled. Should she stay, or get up and leave? Had she sat there by mistake? Surely it was a mistake.

Lady Astley fluttered her fan in front of her face, even though the ballroom was not hot. "Do you know we are related, my dear?"

Charis nodded, unable to clear her throat to say anything.

"I will not stay long. Only to say you look exquisite. I see Lady Hartley gave you the necklace as I instructed."

"Oh. She did not mention it was from you." Was nothing as it seemed on this infernal trip, or must everything have a hidden meaning?

"A good friend always keeps secrets." She fluttered her fan a little harder.

Had Charis detected a slight French accent on the word *exquisite*? Or was it just an affectation? Whichever it was, Lady Astley's offhand tone had the hairs on her arms standing on end. "You have nothing in the world to be sorry for, madam. But if you are proud of anything, let it be my determination to save my family from penury, and not that I look fine in a borrowed dress."

"Penury? Surely you exaggerate?"

Charis kept her voice perfectly modulated, as though she were speaking of the weather. "My father has suffered an apoplexy, and recovery has been slow and costly. We have therefore lost our income." She smiled brightly as Lady Astley's face fell. "My mother works herself to the bone, cleaning a house that is beyond redemption, and I am seeking a way to earn income to save them from all that because I have not married. No dowry, you see?"

"I see," Lady Astley said softly. "Perhaps I can help?"

Charis wanted to throw the idea back at her, tell her she'd never been interested before and so not to bother now. But how could she do that when they needed the charity so badly?

"Do my parents know you? Have you contributed to my raising?"

Lady Astley shook her head. "No. To my regret, no."

"Well, any small amount would be gratefully accepted, I'm sure. But please don't tell them I know. I have not yet decided if I will speak to them of this."

They sat in silence as the music floated over them and dancers made the floor bounce in time with the Scottish reel they played. Charis's heart beat at twice the pace, and her under arms prickled and spiked in alarm. Why must she do this, on tonight of all nights? This was supposed to be *fun*, not a horrible family reunion that nobody asked for.

"Perhaps through Lady Hartley?" Lady Astley looked the other way, watching her friend introduce another young lady to Ashcroft.

"Perhaps." They both stared straight ahead at the dancers.

Ashcroft bent down to listen to something his partner was saying, but when he straightened, his gaze searched the room until it landed on her. There must have been something in her expression to alarm him because he made his apologies and crossed the room to stand in front of them.

"Miss Eastwood. Would you care to dance?" His outstretched hand was like a rope thrown overboard to a washed away sailor. His eyes darted from Lady Astley to her, a question in them.

Do you need saving?

"I would." She wanted to walk away and not look back. The blood rushed under her skin, causing a blush on her arms and cheeks. She put her hand in his, but before he could lead her onto the dance floor, Monsieur Trellier stood before them with a glass of Champagne in one hand and a hard look in his eye.

"My dear Mademoiselle Eastwood, with my equally dear Lady Astley. Matching beauties." He looked from one to the other and back again, the dawn of comprehension on his face. "*Quelle surprise.*"

Goodness. What now?

––––––

Charis moved away from Lady Astley and stood next to Ashcroft. "Are you enjoying the ball, Monsieur Trellier?"

He tilted his head to one side and ignored her question. "I am enjoying the vision of you both before me. A vision I never thought to see."

"Take your vision elsewhere, Jean-Paul," Lady Astley said, and then under her breath, "I knew it was a mistake to sit next to you." She fidgeted her hands into the folds of her ball gown.

She called him Jean-Paul like an intimate would. But they shot glares at each other that suggested otherwise.

"A mistake, you say? Why would it be so?" He watched Lady Astley closely.

"You can see very well why." Her voice was sharp and a little too high.

Charis looked around. They were attracting attention, and that was the last thing anyone needed. "Perhaps you would like to continue this conversation in the library?"

"It is downstairs and on your right," Ashcroft added. He even used a sweeping motion with his arm, trying to usher them from the room.

Lady Astley and Monsieur Trellier stared at each other. Neither blinked.

"She's my daughter, isn't she?"

Charis gasped, and gasps from people behind them whipped around the ballroom like striking tinder on a fuse.

The dancers stopped, looking around to see what the commotion was about. A few beats later, the music stopped, and then the entire room focused on the four of them.

Her gaze snapped to Ashcroft. *What should I do?*

But Lady Astley and Monsieur Trellier were focused only on each other.

"How dare you!" Lady Astley said, outrage making the feather on her headpiece quiver. "Move away from me."

"No, how dare *you,* madam. Denying me the very thing I grieved for. You *lied.*"

"You did not know?" Charis's voice was quiet but hung ominously in the hush.

He shook his head.

"Oh." The pain of having not one but two parents who did not want her was instantly gone. He had wanted her; he had *grieved* for her. Her breath hitched in her throat, causing her father to glance at her, his expression full of wonder and longing.

"My dear." He reached out a hand, obviously wanting her to take it.

She wanted to take it. But Lady Astley stood, pushing her way between them, knocking his hand out of the way.

"You have ruined me, Jean-Paul," she whispered furiously. "Everything was perfectly fine, and you've ruined it."

"Never my intention," he replied. "Come, let's find somewhere to talk. I am not your enemy."

He picked up Charis's hand and bowed over it, then left them, striding through the watching crowd as though he had an appointment with the devil.

"And he just *assumes* I will follow him," Lady Astley said. But despite that, she rose and followed Monsieur Trellier across the ballroom. "This is a nightmare."

The musicians started up the Allemande, and Charis glanced over her shoulder to see Lady Hartley organizing the lines and moving the attention away from them. The dancers were reluctant, throwing glances over their shoulders, the whispers in the room taking on more of an excited babble now the two instigators had left.

Which left Charis surrounded by people with very hungry eyes.

Being part of society was greatly overvalued.

"What the deuce?" Ashcroft said under his breath, looking at Charis in confusion.

Then her mind flew back to the hidden compartments in the secretaire and the tragic letter that had shaken them both.

She is my light and my love.

He had never married. But Lady Astley had. How long ago had that been? Just over twenty years. Like she herself, just over twenty years old.

Charis blinked rapidly and watched them as they departed. Hadn't he said in the carriage on the way to the theater that she reminded him of someone back in Paris?

The pieces fell into place. "The letter, Ash. Remember the letter we found?"

His eyes widened. "Oh." Then he looked back at Charis. *"Oh."*

"Pure speculation, of course." *What a mess.*

Lady Beatrix and Lady Hartley bore down on them. "Here he is, my dear. Caught up, I dare say." She rapped Ashcroft on the hand with her fan. "Lady Beatrix has been looking for you. You are promised to her for the Allemande, are you not?"

Ash looked at her, then back at Lady Beatrix and his mother. "My fault entirely, apologies, Lady Beatrix. I'll be back shortly, Miss Eastwood, to help you." With a small bow and a look that promised his return, he led Lady Beatrix onto the floor.

She stood there, alone for a few moments, looking for her next dance partner. It was Sir William for the Allemande.

He was nowhere to be seen. But perhaps some other gentleman might come to dance with her, despite what had just happened?

Gentlemen's gazes slid off her, never quite meeting hers.

Not to be, then.

It was as if, despite having a beautiful ball gown and having done nothing wrong herself, she had become entirely invisible. She retreated to the corner of the room to stand next to one of the flowery pillars. Ashcroft and Lady Beatrix danced the graceful Allemande, their arms interlacing as they moved through the figures. She chatted and smiled flirtatiously.

They look lovely together.

Beatrix threw Charis an arch glance. *I know you're watching us. Aren't we lovely?* Then a small smile followed. *He's mine.* It was probably true. She had birth, breeding, and fortune behind her and would be the perfect wife. Why should he bother with Charis and all her messy problems?

Charis just shrugged back in a most unladylike fashion, but it was all she could manage. *I don't care.*

And now she didn't feel like dancing at all, even if someone asked her. The fun had drained from the evening. Her eyes were glazing over just looking at the ballroom, as though she'd been put on ice and couldn't feel anything anymore.

A plate of supper by the comfort of her little hearth and bed was a thought too appealing to ignore.

She wandered out of the ballroom and into the grand drawing room where the supper was laid out.

Lord Hartley was there before her. "Sink me, my dear, you look like a fairy queen, who lost her kingdom. Are you quite well?" He had a plate piled with sandwiches and little tarts. "Take a lemon tart. They will cure any disappointment."

For once, she was not in the mood for his light pleasantries. But there was not much to be done about it.

"Good idea." Charis took a plate and followed suit, taking several of the lemon tarts he'd suggested. Sometimes shock made her appetite flee, but not tonight. Tonight, she needed all the cake she could find.

"Spoke to m'son before. It seems he wants to marry you." His tone, now, was entirely serious. Gentle, but serious. He tilted his head to one side. "He also said he told you about Althea. Rotten

226

business back then." He inspected his lemon tart, then put another one on his plate.

"He did, but I did not accept." A chocolate ganache tart found its way onto her plate.

"You didn't? Brave girl. Nobody says no to Ash. Do him the world of good." He laughed softly to himself.

"And I'm leaving tomorrow." Two sandwiches and a wedge of cheese.

His eyes widened. "Even better. It'll drive him wild. I haven't been so diverted in a long time. I should stay in London for a while. Good evening, Miss Eastwood." He wandered off, leaving Charis to stare after him, more confused than ever.

"One moment, Lord Hartley, if you please?"

He turned, curiosity lighting his gaze. "Yes, m'dear?"

"Monsieur Trellier, is he my father?"

His plate wobbled, a tart threatening to fall off the side. "What would make you think that?"

He had obviously missed the scene in the ballroom. "He and Lady Astley just confronted each other about it in front of the entire ballroom."

He shook his head. "Did they? A shame. No point dissembling, then. It was twenty years ago. I knew Althea was in a delicate way when she came to us. Jean-Paul had sent me a letter asking me to fetch a priest to marry them as soon as he landed."

"What happened?"

He exhaled a long and sad breath. "He never came. She waited so long for him, and there was not a word. We assumed he'd been caught by Madame Le Guillotine, and we mourned. For we all loved him."

"She married." It wasn't a question.

He nodded. "She gave birth to you in secret. She'd waited too long for Jean-Paul, leaving no time to find someone who would pretend the baby was theirs. So, she gave you up and married. Then sink me if he didn't turn up, looking like a convict, starved almost to the bone. Penniless, homeless, and the woman he loved married to another man. Althea made us promise never to tell him."

"And she never told him, either."

"They have a severe distaste for each other. Have for years. Normally can't get them in the same room."

"What fine, upstanding parents I have," Charis said darkly.

Lord Hartley smiled, his gaze warm. "Why yes you do, my dear. Captain Eastwood and his lovely wife. Picked 'em out myself." He took her arm. "Now let's pile your plate a little higher, and you can sit with me a while and gather your thoughts. Such dramatic people, the French. They'll be somewhere having it out as we speak. Best we stay out of their way."

She curtsied. Carefully, because her plate was a mountain of food in danger of an avalanche. "Thank you. Both for my parents and the morsels. But I think I shall retire for the evening and enjoy this by my own small fire upstairs."

He nodded and waved his hand. "As you wish, my dear. I am always here if you need me."

Charis made her way upstairs to find Mary slumped in a chair by the fire. She straightened as Charis entered. "There, miss, you're early. I expected you well after midnight!"

The maid's eyes widened when she spied the plate of food, and her stomach rumbled.

Charis smiled, despite the woeful evening. "Let's get me out of this dress. Could you make sure it gets back to Madame Le Favre tomorrow? Lady Hartley knows the details."

Mary nodded, her eyes darting to the plate of food as she silently worked on the fastenings of the magical gown, one by one.

When the dress was folded gently back in its box with tissue paper, Charis offered the plate to Mary. "Come, share this plate of deliciousness with me."

"Truly, miss?" But she didn't wait for an answer, sitting on the side of the bed and picking a cream puff from the plate. "You're awfully quiet, miss. Did something go wrong?"

"It was not quite what I had hoped for, but I'm sure you'll hear about it in the kitchens." On reflection, at least the anvil of her parentage was held over her no longer. Now it was out in the open for everyone to know, and Ashcroft could see what a bad idea courting her had been. She only hoped the news did not travel to Hartley Green. It was a conversation she certainly did not want to have with her parents.

If only everything could just go back to how it was before she came to London. When she had pretty paintings and dreams to pour into them.

They sat on the bed and ate every crumb. Then Charis bade Mary good night and blew out her candle.

This was not the evening where she danced with handsome gentlemen until the wee hours of the morning. This was the night she realized she was destined for the cellar hearth and put herself to bed.

But it was a long time before she fell asleep.

CHAPTER 22

WHEN THE ONLY THING TO DO IS LEAVE

The next morning Charis woke before sunrise, so early that none but the servants were up, and Ashcroft and his mother were still fast asleep in bed.

At seven there was a hushed knock at her door, and she was told the carriage was ready. They had packed a breakfast box for her to eat while traveling, showing Lady Hartley was happy for her to depart before the house woke. Goodbyes would be torture in any case.

It still felt like a punishment. As though the troublesome houseguest was being sent away under a cloud.

At least she would be far from London when the scandal broke. That was a blessing.

She left Lady Hartley a letter of thanks, along with the last painting she had done for the main bedroom of the lady of the house. It was decorated in the azure Lady Hartley had admired that first day in Hartley Green.

She had also painted one for Lord Ashcroft's bedroom, much as it may be inappropriate for her to do so. It had a comfortable leather reading chair in the corner, a table where he could shave in the morning, a dressing area, and a painting she hoped looked like Turner on the wall. It felt intimate to imagine him there, in the room she created.

With a lump in her throat and a heavy heart, she wrote Ashcroft a note, too.

Dear Ash,

Forgive me for not waiting until you rose to bid you goodbye. Thank you for always being my friend.

Ever yours,

Charis.

Her bags were put into the carriage, Mary was overjoyed at the gift of very fine lawn handkerchiefs from Madame Le Favre, and there was nothing more for Charis to do but leave.

She looked up at the house one last time, the most elegant and luxurious house she would ever stay in.

She stepped into the carriage. Someone had stacked the periodicals and catalogs that the manufacturers had given Lady Hartley. There was a note on top. "Thank you," and signed by her ladyship.

Charis sighed. They would come in very handy.

Sometimes things just didn't work out, even when the stars aligned.

Sometimes dreams didn't end in fireworks, but with the quiet fizzle of a candle burned to its gutter.

Ashcroft woke the morning after the ball with a vague sense that something was wrong, a notion that was only compounded when his valet told him that Miss Eastwood had left less than an hour before.

"Damnation," he said, rolling out of bed and shoving his feet into his slippers.

He had hoped to try to stop her even if it was fighting a losing battle. He smiled to himself. Think she could leave him, did she? Think that his love for her was something that would easily fade? *Ha.* Anyone with any military experience, of which he had precisely none, knew that battles could be lost but wars won.

He had not yet given up hope.

He passed her bedroom door where her maid was inspecting a large white box. "What is to happen to the dress, Mary?"

"Mrs. Douglas has given me permission to deliver the dress, and the letter Miss Eastwood wrote to her modiste, this morning. I was just taking one last look at it. She looked so beautiful, didn't she, my lord?"

He swallowed. "She did indeed." He should take it there himself. Spending an hour in the company of the dress she had worn was as close as he was going to come to Charis herself for a long while. "Allow me to undertake this small errand for you," he said.

Mary tied the ribbon on the box, tucked the letter under it, bobbed a curtsy, and left the room.

Ash stood in the doorway, looking at the bed she had slept in only hours before. At the window she had looked out of and the looking glass she'd sat before. He walked into the room, and put his hand under the blankets. They were still warm. From her. His love.

He turned to see his father standing in the doorway, dressed in the floral embroidered silk robe he so loved. "Gone then?" There was nothing but kindness in his eyes.

"She's so lovely, father." He ran a frustrated hand through his hair.

"Indeed, she is. But this has all been quite a shock for her. It might not be the best thing to whisk her away until she's come to terms with it all."

"I'm not sure she ever will. She's so determined to do the right thing by me."

"Admirable if misguided."

He shook his head while his father laughed softly. "It will come about, Son. We Hartley's don't give up easily."

"You support me? Mother doesn't."

"Well then, I suppose you will have to live with the support of one parent and not the other. She's wrong. And I'm right, as always." He sauntered out of the room.

Ashcroft picked up the box and made his way to Madame Le Favre in Covent Garden. He had seen through the window of the shop on previous visits but upon entering, he saw the painting Charis had shown him come to life.

What a gift she had. Madame Le Favre entered the room, her face breaking into a broad smile when she recognized him.

"Ah, but you have returned the dress from my dear Miss Eastwood."

"Can I purchase it?" It was a sad thing to want, as though keeping it close would somehow keep her close too. That if he held it, he might lure her back.

"I'm afraid not. Loaning it to her was a small token of my thanks for everything she has done for my business, but the dress is needed this week for another client. I cannot remake another in time."

"Ah. I see." Ashcroft looked around at the beautiful room she had designed. "She has a habit of changing the surroundings of wherever she is for the better." The house would be quiet without her. His life would be lesser.

The dressmaker arched an eyebrow as though she knew there was more to the story than he was telling. "I look forward to helping spread the news of her talent far and wide. The idea of painting her interiors and receiving commissions by mail was inspired if I do say so myself."

"I must agree with you, although I am sad to admit the dream of running her own enterprise has perhaps dissuaded Charis from accepting my hand in marriage."

There. Now he had said far too much, and if this lady had no integrity the news would be spread over the scandal rags in less time than it would take him to eat his breakfast.

"Refuse *you*, did she?" Madame Le Favre's mouth pursed, and her eyebrows drew together. "Ah, well. I'm sure she had her reasons."

"There is a letter too." Ashcroft fished it from the pocket of his coat where he had put it for safekeeping.

Madame opened it and scanned the contents. "It is her thanks, and instructions for the advertisement she would like placed with Mr. Ackermann. She directs me to list her only by her initials. Clever girl." A smile played at the corners of her mouth. "I will try and put in a good word with him so he accepts her. I hope it is enough."

"I could make it enough, if you let me do it." He held out his hand for the letter. The Ashcroft title was good for just this kind of thing. "I'll pay a visit to Mr. Ackermann this afternoon and show him the designs we have installed in Grosvenor Square. I'm sure he will be impressed. I don't think I shall tell him C. A. Eastwood is a young lady."

Madame Le Favre put the letter in his outstretched palm. "If her designs arrive by mail, nobody need know."

They shared a smile of understanding. "We are in accord, madame. May her new business thrive and prosper so her family may thrive and prosper too."

"And once that happens you can go and ask again, perhaps. Some ladies don't like to be rescued, you see. They are headstrong and obstinate."

"Sometimes the chase takes a little more, and a little longer than you originally thought."

"But you are prepared to take your time." She smirked.

Ashcroft returned her smile. "I am."

That afternoon he did everything he'd said he would. He visited Mr. Ackermann in person, and after showing him the paintings, then asked him to list the advertisement and send him the account.

If he couldn't marry Charis right now, then the next best thing to do was to help her in her endeavors however he could.

Even though everything he did took her further away from him. But who wanted a wife who was only there for the title and the money? Not he.

CHAPTER 23

IN WHICH A LADY MAKES HER WAY IN THE WORLD

A rriving home was like putting on an old pair of slippers. Charis slipped into her daily routine as though she had not spent all those weeks in London.

Each time she looked at Mother or Father, it was hard not to tell them what she had learned, or that she would dearly like to deepen her acquaintance with Monsieur Trellier and would they countenance such a thing? But it felt like the right decision. No word had drifted from London, and until it did, she would keep the secret.

If they had spent the first twenty years of her life pretending otherwise and being perfectly happy with their lives, then it wasn't for her to ruin the illusion. Nothing had to change. And if, now and then, she stopped to wonder about the small fibs her parents had told through the years, it was only to be expected. For example, all the times she had asked her mother how she had dark blonde hair, even though both Mother and Father had brown. Or why her eyes were blue when theirs were brown. The answer had always been that Charis looked mightily like her grandmother, so the looks must've skipped a generation. And what a comfort it was to her mother that she looked just as she did. They were white lies to make a child feel part of a family. But now she saw them in a slightly different light.

Oh, that she had never gone to London.

But then the wonderful memories with Ashcroft would be gone, too. Thoughts of his smile, so rare and yet so transformative, would come to her unbidden, clutch at her heart, and squeeze. But they soothed her when she couldn't sleep at night.

His letters started arriving at the end of her first week at home. The first one gave her a great surprise and made her exclaim out loud when she read it. Luckily, she was sitting down or she may have fallen over with the surprise.

"What is it, my dear?" Mother asked as she squinted to thread her needle.

"A letter from Lord Ashcroft. He says he returned my dress to the modiste and has taken it upon himself to visit Mr. Ackermann and request an advertisement for my room refurbishment skills." She looked up at her mother. "He was a great believer in my talent once he saw the results. He also showed him my paintings and"—she drew a shocked breath—"Mr. Ackermann is to run a small section expounding on my services in the May issue. A whole section! Lord Ashcroft promises to send me a copy." She looked up, her heart hammering. "Only think, if I could get commissions to design people's rooms, we could have the money to lease a better house."

Mother dropped her needlework into her lap and pressed her hand to her chest, blinking fast. "Can you do that?"

"Lord Ashcroft believes I can so I must agree with him. Only no one must know I am female. I asked for the advertisement to be under the name C. A. Eastwood."

She nodded slowly. "I suppose if anyone asks, we can say it is your father. His initials are the same as yours. Although he can't paint to save himself."

"I'm sure nobody in Hartley Green will purchase our services. I think I should do this. Or at least try. There is too much to lose from me not trying."

"It is lucky you have supplies enough to last you a year with what Lady Hartley gave you."

Charis had not confided it was Lord Ashcroft who had purchased her supplies. She had also not told her mother how deeply she had fallen in love with him in such a short period. With any luck, her memory of him would grow fainter and fainter. Then, someday in the future, she could think of him without the sharp pain in her heart she felt right now.

But when his letters arrived faithfully each day, she knew it would not be so easy. *My dear Charis*, they always began, and her heart flipped a little each time. They detailed what he was working on, or whatever small thing he had seen in London that he thought might amuse her. There were tales from the balls he attended with his mother, trips to Parmentier's, telling her in minute detail about the *papillotes avec devises*, which were sweets wrapped in paper printed with a joke. Apparently, the jokes were all bad.

He finished each letter by signing himself as her faithful servant. She wrote back because it was not polite to ignore a missive. Her letters were about the inhabitants of Hartley Green and whenever there was not much to say, she would sketch something small and fill it in with watercolors. Sometimes it was a red squirrel, sometimes a bird or a quick sketch of her mother bent over the border of her embroidered tablecloth. Never what she truly felt. That the color had been leached out of her life, and every day seemed just like the last.

Mother was intrigued, although felt it her duty to point out the impropriety of an unmarried gentleman writing letters to an unmarried lady.

Charis assured her they would stop soon enough.

The orders from the advert placed in the May copy of *Ackermann's Repository of Arts* started as a trickle, quickly progressed to a stream, and after a month had become the kind of river that it took a boat and a great deal of courage to cross.

Charis had taken to painting all morning, all afternoon, and into the evening by candlelight, just to keep up with the demand.

The payments had also started as a trickle, but were now a very handsome income that was more than enough for the small family to find a new abode.

Certainly, Father had taken umbrage at the fact they were using her income to rent a new house on the picturesque Oak Street, but as Charis pointed out, she no longer wanted to live in the damp, and why shouldn't she use her money to increase their health and happiness?

He had grumbled, but soon enough they were installed in a neat cottage that the previous incumbents had thoughtfully planted with apple trees and berry bushes. Mother was already planning all the preserves she would make come summer.

Charis wrote to Ashcroft to tell him as much, thanking him once again for the vital service he had offered her. The reply came back quickly.

"I would offer you anything. My heart still belongs to you, and my hand, if you should ever wish it."

How was she to reply to that?

To make light of it was to diminish the genuine feelings he had risked putting onto the page. She started her letter of reply five times until finally, not wanting to waste precious paper, she fetched the drafts from the bin and practiced on the reverse side.

In the end, she settled for:

"I think we both established that ours was to be a friendship. You have my highest regard, and I could think of nothing worse I could do

*for you than to accept the offer of your hand in marriage. I would do
you the gravest disservice, as we both know."*

After that, there were no letters for a fortnight. Perhaps he
truly had given up this time. The thought should make her happy,
but, instead, it felt like her heart was a shriveled old walnut.

And then one day, her tidy world where nothing had changed
and her parents looked at her as their beloved daughter came
crashing down when she walked into her bedroom to find her
mother sitting on her bed with one of her drafts to Ashcroft open
on her lap.

She looked up as Charis came into the room, and her warm
brown eyes were full of unshed tears.

"He asked you to marry him? And you said no, because you
would do him the *gravest disservice*. How could our daughter, a
gentleman's daughter, think she would do a grave disservice to
Lord Ashcroft? You refused him, and you refused him based on
who you are, not what your heart wanted. Help me understand."

Charis sat down next to her. Perhaps it had been silly to
suppose they could avoid this conversation. She took a deep
breath. "In London, I met a lady who seemed familiar to me. Her
name was Lady Astley."

Mother closed her eyes as though by closing them she didn't
have to hear what came next.

"Apparently Lady Hartley thought we might like to meet,
since she lost her son in the Salamanca battle."

Mother clutched her heart and burst into tears. She rocked
back and forth. "I should have told you. It should have come from
me. A pox upon her!"

"If there's one thing I learned from my stay in London, it's
that Lady Hartley really only ever pleases Lady Hartley." She took
her mother's hands. "But we must admit, she showed excellent
taste when she chose my parents for me."

"You're not angry?"

Charis put her arms around her. "If I were you, I would not

want to admit anyone had a claim on my daughter but me. It was a shock, to be sure, but I think I understand."

Her mother looked up through watery eyes. "There was a time I could have told you. When you were five, and kept asking why you couldn't have a brother or sister. But I didn't." She pulled Charis tighter. "I'm so sorry. I tried so hard. Lady Astley stayed sequestered. I made sure my midsection grew with wadding every month before you were born. Everyone thought it was a miracle pregnancy. I wanted nothing to hold you back, whether you were a girl or a boy."

So that meant ... everyone thought she was legitimate? But she wasn't. What a mess! "Lord Ashcroft told me she didn't want to acknowledge the relationship, but she sat down next to me at Lady Hartley's ball and entirely ruined my night."

Mother took her handkerchief from up her sleeve and wiped her eyes. "How dare she sit next to you! She who refused to wed and make her daughter legitimate. She doesn't deserve to breathe the same air as you."

Charis shook her head. "It was more complicated than that. My natural father was imprisoned during the French Revolution and she married another before he could reach her. We must be kind. It would have been a difficult time." She had liked him immediately, and was thrilled when the tentative letter she had sent him, received a swift reply and a promise to visit Hartley Green when the time was right for her.

"Is that why you can't marry Lord Ashcroft? Does knowing you have proper certificates make it any better?"

"He knows, his family knows. And there were witnesses at the ball. It feels wrong somehow. His mother doesn't want it, and I look too much like Lady Astley for there to be no family connection."

Mother nodded. "I see. Well, for what it's worth, half of the Ton is related in one way or another. And many of them do not have the parents they think they do. If Ashcroft doesn't see a problem, I'm not sure why you should. That lady was the daughter of a marquess in France, did you know? Your blood is just as blue as his."

"And her love was a French comte." Charis laughed, because finally it felt funny. "But you'd never know from how well I can scrub a kitchen."

Charis thought about Ashcroft every time she saw a wren that looked like Mr. Lark and every time sparrows flitted around her in the garden. He was never far from her thoughts, and his letters resumed again and continued to arrive with such frequency that he made it nigh on impossible to forget him.

Mother looked at the letter unopened in Charis's hands with the now familiar charismatic and loopy handwriting on the envelope. "He has not forgotten you, it seems," she commented with a small smile.

Charis sighed. "We became friends. His letters are not a declaration of love, but just a recounting of the things from his day. I thought he was lonely when we arrived, and I think he assuages his loneliness by writing to me. There is nothing more to it, I am sure."

Her mother didn't respond but continued to sort through her recipes, which she was compiling in a new scrapbook. "I seem to have lost my fruitcake recipe."

"Fruits, flour, sugar, butter and half a bottle of sherry, if I remember correctly. No measuring required."

Her mother smiled. "Close enough."

Charis put Ashcroft's letter to the bottom of the pile and started opening what were likely five additional requests for room refurbishments. The last one was the most interesting.

"Why, this one is less than ten miles from here. Listen to this. *I am the happy purchaser of Linton Hall, and would appreciate it if Mr.*

Eastwood could visit this residence to give me a more thorough recommendation than can come by mail." Her eyes opened wide. *"I enclose ten pounds for your travel costs and await your reply with a time mutually convenient to us both. However, if you read this and can visit Linton Hall on Wednesday afternoon, tenth of June, I will be at home. Yours sincerely, Mr. T. Francis."*

Charis let her hand fall. "What are we to do?"

Mother shrugged. "What we originally agreed upon. Take your father along and pretend that he is C. A. Eastwood, which, in fact, he is, being Charles Anthony. Introduce yourself as his assistant and no one need be any the wiser. Then you can be a party to the meeting, and your father can lend you the countenance you need."

Charis nodded. "A good plan. Very well. We will visit on the tenth. I will reply."

The thought of giving her opinions in person to a complete stranger brought flutters of nerves the entire week. At least she had her beautiful day dress from Madame Le Favre to arm herself with. She *looked* the height of fashion.

The next Wednesday she and Father took the gig and made their way the ten miles to Linton Hall. Charis drove them, having practiced a little with Sally every day since she returned from London.

He watched with a smile as she handled Sally gently and guided them down the road. "I must admit, I never expected you to bring back driving skills when you went to London. A husband, perhaps, but not driving skills and a new business."

"I hope you're not disappointed."

He barked a laugh. "Disappointed? Proud more like. You're showing the steel I bred in you. None of this claptrap about not being my natural daughter. You'll get no tears from me. You're an Eastwood through and through. It's upbringing, my love, it always tells true. You held your head high in London with none of us around you, stood firm, came home from war with a trophy chest that's made our lives better. I could not be more proud."

She turned to see his eyes watery, never mind about him saying "no tears."

"Oh, Papa, you are the very best. I must have used up all my luck getting both you and Mama."

"Bosh. You've plenty of luck to come. You make it yourself, don't you know?"

They arrived by two in the afternoon on a blustery spring day, where the clouds raced across the sky, and the wind threatened to take her bonnet to meet them.

Linton Hall was a charming mansion made of the red brick so often used in houses that were built eighty years previously. There were scaffolds around the outside, and workers were currently covering those bricks in stucco.

Along with beautiful new frames around the windows and a new portico being constructed at the front, the stucco would revitalize the exterior of Linton Hall and bring it into the nineteenth century.

The landscape around the hall needed no help at all. The gig made its way down the long drive that cut over acres of farmland and the natural beauty of fully grown trees.

"My, what a lovely residence." As they pulled up in front, the door opened, and a man stepped out to greet them.

He was tall, with long legs and a mop of dark hair that could not belong to anyone else.

Charis's eyes widened and her mouth fell open.

Ashcroft.

He walked toward the gig, his hands held out in front of him. "Welcome to Linton Hall," he said, his face breaking into one of those rare smiles that made her heart skip a beat.

She stepped out of the gig, and took his hand. "Did you think I would not come if you signed the letter with your own name?"

"I did. My first name is Theodore and my second name is

Francis. But come inside." He turned to Father. "Mr. Eastwood, I know you are more than likely here to lend your daughter your consequence, but I have a lovely fireplace and a very comfortable armchair in front of it if you would prefer to stay there."

She followed him into a front drawing room where paint was peeling off the ceiling, and the floorboards had seen better days. "This needs some work, doesn't it?"

He nodded. "It will be a challenge."

He was right about the cozy spot by the fireplace, though. Father wandered over to sit in it, picking up the newspaper from the small table next to the chair.

"I will call for tea," Ashcroft said, and pulled on a bell rope near the door.

Mary arrived and bobbed a curtsy, her face lighting up when she spotted Charis. Her hopes took flight a little more. He'd brought her maid from London; surely it was a sign?

"Am I to renovate it?" *Who for?* As the heir to the Hartley marquisate who would likely not inherit for many years to come, it was fair he had purchased the country house, but did it mean he had found a wife and this was the house they would raise their children in?

Or, was this, could this be for her? Hope was a treacherous thing, and it escaped its chains and flew toward the sky. He had never stopped writing. Did it mean he had never stopped loving her?

"Of course you are to renovate. You would be amazed at the number of people paying morning visits on Mother to see your refurbishment. The house is a joy to live in."

"She's talented, my girl," Father rumbled from his chair.

Ashcroft nodded. "That she is. Would you mind if I borrowed her for a few minutes?"

"With my blessing," Father replied. He and Ashcroft exchanged a knowing glance.

Ashcroft then took Charis's arm and led her to the back of the house, overlooking a formal garden with a fountain. Birds flapped their wings in the water, bathing. Late spring had turned the trees to leafy havens. Ashcroft opened the door, and the sounds of the country came inside. It was beautiful.

"How is Mr. Lark?" It felt so right to be with him again. Like the missing part of herself had been found, and now she was whole.

"Very well, indeed. In fact, I believe there may be eggs in the nest, for he is very protective of it. Or she. How can we tell?"

She couldn't think what else to say. The words dried up in her mouth.

But Ashcroft reached out and took her hands. "I'm sorry, Charis, but I can't dissemble. I have asked you here to see if there is any hope you'll marry me. I promise I looked at all the other ladies as you asked me to. I spoke to them. I even took a few to Gunter's. But they didn't tease me and weren't even slightly mischievous about my flirting skills." He closed his eyes and when he opened them, they were shining with love. "Please tell me there is hope. I wrote to your mother, and she said you were a sack of sadness and read each of my letters until the edges frayed."

She smiled up at him, brushing her knuckle over his cheek. "I thought you were just swayed by having me in close quarters, and could not see the other, much more eligible, young ladies."

"Perhaps I would never have known how wonderful you were if you had not come to stay with us. That much is true. But how could I look at another lady when there is you?"

It was a crazy idea, and there would be hurdles ahead for them, the least of which was her birth. "But the scandal. It could ruin your political career."

He shrugged. "There's nothing more to tell, all your secrets are out in society, and if you're willing to brave them, I will be by your side as you do."

"I won't look forward to standing up to them, but ..."

"Please say I'm worth it." He leaned in and touched his forehead to hers. "Because marriage to me will not always be peaceful. I'm always crusading on one thing or another."

"You are so very worth it." It would be a full life, a challenging life, but there was nobody else she wanted to go on the adventure with more. "Then yes, yes I—"

She was cut off by him lifting her off her feet and carrying her to a nearby lounge where he sat her on his lap and proceeded to kiss her in a way that showed her just how much he'd missed her.

"Oh!" she said after a few minutes, breathless and more than a little disheveled.

"Do you feel shortchanged?" He laughed. "I'll never forget you saying that after I kissed you for the first time."

"Well, the second time is obviously the charm."

He picked her up and put her on her feet. "Let's go and tell your father."

They found him halfway through the newspaper with a cup of tea and a plate of shortbreads. He looked around. "Well?"

Charis curtsied. "We are to be married, Papa."

His deeply lined face broke into a smile. "Thank goodness! I wondered when you would come to your senses. Men like Lord Ashcroft don't fall at your feet every day."

"I plan to fall at her feet every single day from here on out," said Ash. "Is this house good enough to be your dream dilapidated country house? There is even a litter of kittens in the barn."

Charis tilted her head to one side, pretending to think about it. "Well, if you say there're kittens ..." she said, and threw her arms around him.

THE END

Thank you for reading *A Lady Made for Mischief*. If you enjoyed this regency romance, you a might also enjoy *A Whiff of Scandal* in which Miss Daphne Davenport risks all to save her family from ruin.

Or *A Dash of Daring* in which Miss Diana Kingsley enters a curricle race to win back her favorite horse, but ends up with more than she bargained for!

Or maybe *A Song of Secrets* in which opera singer Sarah is the very last person the vicar of Seven Oaks should fall in love with.

ALSO BY ROBYN CHALMERS

OTHER BOOKS IN THE SPIRITED SPINSTERS SERIES:

A Song of Secrets

The Lost Bride (free short story)

A Whiff of Scandal

A Dash of Daring

A Lady Made for Mischief (Oct 2022)

A Talent for Trouble (2023)

ABOUT THE AUTHOR

Robyn Chalmers is an emerging author of sweet regency romance.

She lives in a country town in southern Australia with her family and a white fluffy dog. She reads a lot, walks a lot and has way too many books.

When not reading, you can find her writing her favorite kind of novel – Regency romance.

She loves hearing from readers and you can find her on Facebook, Twitter and posting bad photos of donuts on Instagram.

facebook.com/authorrobynchalmers
twitter.com/regencygal
instagram.com/robyn_chalmers_author

Printed in Great Britain
by Amazon

24308747R00148